Something Read, Something Dead

Also available by Eva Gates

Lighthouse Library Mysteries

The Spook in the Stacks
Reading Up a Storm
Booked for Trouble
By Book or By Crook

Writing as Vicki Delany

Sherlock Holmes Bookshop Mysteries

A Scandal in Scarlet
The Cat of Baskervilles
Body on Baker Street
Elementary, She Read

Ashley Grant Mysteries

White Sand Blues
Blue Water Hues

Year Round Christmas Mysteries

Hark the Herald Angels Slay
We Wish you a Murderous Christmas
Rest Ye Murdered Gentlemen

Constable Molly Smith Mysteries

Unreasonable Doubt
Under Cold Stone
A Cold White Sun
Among the Departed
Negative Image
Winter of Secrets
Valley of the Lost
In the Shadow of the Glacier

Klondike Gold Rush Mysteries

Gold Web
Gold Mountain
Gold Fever
Gold Digger

Also Available by Vicki Delany

More than Sorrow
Burden of Memory
Scare the Light Away

Something Read, Something Dead

A LIGHTHOUSE LIBRARY MYSTERY

Eva Gates

NEW YORK

Copyright © 2019 by Vicki Delany

Published in the United States by Crooked Lane Books, an imprint of The Quick Brown Fox & Company LLC.

Crooked Lane Books and its logo are trademarks of The Quick Brown Fox & Company LLC.

Library of Congress Catalog-in-Publication data available upon request.

ISBN (hardcover): 978-1-68331-950-4
ISBN (ePub): 978-1-68331-951-1
ISBN (ePDF): 978-1-68331-952-8

Cover illustration by Joe Burleson

Printed in the United States.

www.crookedlanebooks.com

Crooked Lane Books
34 West 27th St., 10th Floor
New York, NY 10001

First Edition: March 2019

10 9 8 7 6 5 4 3 2 1

Welcome to the world,
Nolan Arthur Hartley Webb

Chapter One

"I've decided to elope."

"You are not going to elope."

"Yes, I am. Jake and I will go someplace in the Himalayas. We'll take days to hike in. We'll be married by a hermit in a cave."

"I don't think hermits do weddings," Stephanie said. "Lucy, do you know if Buddhist hermits conduct weddings?"

"I don't even know if Buddhists have official hermits," I said.

"Harrumph," said the bride-to-be.

"I know it all seems difficult now, Josie," I said. "But when the day arrives, everything is going to be marvelous. You've got a great guy, and you're a pretty great person yourself."

My cousin sighed. "Aside from the part about me, you're right, Lucy. As always."

"I'm always right too," Grace said, and we all laughed.

We were on the deck of Josie's parents' beach house in Nags Head, North Carolina, planning her forthcoming wedding. Josie's mom, my Aunt Ellen, had gone into the kitchen to put together the fixings for a sandwich lunch. In her mother's absence, Josie had announced that she'd decided not to go through with the wedding after all.

"You'd break your mother's heart," Grace said. "No wedding for her only daughter?"

"Never mind Aunt Ellen," I said, "you'd break my mother's heart. No chance to spend a weekend in New York searching for a new dress."

"I wouldn't worry about that," Josie said. "About Aunt Suzanne, I mean. She doesn't need an excuse to spend a shopping weekend in New York."

"That's true enough." I closed the magazine on the table in front of me. "To avoid complications, and thus elopements, why don't we coordinate our colors and leave it at that. No need for matching bridesmaids' dresses."

"I'm good with that," Steph said. Grace nodded in agreement.

"Blue," I said.

"Green," Steph said.

"Yellow," Grace said.

Josie threw up her hands.

"Yellow isn't exactly a winter color," I said.

"True," Grace said, "but I look good in yellow."

"You look good in everything," Josie said. "Which is why I hate you."

We all laughed. Josie, currently dressed in torn jeans and a baggy T-shirt, face scrubbed clean, hair in a wind-tangled mess, is no slouch in the looks department.

"Let's wear black," Steph said. "It's winter. It's an evening wedding. Everyone looks good in black. Josie will be in white, so she'll stand out."

"Josie'd stand out in a paper bag," I said.

"She would definitely stand out in a paper bag," Steph said. And we all laughed again.

"Thanks, guys," Josie said. "With your help, I might actually get through this."

I put my hand on hers. "That's why we're here."

She smiled at me.

"Remember, everyone," Grace said. "Small and simple is our mantra."

"Small, simple, and perfect in every way," I said.

"Ready for lunch?" Aunt Ellen eased open the sliding door with one hand and a jutting hip while the other hand balanced a tray piled high with sandwich fixings and a pitcher of tea clinking with ice. I leapt to help her and grabbed the wobbling jug.

"I know it's stressful." Ellen put the tray on the table. "That's because you want everything to be perfect, honey. And it will be. Even if the occasional little thing goes wrong, no one will notice." She took her seat.

Josie smiled at her mother and piled ham onto her sliced baguette. We all dug in.

"I hope the weather's as nice on your wedding day as this." I leaned back in my chair, nibbled on my sandwich, and looked out over the beach. It was early January in the Outer Banks, but unseasonably warm. No one was brave enough to attempt a swim, but people walked barefoot through the surf. Gulls circled overhead and sandpipers darted in and out of the waves. There wasn't a cloud in the sky, and the ocean rose and fell in calm, gentle swells. On the deck, out of the wind, we were comfortable in sweaters and woolen throws.

"A sunny day would be nice for the pictures," Ellen said. "But otherwise we're weatherproof. Compared to some of my friends' daughters' weddings, we're pretty much good to go. The church is booked, the dinner is out of our hands. Lucy, the cake?"

"All taken care of. I've ordered an arrangement of cupcakes in three flavors, French vanilla, carrot, and chocolate fudge, like Josie wanted." Josie had wanted to make her cake herself, but I'd managed to convince her that she'd have enough to do in the days leading up to her wedding. She'd finally given in and provided me with the name of a baker friend of hers in Kill Devil Hills whom she referred customers to if she couldn't accommodate them at her own bakery.

"We need to plan flowers for the church and the table settings at the restaurant," Ellen said. "You three sort out your dresses. And that's about it."

"Have you got your dress, Ellen?" Grace asked.

"I've had it for months. It cost far more than I planned on spending, and when Amos saw the price tag, I thought he was going to have a heart attack on the spot." She smiled. "But it's worth every penny."

"How many guests are we expecting?" Steph asked.

"About eighty. Almost everyone we invited has accepted."

Small and simple was what Josie and her fiancé, Jake Greenblatt, wanted, and small and simple was what we were determined my cousin's wedding would be. They didn't want to spend a lot of money; they didn't want a lot of gifts. They only wanted to celebrate their love in the presence of their closest friends and family.

Fortunately, the mother of the bride, Aunt Ellen, was on

board with that. Jake, the groom, was the owner and head chef at Jake's Seafood Bar, a restaurant in Nags Head. The reception would be held at the restaurant, and he and his staff would handle all the details of the food and drinks. That took an enormous burden off Josie and her bridesmaids: me, Stephanie, and Grace. Josie's cousin from her father's side, Mirabelle, was also going to be a bridesmaid, but she lived in Louisiana and I hadn't met her yet.

"You're wise not to worry about matching bridesmaids' dresses," Aunt Ellen said. "You have your own individual taste, and I trust each of you to make the perfect choice. So there's no reason, dear, for you to run away to the mountains."

I hid a grin as I glanced at the kitchen window, open to let in the soft breeze. Like most mothers, Aunt Ellen always knows what's going on in her house, even when she isn't supposed to be in hearing range.

Josie leaned over and gave her mother an enthusiastic embrace. The rest of us leapt to our feet and gathered around for a group hug.

When we were seated once again and enjoying our lunch, Steph said, "I'm thinking of a beach wedding."

Even Aunt Ellen squealed.

"You're getting married!"

"When?"

"Did Butch propose?"

"Calm down, everyone," Steph laughed. "I'm talking when I get married. If ever I do. I have absolutely no plans for that at the moment. I think an outdoor wedding is nice. And here"—she waved her hand to encompass the beach spread out

below us, stretching off into the distance in both directions—
"is the perfect place. Weather permitting, of course. I've been
to some pretty soggy outdoor weddings."

"I like a winter wedding," I said. "My oldest brother got
married in January at a resort at Lake Placid. It was absolutely
magical with the freshly fallen snow. The bride wore a dress in
winter white. The sleeves were trimmed with fake fur and she
had a big furry hood. It was so beautiful."

"About all I remember of that wedding," Aunt Ellen said,
"is freezing my extremities off standing outside while they took
the blasted pictures, and then being close to busting into flames
inside that crowded room for the reception. Something about
the furnace not working properly, I recall."

"Oh, yes," I said. "That. And the frilly pink dress I was
forced to wear as a bridesmaid. She never did like me."

"How's their divorce coming along?" Aunt Ellen asked.

"It seems to be off. At least for now. I suspect substantial
sums of money were mentioned as an incentive to keep her in
the family."

"Poor Amos." Aunt Ellen smiled at the thought of her husband. "He just about died in New York in January. I overheard
him several times muttering something about not knowing
how human beings can live at those temperatures."

Uncle Amos is originally from Louisiana. To him, North
Carolina is as far north as any civilized person should venture.

"Didn't my dad talk him into trying cross-country skiing?"
I asked.

"Don't remind her," Josie said. "I went with them. I enjoyed
it, but I didn't know Dad knew so many bad words."

We laughed.

"Believe me," said Stephanie, who is Uncle Amos's law partner, "he knows plenty."

I reached for the pad of paper in front of me. One of my jobs was to coordinate everything. "Let's remind everyone of their tasks. Once assigned, Josie doesn't have to think about it again."

"That sounds good to me," Josie said.

"Grace, you said you'd do the flowers?"

"I've been collecting mason jars, and my mom's asking all her friends to give her their extras. I'll tie silver ribbon around the jars and fill them with flowers. Nothing expensive, as y'all keep saying. Large jars for the church and small ones for the restaurant tables."

"Steph. The signature cocktail for when people arrive at the reception."

"You can count on Butch and me to spend the next month making and tasting samples. Butch says it's a tough job but someone has to do it. I got two big old-fashioned punch bowls at the charity shop, and that's what we're going to use. We'll have a nonalcoholic option as well."

"Aunt Ellen. The toast."

"We've found a very nice, not too expensive sparkling wine from Washington State that will do the trick perfectly."

"Josie," I said. "You have one job and one job only."

"To show up on the day," Steph said.

"Other than that. The dress. When are you going to get your dress? Time is running out. The wedding's less than a month away."

"I know, I know. But we've been busier at the bakery since Christmas than I expected. Then Alison got sick, so I'm short-handed out front, and . . ."

"And on it goes," Grace said. "The ideal time will never arrive. Pick a day. Now. We'll put it on our calendars."

"Not this week," Steph said. "I'm in court, and that'll probably last most of the week." She pulled out her phone and checked her calendar. "Then the following Monday, I've a deposition to make . . ."

"Pick a date, Josie," I said. "Those of us who are free to accompany you will do so."

"Okay, okay. I have to check the calendar at the bakery first. I'll do that tomorrow and send you a text."

"If I haven't heard from you by the time I open the library in the morning, I'll call to remind you," I said.

"You still don't want to go to Raleigh, dear?" Aunt Ellen said.

Josie shook her head. "Heidi got a perfectly nice dress at that shop in Kill Devil Hills. At a good price too. So that's fine for me."

Keeping the cost of the wedding down was important to Josie and Jake. They owned their own businesses—Jake's restaurant and Josie's bakery. Both sets of parents had helped their children get their start, and Josie had told them that was enough. She and Jake wanted to pay for their wedding themselves.

"About a bridal shower," Aunt Ellen said. "There's still time to organize one."

"No shower," Josie said firmly. "Jake and I don't need silly frivolities, and I'm not the sort to wear a funny hat. I don't have the time anyway."

"As you like, honey."

I read the disappointment on Aunt Ellen's face. "Maybe something small," I said. "An afternoon tea. I can make sandwiches and a few desserts. Something for your circle of friends, Aunt Ellen, so they can congratulate the bride."

"I guess that'd be okay," Josie said. Aunt Ellen gave me a grateful smile.

"I can help with the desserts," Grace said.

"You don't want me to bake, believe me," Steph said.

"I'll host it," I said. "We can have the shower at the lighthouse. We'll do it next Sunday afternoon when the library's closed. At this time of year, it won't matter about short notice. People don't have a lot on. Aunt Ellen, you work up the guest list, and we can send the invitations by email."

"As Steph said, we don't want her to bake," Josie said. "You guys do the sandwiches and I'll provide a dessert tray."

"No!" we shouted. "You're the guest of honor. You can't be working for your own party."

"It's no trouble for me to whip up a few extra squares and tarts on Sunday morning," Josie said. "As I'm baking anyway."

"You're not going in to work the day of your shower?" Aunt Ellen said.

"Of course I am. Why wouldn't I? I'll leave the bakery in time to go home and change. I promise you, I'll look respectable enough for your friends, Mom."

"In that case," Steph said, "as I'm relieved of baking duties, I'll provide sparkling wine for a toast."

"We have plenty of party glasses at the library, and I'll buy fancy decorated paper plates and napkins," I said.

Inside the house, the phone rang. Ellen got up and hurried to answer it.

I checked my list. "Anything else?"

"Sounds like all's under control," Steph said.

"I take back what I said about eloping," Josie said. "You are so great to do this."

"Of course we're great," Grace said. "Because we love you."

Aunt Ellen came back outside, her face set into a tight line.

"Is something wrong, Mom?" Josie asked.

"Not wrong as in the impending arrival of the zombie apocalypse, but . . ." Her voice trailed off.

"But?" we chorused.

"That was your grandma calling, honey." Ellen meant Uncle Amos's mother. Josie's and my maternal grandmother had died some years ago. "She and . . . uh . . . an unspecified *rest of the girls* are at the New Orleans airport about to catch a flight."

"Not to Raleigh, I hope," Josie said.

"I'm afraid so. Gloria thinks the wedding plans are not progressing fast enough. She is bringing, and I quote, 'a suitcase full of wedding magazines.'"

"Shoot me now." Josie groaned and put her head in her hands.

Chapter Two

At one minute after nine the following morning, I unlocked the library door. We did not have a rush of patrons, so I was free to call Josie.

I'd given her until opening today to set a date for dress shopping, but I knew she wouldn't get around to it. Once she arrived at work, all my cousin would have on her mind would be making bread, ordering flour, managing staff, arranging deliveries, and getting herself elbow deep in bread dough and pastry and sliced fruit.

She and Jake are the hardest-working people I knew. As well as supplying many of the hotels around Nags Head with bread and desserts, Josie's Cozy Bakery was fast becoming the Nags Head in-spot for coffee and light lunches and takeout treats. Jake's Seafood Bar is the hottest restaurant at this end of the long strip of sand that makes up the Outer Banks.

"Good morning," I said cheerfully. "This is your cousin with a friendly reminder that you have to make an appointment at the bridal shop."

"No, I don't," she said. Something was wrong with her voice.

"Yes, you do. Remember what we decided yesterday?"

"I remember. But Grandma Gloria has other plans. Tomorrow we're going to Raleigh. She made an appointment at a bridal shop. I looked it up on the Internet. Dress prices start in the thousand-dollar range."

"Can't you tell her you want to use a local store?"

"I can tell her until I'm blue in the face. Doesn't do any good. I spent a good part of yesterday evening being shown bridal magazines. Dresses, flowers, place settings, lighting arrangements." She groaned. "It was awful. When I could finally get a word in edgewise, I made an excuse and left."

"I understand," I said. And I did. My mother could sometimes be the same. She'd had my china pattern picked out before I was even engaged. She'd had the nursery bassinet chosen before that.

Not that the engagement she'd so hoped for happened. Nor had the need for a bassinet. I'd left my erstwhile fiancé (chosen more by my parents than by me) on bended knee—literally— and escaped to my favorite place on earth. The Outer Banks of North Carolina.

"You're her only granddaughter, right?" I said.

"Yes. Grandma and Grandpa had three children, two boys and a girl, but all of their progeny, except for me, are boys."

"Then this wedding is particularly important to her. I don't really understand why the wedding of male offspring is of less significance, but it is. All you have to do is nod and smile and agree. And then do it your own way."

"Oh no, Lucy. You don't understand. No one is allowed to do things their own way when Grandma Gloria has made up your mind for you."

"Really?"

"As you are about to find out."

"Me? You mean dress shopping? I can't make it tomorrow. Not all the way to Raleigh and back. It's Ronald's day off, and a team from the University of Bristol, in the UK, are coming to work with Charlene. Go ahead without me. We told you you're the only one who matters and you'll have to work around us."

"I am not buying my wedding dress without my favorite cousin and maid of honor to help me. And that's that. But I meant you're about to find out in a more immediate sense. Prepare for incoming." She hung up. I was left staring at the phone in my hand wondering what that cryptic comment meant.

"I can work tomorrow if you need me to, Lucy," said a voice from behind me. "I have nothing in particular planned. We can swap days."

I turned around. "I didn't know you were standing there. I didn't mean for you to overhear."

"But overhear I did," Ronald said.

Charles, the library cat, leapt onto the shelf next to me, and I ran my fingers through his thick tan-and-white fur. "Thanks, Ronald. I would like to be with Josie when she gets her dress."

"She's cutting it rather fine, isn't she?" Ronald said. "The wedding's what, less than four weeks away? Don't these dresses have to be altered and fitted and all that? That's what happened for my sisters' weddings."

"Josie wants something simple. Just a long white dress. You

know Josie. She'll look absolutely perfect no matter what she wears. Everything fits her immediately, and everything suits her." My cousin is the most beautiful woman I know, with thick, long glossy hair streaked gold and caramel by the sun, an oval face dotted with freckles, and cornflower-blue eyes that sparkle when she laughs, which is often. Her mouth is wide, her lips pink and full, and her teeth perfect. To prove that life is even more unfair, she is five foot ten and as thin as the sandpipers that dart around on the beach. Imagine, a woman who makes cookies, pies, and tarts all day being reed thin.

If I didn't love her so much, I'd hate her.

My mother is also beautiful, but the women in her family are short and inclined to put on weight. I got my lack of height from my mother and the round face, plump cheeks, and always-out-of-control curly black hair from my father. Oh, well. Who said life was fair?

"What did Nan wear to your wedding?" I asked Ronald. "I've never seen any of your wedding pictures."

Ronald Burkowski is our children's librarian. Today he wore beige chinos, a blue checked shirt, and an excessively wide tie festooned with Star Wars characters. "We rented costumes from a theater company and went as Romeo and Juliet."

I grinned. "I can see you two doing that. But weren't you tempting fate? That romance didn't exactly end well."

"We were young and foolish. Maybe we had reverse-karma. Nan and I have been married for twenty-one years now. And very happily, too."

The door opened, and we turned to greet the first patrons of the day.

Something Read, Something Dead

A wave of Chanel No. 5 hit me as four women marched in, led by a lady in her eighties who was pretty much the dictionary definition of a southern matron. She was overdressed for the time of day—nine AM—and the place—the Outer Banks on a Monday—in a pale-blue skirt suit that came to her knees, pantyhose, and pumps with one-inch heels. Her well-ironed and heavily starched white blouse had a big blue bow tied in perfect folds at her neck. Small gold earrings were in her ears, and large diamonds glittered on her fingers. Her dark-brown hair appeared to have been sprayed on, as had her somewhat excessive makeup. She was close to six feet tall and probably weighed a hundred pounds after a big meal. Enormous cornflower-blue eyes, rimmed in eyeliner, the lashes thick with mascara, studied me. I'd never seen her before, but something was familiar about the shape of her chin and the color of those penetrating eyes. Her cheekbones were so sharp you could cut cheese with them, and her chin came to a small point. Her skin was almost translucent, but age had taken its toll, and the folds were numerous and deep. She must, I thought, have been a great beauty in her youth. She leaned on a black cane topped with an image of a falcon in brass. The three women following her were younger, ranging from their early thirties to late fifties. They were slightly more casually dressed, but not by much.

The door swung shut behind them, hit something, and a voice said, "Oof." It opened again to reveal Aunt Ellen, grimacing and rubbing her arm.

The elderly lady could only be Josie's grandmother. That was where I'd seen that shade of eyes and those features—on Josie herself.

I stepped forward. "Welcome to the Bodie Island Lighthouse Library, Mrs. O'Malley. I'm Lucy Richardson."

"Then it is you I am here to see," the elderly lady announced. "As you have surmised, I am Mrs. Gloria O'Malley." She glanced around the room. It was a library, just a library, but to us it was a very special place.

Mrs. Gloria O'Malley didn't look particularly impressed. "Is that a cat I see?"

Charles preened, and I said, "This is Charles, named after Mr. Dickens."

"I don't care for cats myself," she said. "Nasty creatures."

Charles deflated.

Ronald stepped forward. "Pleased to meet you, ma'am. I'm Ronald Burkowski, children's librarian."

Gloria extended her hand. Ronald touched her fingers as though she were a newly hatched robin. She gave him a radiant smile. "A librarian! So nice to see men doing nontraditional occupations, isn't it, girls?"

"Yes," her followers chorused.

"We're sorry to bother you at work, Lucy," Aunt Ellen said. "My mother-in-law wanted to talk to you in person. She has some . . . suggestions about the shower on Sunday."

"I certainly do," Gloria said. "In a library! That doesn't seem at all suitable to me."

"We're closed on Sunday," I said, "which is why I suggested it. We host many events here, so we're used to accommodating people." I looked at the three women clustered behind Gloria. "Welcome."

"Lucy," Ellen said, "let me introduce you." She gestured to

the eldest of the group. "Amos's sister Mary Anna." Mary Anna was a paler, washed-out version of her mother, as though a duplicate Gloria had been left out in the rain and most of the color had run out. She nodded politely at me and mumbled something about being pleased to meet me.

"This is Mirabelle, my . . ."

"Mirabelle," Gloria said, "is the granddaughter of my late, and not at all lamented, brother Clive."

"Mama!" Mary Anna said. "You can't be sayin' things like that in front of outsiders."

"Nonsense. I believe in telling the truth at all times," Gloria said proudly. "That Clive always was a rapscallion."

I didn't know what a rapscallion was, but I could guess. "Pleased to meet you," I said to Mirabelle. She was about Josie's and my age, early thirties. She had the O'Malley family height and traces of her grandmother's beauty, but on her it was ruined by the sneer on her face and the narrowness of her eyes as she studied first the library and then me. She wore tight jeans, artfully distressed and shredded in places, a red T-shirt with an excessively low neckline under a short denim jacket, and killer stiletto heels. Her blonde hair fell to her shoulders and flipped at the ends. Her long nails were painted bright red, the same color as her lipstick.

"Soooo pleased to meet you," Mirabelle drawled. "A library in a lighthouse. How clever."

"We like it," Ronald said.

Her eyes passed over me, and she turned the full force of her smile onto him. "It's absolutely charming. I simply adore your tie."

Ronald—calm, sensible, happily married Ronald—blushed.

The third woman stepped forward and thrust out her hand. "As it looks like no one's going to introduce me, I'll do it myself. I'm Florence." She was also in her thirties, with a prominent nose and square chin. She peered at the world through glasses with heavy frames and thick lenses. Her brown hair hung limply to her chin, and the bangs were cut in a sharp, straight line one inch above her eyebrows. She was about five foot nine or ten, even wearing flats. I was beginning to feel as though I'd accidentally wandered into a tall people's convention. Not a place I, all five foot three of me, am ever comfortable.

"Florence," Gloria said, "is Mirabelle's business partner. She is the youngest daughter of my youngest brother by his third wife. Florence was a late-in-life . . . gift to him."

There was a story there, but I had no time to think about that right now. I threw a quick glance at Aunt Ellen. She grimaced in return.

"How nice," I said. "What business are you two in?"

"Event planning," Florence said. "My company's called Festivities by Fanshaw."

"Which," Gloria said, "is why we are here."

"To help y'all out," Mirabelle said.

I had a bad feeling about this.

"Now, about this shower," Gloria said.

Behind her, Aunt Ellen beseeched the heavens with her eyes.

"It's nice to meet you," I said. "But I can't talk about private matters right now. I'm at work. You're welcome to tour the library, if you like. The view from the top of the lighthouse tower is worth seeing."

"I didn't come all this way to look at a bunch of books," Gloria said. "We will sit ourselves down right here and have a nice chat. I'm sure Mr. Burkowski won't mind."

"Me? Oh, I'm not the boss," Ronald said. "I'm the . . ."

"Children's librarian, yes." Gloria arranged herself in the wingback chair by the magazine rack, gripping her cane with both hands. She sat as though she were holding court. Mary Anna and Florence took places on either side of her, like ladies in waiting.

"Sorry," Aunt Ellen whispered to me. "She won't leave until she's said what she has to say, so let her get it over with."

"What brings you to Nags Head, Mrs. O'Malley?" Ronald asked politely.

"Yesterday morning, when I got home from church, I checked my calendar for the forthcoming month, as is my custom of a lifetime. I noticed the date of Josephine's wedding clearly marked, and then I realized, to my absolute horror, that I haven't received my invitation."

I looked at Aunt Ellen. I'd checked the guest list only yesterday. Gloria's name was right at the top. With a tick mark beside it, indicating that she'd accepted.

"Gloria, we've discussed this," Ellen said. "The invitations were sent by email."

"And I could scarcely believe it," Gloria said. "Emailed invitations for my granddaughter's wedding! In this one thing only I'm glad my mother isn't alive to see Josephine finally wed."

"So, what does a children's librarian do?" Mirabelle asked Ronald. She'd picked Charles up and was stroking him while staring deeply into Ronald's eyes. Ronald blushed some more. Charles purred. I've always thought Charles a great judge of human character. Today he seemed to have fallen down on the job.

"I help children develop their love of reading." Ronald fiddled with his tie.

"Once I realized that proper invitations, gold engraving on sturdy card stock delivered by hand by the United States Postal Service, were not forthcoming, I decided I had to take matters into my own hands. And then I found out that Florence, her parents, and my great-niece Crystal didn't even get invitations by email!"

"Josie and Jake want to keep the wedding small," Aunt Ellen said meekly. My strong, confident Aunt Ellen seemed to have suddenly lost her spine.

"There's small and then there's unseemly," Gloria said. She looked at me. "I made a few changes to Ellen's guest list last night."

"Was Josie all right with that?" I asked.

"I'd scarcely arrived when she had some emergency at the bakery and had to rush away. You'd think she could take time off when her grandmother comes to visit. Imagine my shock when I realized that with less than a month to go, she doesn't have her dress yet."

"About that," Ellen said.

"You needn't worry, dear," Gloria said. "It's all in hand. Our appointment is at eleven tomorrow."

"I'm getting the day off work so I can come with you," I said.

Aunt Ellen's face was a picture of relief.

"Your wife must be so proud of you," Mirabelle said to Ronald.

"She is," he said. "Very proud. As I am of her. Her name's Nan." He reached into his pocket. "I have a picture here somewhere."

"How nice for you." Mirabelle put Charles down and wandered over to the magazine rack.

One of Charles's duties as library cat is to keep patrons company. One of his favorite places to do that is in the wingback chair. He studied Gloria's lap. He braced himself, ready to leap. She turned her penetrating eyes on him. He turned and slunk away.

"Tell me again why you are having Josephine's bridal shower in this library," Gloria said.

"Because I live here, and I'm hosting it," I said.

"You live here? You mean on the grounds? I saw no houses nearby."

"I have rooms upstairs."

"Oh. That must be . . . small. Is there an elevator?"

"No. I walk all one hundred steps several times a day. Saves me money on a gym membership." My apartment's on the fourth floor. It's tiny and beautiful and suits me perfectly. At this stage in my life, anyway. I call it my Lighthouse Aerie.

I didn't plan to have the bridal shower in my apartment; I own only two chairs. We regularly use the main room in the library for fund-raising events or hosting visiting authors and historians. It's more than suitable for Aunt Ellen's friends, most of whom are library volunteers. I explained that to Gloria.

"A restaurant would be better. Mary Anna, start making calls."

"Yes, Mama."

"A restaurant will charge," I said. "The library's free, because Aunt Ellen is one of our volunteers. All we ask is a donation. My friends and I are going to prepare the food ourselves to keep the costs down."

"Nonsense," Gloria said. "My son and his wife can afford to pay for a proper shower for their only daughter."

"I told you, Gloria. Josie doesn't want to accept our help," Ellen said.

"Ridiculous. A man pays for his daughter's wedding."

"But . . ."

"I'm giving the shower," I said. "As the maid of honor, that's part of my role. I want to have it here. I'm sure you understand."

Mary Anna and Florence exchanged worried glances over the matriarch's head. Gloria took a deep breath. Mary Anna, Florence, and Aunt Ellen braced themselves. Charles leapt onto the top shelf of the magazine rack to watch the drama.

"Will you look at the time," Ronald said. "I'd better get to work. Nice meeting you, ladies. Mrs. O'Malley." He fled. The coward.

"Very well," Gloria said. "If you insist." We collectively exhaled. "Mary Anna will help you plan the games."

"I wasn't going to have games," I said.

She waved her hand. "Mary Anna will help."

Mary Anna nodded.

"As this event is on Sunday and it's already Monday, we are too late to send out proper mailed invitations. Email will have to do. You will handle that, Laura."

"Who? Oh, you mean me. I'm Lucy. I'm already on it."

Gloria rose from her chair like a great ship being launched from dry dock. All that was missing was the breaking bottle and the splash. "We're having dinner tonight so I can meet Josephine's young man. You will join us, Laura. I have further arrangements to discuss with you. I didn't see the florist listed as a supplier for the wedding, and we need to pay a call on them."

"We're not . . ." But I was talking to her back.

While the rest of us discussed wedding plans, Mirabelle had spent her time flipping idly through magazines. She picked up a copy of the latest edition of the local newspaper. "Will you look at this," she said. "Maybe this place isn't such a backwater after all. Not if someone this hot is the mayor."

She held up the paper for Florence to see.

"Not bad," Florence said.

The picture showed the mayor of Nags Head, Connor McNeil, shaking hands with an award recipient from a service club. The mayor did look good in that picture. It emphasized his strong jaw, his attractive blue eyes, his excellent bone structure. "Any chance we can send an invitation to this mayor for Josie's wedding?" Mirabelle said.

Aunt Ellen broke into a coughing fit. Mary Anna slapped her back.

"It's all taken care of," I said. "He's already confirmed his attendance."

"Cool," she said. "I hope he's not married."

"He isn't." I did not add that he was coming to the wedding not only because he was a close friend of Josie and Jake's but also because he was my date.

Chapter Three

"**I**'m eloping. And this time I'm not kidding."

"I might join you," I said. "A hermit's hut in the Himalayas sounds mighty attractive right about now."

Josie patted Charles. He leaned up against her and purred loudly. Josie had come to pick me up for dinner. She'd come alone, probably not a good sign.

"Mom called Dad as soon as they got back from the library this morning." My uncle was at a legal conference in Houston. "He said he'll come home when he can get away, but that might not be for a few more days. Liar. I bet he's grabbing the next flight to Kathmandu."

"How does your dad get on with his mother?" I asked.

"They get on fine because he fusses over her and flatters her and then goes his own way. Grandma rules the women in the family with an iron fist. Things she considers male pursuits she says are not her concern." Josie burst into tears. "She's going to ruin my wedding!"

"You're simply going to have to put your foot down," I said. "Tell her to go back to New Orleans until the wedding."

"If I do that, one of two things will happen. She'll ignore me and my wedding will be ruined. Or she'll storm out, dragging all of Dad's side of the family with her, creating a huge family rift, and my wedding will be ruined."

I gave her a hug. What could I say? I'd met Gloria.

Charles wiggled between us, enjoying the hug.

"Bad enough Grandma's putting her oar in, but she's dragged Mirabelle and her friend into it. They spent the afternoon visiting florists. And you can bet the word *budget* didn't come up."

"Someone said something about them having an event-planning company?"

"Of all things. Florence went into the hotel business as a hospitality manager when she finished college. A couple of years ago she started up her own company. I don't know what happened next, but now it seems as if Mirabelle's involved with it. Mirabelle knows as much about event planning as I know about captaining an aircraft carrier. Less, probably. Aaron was planning on going into the Navy when he was younger, and all he talked about for a year was boats."

"I think an aircraft carrier is called a ship. Not a boat."

"My point exactly. If I don't know what to call it, I can't run one. And Mirabelle is calling my wedding the social event of the season." She groaned.

"Did she really say that?"

"Yes. Jake's furious."

"What? Why?"

"Gloria phoned him. She weaseled his phone number out of Mom. In the face of her mother-in-law, Mom turns into a quivering piece of jelly. Everyone in the family says that when my parents married, Mom couldn't bear to move away from the Outer Banks, so Dad set up his law practice here. I don't think that's it at all. I think she told him she couldn't live anywhere near his mother."

"Funny to think that if that hadn't been the case, we might not have OBX in our lives," I said, using the popular term for the Outer Banks. "And wouldn't that have been a tragedy."

"Doesn't bear thinking about," Josie agreed.

Charles meowed in agreement.

"What did Gloria say to Jake?"

"She wants approval of his wedding attire."

"You're kidding."

"Need you ask? You've met my grandmother. Now that I have, in her words, decided to get a *proper* wedding dress, she needs to make sure he's also suitably dressed. Mirabelle and Florence have been instructed to take him shopping. She did say he needn't go as far as a morning suit."

"That's something to be thankful for. What did he say to that?"

"I don't know what he said to her, but he had a few things to say to me later. Starting with, what's a morning suit?" Josie shook her head. "Do you know?"

"In *The Busman's Honeymoon*, Lord Peter Wimsey wears a morning suit to his wedding."

"Yeah, but I thought that was what the English call a suit a man puts on in the morning, to wear to the office. Not something special. What am I going to do, sweetie?"

"Call your dad," I said. "Tell him you need him."

"This conference is important to him."

"His daughter is more important," I said.

She smiled sadly at me. "Let's go. I want to be at the restaurant before the Louisiana Mafia descends. Poor Jake doesn't need to be alone with them. You're sure Connor can't make it? Jake's going to be the only man at the table. I wish the boys were closer." Josie is the middle child in the family. At the moment, Aaron was in his freshmen year at college, and Noah is an accountant at a big firm in Raleigh.

"Sorry, but Connor has a dinner meeting with the other Outer Banks mayors. Speaking of Connor, what's the story with your cousin Mirabelle?"

"Why does mention of Connor make you think of Mirabelle?"

"No reason."

"She's the same age as me, as us, and she's already been married twice, divorced twice. No kids. I must say, each time she's landed on her feet. Meaning bigger and better divorce settlements. Maybe that's why she joined Florence's business, if she put some of her ill-gotten gains into it. I've never liked her much, even when we were kids. I didn't want to have her as a bridesmaid, but Mom sort of insisted. She said if I'm having a cousin from her family, meaning you, I need to have one from Dad's side too."

"That's only fair."

"I didn't mind too much, because at least I know her. Mirabelle's family came to Nags Head a few times to visit us over the years, and we once spent Christmas at her parents' place in New Orleans. I haven't seen or been in touch with Florence since primary school. Not until yesterday. And as for second-cousin Crystal who Grandma mentioned, I've never even heard of her before."

"How many people got added to the guest list?" I asked.

Josie sighed. "More than I wanted. Okay, Florence is here and has met me, so she can come. Florence plus one, of course. And now Mary Anna's three children and their partners need to be invited. I couldn't say no to her face, but I crossed out all the others Grandma added. Second cousins and third cousins once removed. She has some distant relatives living in France who would just love the chance to get reacquainted with their American roots. I don't trust her not to go behind my back and invite them all anyway."

"Chin up," I said. "You can get through this. We can get through it."

"If Jake doesn't call the whole thing off first. He's going to be beyond furious if I have to tell him a whole pack of my relatives are coming. He's been ruthless about telling his parents he's not entertaining their friends or inviting long-unseen relatives."

"Jake's a sensible guy," I said. "And he loves you. He's not going to call anything off."

She sighed. "I just wish they'd listen to me. It is supposed to be *my* wedding."

"Why don't I speak to your grandmother? I'll be calm and straightforward and tell her what's what. We can find something for her to do that'll make her think she's involved and keep her happy. She can design the table decorations or come up with ideas for wedding favors."

"That would work if it was only Grandma to worry about. She makes declarations, puts her foot down, and then realizes she's gone too far. She can't back out without losing face, and all she needs is a way of giving in graciously. That's how Dad's always dealt with her. But it's different with Mirabelle sticking her nose in. She and Grandma are feeding off each other. One of them has an idea, the other writes it down, and next thing I know Florence is making phone calls. My opinion isn't wanted or needed."

"Let me try, anyway," I said.

"Thanks, sweetie. It certainly can't hurt. Oh, about your dresses. Mirabelle doesn't want to wear black to the wedding. She wants all the bridesmaids to go shopping together and pick out matching outfits. She showed me some examples in wedding magazines. Her taste, what there is of it, is either pastel-colored and puffy or suitable for an adult movie about weddings gone wild."

I shuddered. "Not gonna happen. Maybe we should sic Stephanie on her."

"That I'd like to see. But you don't want my dear cousin to get a look at Butch."

"Why not?"

"Mirabelle's a man-eater, always has been. Watch out for her."

I thought of the way she'd latched on to Connor's picture in the paper. I was confident that Connor wasn't the sort to be attracted by a "man-eater." But our relationship was new and we were at that carefully-feeling-our-way stage and my insecurity was bottomless. I mentally shook my head. Right now,

I had more important things to worry about. "I can do something about the bridesmaids' dresses. I'll call Steph and Grace and fill them in, and we'll simply never be available to go shopping with Mirabelle. We'd better get going. I'll phone them from the car."

Charles leapt onto the returns shelf to wave us off and wish us a pleasant evening. Josie gave him a pat. When she saw the book he was sitting on, her smile died. "Tell me that's not an omen."

Great Expectations, by Charles's namesake, Mr. Dickens. A doomed engagement; an abandoned bride gone mad.

"You're safe," I said. "If Miss Havisham had a grandmother, Dickens never mentioned her. Miss Havisham managed to ruin her life all by herself. Speaking of books, have you finished *The Busman's Honeymoon?*" That Dorothy L. Sayers novel, part of the Lord Peter Wimsey mystery series, was the title we'd chosen for the next meeting of the Bodie Island Lighthouse Library Classic Novel Reading Club.

For the first time this evening, Josie smiled. "Almost, and I'm enjoying it. Why is it called that? There aren't any bus drivers in it that I can see."

"A busman's honeymoon means a working vacation. Which Lord Peter and Harriet Vane's turned out to be when someone turned up dead in the place they were staying."

"Talk about interfering families." She laughed. "His is almost as bad as mine. Hey, that's an idea. Lord Peter lets his sister-in-law Helen make all the snooty arrangements she wants, for the wedding *and* the honeymoon, and then he and Harriet do things the way they want and at the last minute they invite Helen. They tell her she can come or not. That might be an idea."

I didn't like the look on Josie's face. She was not joking.

"May I remind you," I said, "you don't have the money to book a luxury European honeymoon and then give it to a deserving employee so you can escape to the countryside for the quiet vacation you wanted all along."

"Things can be arranged," she said.

*   *   *

We were having dinner at Jake's Seafood Bar, and the groom-to-be himself met us at the door. He gave me a quick hug and Josie a long kiss. "Sorry about what I said on the phone, babe," he said to her. "Your grandmother annoyed me, but I never should have taken it out on you."

She put her arm around him. "I understand. Grandma can be difficult. To say the least."

"Simply agree with everything she says," I said, "and then go ahead and do what you want, in the manner of Lord Peter Wimsey."

"Who?" Jake was not a member of our book club, as he worked most evenings.

"Never mind. Gloria O'Malley is a formidable southern matriarch of the old school, and that means a handsome, charming man can get away with almost anything."

He grinned at me. "Thanks for the tip, Lucy. What's a morning suit?"

"Men's daytime formal wear. Very formal. Extremely formal.

Not to be confused with white tie, which is formal evening wear. You see morning suits at royal weddings."

"Which is sort of what my grandmother thinks we're having," Josie said.

"Let's go in," Jake said. "Our table's ready."

"Nervous?" I asked him.

"Oh, yeah. Meeting the Louisiana clan for the first time is not for the faint of heart."

"Just be your charming self," I said, "and you'll be fine."

He gave me a crooked grin. He was a good-looking man, my cousin's fiancé. He was also smart, kind, funny, and hardworking. Josie was lucky to have found him. And he was extremely lucky to have found her.

I gave him an impromptu hug.

"Before we go in . . ." Jake's smile died as he turned to Josie. "Another three calls this afternoon."

"Oh, no," Josie said. "Did you speak to her?"

"I let them all go to voice mail. Three calls, three messages imploring me to get in touch right away."

"What's this about?" I asked.

"An old girlfriend of Jake's has arrived in town," Josie said.

"She followed me from New York," he said. "We weren't much of an item; we only went on a handful of casual dates. We were finished before I moved back here. That is, I thought we were finished. I never gave her another thought, and then, a couple of weeks ago, she showed up here to tell me she was ready to get back together."

"I assume you told her you'd moved on?" I said.

"I told her. And I told her. And I told her. She doesn't seem to be getting the hint. She's done nothing to cause trouble, not yet anyway, just phone calls and texts and hanging around. Here." He pulled out his phone. "I showed Josie this, wanting her to be on the lookout in case Toni approaches her. I took this about a year ago and never deleted it." He showed me the picture. The young woman was moderately pretty, smiling broadly into the camera. The picture had been taken outside, pine trees drooped under a load of fresh snow in the background, and the woman wore a gray coat and white scarf. She had short black hair that stood up in spikes, a wide mouth, and a row of silver rings through her ears. "I haven't seen her," I said. "But if I do, I'll let you know."

"Thanks. Not a word to Ellen, please. Now, let's go in. They'll be here soon."

The outdoor bar and seating area was closed for the season, but Jake had reserved a large round table next to the wall of windows for his guests. I love this restaurant, and I never tire of the view. It sits on Roanoke Sound, overlooking Roanoke Island and its small-boat harbor. At this hour, at this time of year, it was fully dark outside. Lights twinkled on the island or bobbed on boats moored in the calm waters of the Sound. The fourth-order Fresnel lens of the reproduction Roanoke Marshes Lighthouse flashed its rhythm. The restaurant was about a quarter full. Not bad for a Monday night in January.

"Now remember," Josie said. "As Lucy said, Grandma is a southern lady of the old school. Manners are everything to her. You can literally get away with murder if you're gracious about it."

"I'll try not to dribble soup down my front," Jake said.

"I'm serious," Josie said.

He planted a kiss on the top of her head. "So am I. I have trouble with soup."

"She tells people the family lost our land and status in the War of Northern Aggression, as she calls it. According to her, our plantation rivaled Tara in its grandness. My dad says that's absolute nonsense. Our family was nothing but hardworking fishing folk. And proud of it. Although he never says that in her hearing."

We took our seats, and waiters arrived to fill our water glasses. "Do you want to order drinks now, Jake, or wait for your guests?"

"We'll wait, thanks." Jake turned to Josie. "Too bad your dad's not able to come. I managed to get a couple of bottles of that Oregon Pinot Noir he likes so much."

"I'm sure it'll keep," she said.

The table was set with nine places. "I would've liked to have my brother here to give me moral support," Jake said, referring to Butch, Stephanie's boyfriend. "But he's still on night shift." Butch Greenblatt was a police officer.

"Here they are now," Josie said, and the three of us leapt to our feet.

The hostess led the new arrivals to our table. Gloria marched in front, tapping the floor with her cane as she walked. Aunt Ellen was a few steps behind her, followed by Florence and Mirabelle walking together. Mary Anna scurried along behind. It really did look like a royal procession. Gloria had changed into a knee-length pink dress that was all sparkles and sequins. The rope of pearls draped around her neck matched the earrings in her ears.

"Let me look at you," she ordered Jake. She studied him, head to toe. He changed color several times. Then she gripped him by both arms and stared into his face. He threw a panicked look at Josie. He'd dressed for the occasion in blue trousers, white shirt, and a blue tie. He'd shaved closely and combed his hair, and he smelled of shampoo and good soap.

"You'll do," Gloria said. She turned to Josie. "I can always tell an honest man when I look him in the eye. This one is honest. Not bad-looking either. I want you to know that I'm expecting great-grandchildren before much longer. I'm not getting any younger."

Jake changed color once again. Josie's eyes widened. Gloria settled herself in a chair facing the windows while Aunt Ellen introduced the others to Jake. Formalities over, the new arrivals fanned out to find their own seats. Josie and Jake sat together, with me opposite Josie. Mirabelle shoved Mary Anna out of the way to snag the seat next to Jake. She gave him a huge smile. "Welcome to the family, honey. I'm Mirabelle and I'm soooo glad we're going to be cousins."

Jake smiled back at her. "Nice to meet you, Cousin Mirabelle."

"Kissing cousins, perhaps?" She threw back her head and laughed. Jake's gaze slid to her ample cleavage, barely contained by her tight red dress.

Josie noticed. Her smile stiffened.

Aunt Ellen politely asked Florence for news of her family.

A waiter passed out menus while another put the bread

basket on the table along with little bottles of olive oil and balsamic vinegar.

"Is that bread gluten-free?" Gloria asked the waiter.

"Sorry, no," he said. "I can bring you some gluten-free crackers if you want."

"Yes, please."

"Thanks for thinking of me, Aunt Gloria," Mirabelle said. "I'm feeling so much better since I've started eating gluten-free."

"I didn't . . ." Gloria began.

But Mirabelle had turned to Jake and gave him a big smile. "Josie tells us you own this marvelous place. Aren't you the lucky one?"

"No luck about it, Cousin Mirabelle," Josie said. "Jake worked in New York City for years, making his way up the food chain in the brutal restaurant world. That, and years of hard saving, allowed him to come back to Nags Head and open this place over the summer."

"I've always said a good man makes his own luck," Gloria said.

"Wouldn't you agree with Great-Aunt Gloria, Jake honey?" Mirabelle said.

"I sure would," he replied.

"I hope you have an excellent chef."

"I'm the head chef. And my staff is excellent."

"Oh, my goodness." Mirabelle clutched the approximate vicinity of her heart. "I have always simply *adored* a man who could cook. Neither of my husbands could boil water. Now that I'm free again, I've told everyone that before I marry again,

I'm going to test out his skill in the kitchen. Didn't I say that, Aunt Gloria?"

"You might have," Gloria said dryly. "Right after you check out his bank account."

Mirabelle's laugh was slightly strained. Josie grinned. She wiggled her chair closer to Jake's. Aunt Ellen buried her head in her menu while the waiter brought a basket of crackers and then prepared to take orders.

"I'll have a Jack Daniels. Straight. No rocks." Gloria helped herself to a cracker.

"Certainly, madam," the waiter said.

Drinks were served and the menu discussed. Mirabelle said, gazing into Jake's eyes, that she'd have whatever he, the head chef, recommended.

He gave her a warm smile and suggested the sea scallops.

Josie tore a hunk off the bread and stuffed it into her mouth.

"One of Josie's friends wants us bridesmaids to wear black," Mirabelle told Jake as she nibbled daintily on a cracker. "Isn't that just the silliest thing you've ever heard? Black at a wedding."

"Doesn't seem appropriate," he said.

It was my turn to reach for the bread basket.

"Oh, I'm sorry, Lucy honey," Mirabelle said. "Was that your suggestion? That might be how you do things in New York, but in the South . . ."

"I'm from Boston," I said.

"Aren't they the same?" She took a hearty slug of her wine. Jake laughed.

Support came from an unexpected quarter. "Black can be highly elegant," Florence said. "Particularly in winter. The purple flowers we've chosen for the bridesmaids' bouquets will be stunning against a black background."

"I don't . . ." I began.

"The flowers you've chosen!" Josie's voice rose. "I don't remember authorizing any flowers. My colors are not purple. I hate purple."

Florence threw a panicked look at Mirabelle. "I thought you said . . ."

"Don't you worry about it, Josie honey," Mirabelle said. "That's what professionals like us are for. You'll be impressed when you see how beautifully it all comes together."

"Professionals?" Jake said.

"Aunt Gloria has hired Florence and I . . ."

"Florence and me," I, always the librarian and grammar nerd, muttered under my breath.

"What's that, Lucy honey?" Mirabelle asked.

"Nothing." I took a slug of my own wine. *Where is that food?* The faster we could eat, the sooner we could get the heck out of here.

"As I was saying, before I was interrupted, Aunt Gloria has hired Florence and I to plan your wedding. I know it's awful last minute to put a wedding together, but we regard it as a challenge."

Jake said, "Uh, okay."

"I'll be wanting your mother's phone number. We need to coordinate what the mothers are wearing."

"Sure," Jake said. "I guess that'll be all right."

"It will not be all right," Josie said. "Mom, do you have anything to say? If you don't, I do."

Ellen straightened in her chair. She took a deep breath. "I think this has gone far enough. Amos and I thank you for your help, Gloria, but my daughter and I have her wedding well in hand. Lucy and her friends are full of marvelous ideas."

So there!

Mary Anna excused herself and headed for the restroom at a rapid trot. Gloria's face stiffened. Florence and Mirabelle exchanged glances. Jake looked confused.

"We'd love to get suggestions from you, Gloria," I said quickly. "We have no idea what to do about the favors. I'm sure you've been to plenty of marvelous weddings over the years and have seen some nice, not-overly-expensive gifts."

Gloria's face relaxed. "I will admit, I have some ideas."

"Excellent. Perhaps we can have lunch one day and talk things over."

"That would be lovely, Laura." Gloria lifted her drink. The candle on the table threw sparks from the huge diamond on her left hand and danced through the golden liquid in her glass. "Very well, Ellen. I was prepared to pay Florence and Mirabelle's fee as a gift to the happy couple, but if you insist."

"I do," Ellen said.

Josie winked at me and leaned back in her chair.

"But we need this job," Florence protested. "I've taken time off work to be here. You said . . ."

"There are other things you can do," Gloria said. "You and Mirabelle can organize the reception—for a reduced fee, of course, as you won't be planning the ceremony."

40

Florence's mouth opened and closed, but no sound came out.

"I understand the reception will be held here." Gloria glanced around her. "It seems big enough. I trust you are planning to move some of the tables out of the way to make a dance floor. Can't have a wedding without dancing."

"I've arranged for a live band," Jake said. "Friends of Josie and mine."

"Nothing modern, I hope."

"Fifties and sixties dance music, mostly."

"That should do."

"I'm so glad you approve." Josie grabbed another piece of bread and began tearing it into crumbs.

"Mirabelle and Florence will discuss the meal with Jake," Gloria said.

"What's there to discuss?" Jake said. "Josie and I have decided on . . ."

"Ellen told me there will be canapés. Finger food and circulating waiters. At a wedding! I don't care for canapés. Might as well invite people into the kitchen to stand over the sink and knock back a few beers. This is a restaurant. You are a chef. We will have a proper sit-down meal."

"I can't put on a full dinner," Jake said. "Most of my permanent staff are also my friends and are going to be our guests. Never mind the cost. Josie and I want . . ."

"You will rise, I am sure, to the occasion. Mirabelle and Florence, work with Jake to revise the menu. Three courses, minimum. Although I do like a proper salad course."

"I'd love to." Mirabelle lifted her glass and stared across it into Jake's eyes. "Here's to working together."

For once, Jake did not return her smile.

Josie stuffed more bread into her mouth.

"We're not having a sit-down dinner," Jake said. "I can't manage it. Not here."

"Aunt Gloria," Florence said. "It never works if the wedding planners have different ideas from the clients. The job of an event planner is to give the customers what they want."

"Is it indeed? Well, Florence, as I am the paying customer here, you will give me what I want."

"But . . ."

"Otherwise, I'm sure Mirabelle can manage fine without you. We can always rearrange your flight booking back to New Orleans. At your expense, of course."

Florence mumbled something and dipped her head. Mirabelle smirked. "You will be *soooo* impressed at what we can do," she said to Jake.

"I . . ." he said.

"Shrimp and grits?" asked the waiter.

I raised my hand and he put the plate in front of me.

"We will discuss this later, Gloria," Aunt Ellen said.

"I'm sure we will, dear," the matriarch replied.

Chapter Four

Dinner was not an enjoyable affair. The food was as excellent as always—Jake's makes the best shrimp and grits on the Outer Banks, and that's saying a lot—but I had no appetite. I wasn't the only one. Aunt Ellen barely touched her flounder, and Josie consumed her steak with such sharp, angry bites she clearly wasn't tasting it at all. Florence nibbled on her crab ravioli and avoided everyone's eyes. Mary Anna asked Ellen if Amos was talking about retirement, which allowed my aunt to take a breath and begin discussing their plans. Only Gloria and Mirabelle seemed to be enjoying themselves. Gloria downed several Jack Daniels and pushed lettuce leaves around on her plate, while Mirabelle reduced her mussels to empty shells and flirted with Jake.

Wedding talk over, Jake also seemed to be enjoying the evening. Or the attentions of Cousin Mirabelle at least. He laughed at her jokes, accepted her compliments on the food, and flirted right back.

Josie seethed. I tried to give her an encouraging smile, but she ignored me.

At last the hideous evening approached its end. Coffee and dessert orders were taken. Mirabelle asked for the key lime ice cream, Gloria requested a brandy, and Jake had a coffee.

"The cake!" Mirabelle stabbed her spoon into her ice cream. "I can't believe we've forgotten about the cake. Such an important part of a wedding, isn't it, Flo?"

"It is," Florence said. "Josie, have you ordered your cake yet?"

"Yes, we're—"

"I hope you haven't paid for it," Mirabelle interrupted. "I . . . I mean we . . . can come up with something better. Right, Aunt Gloria?"

"Whatever it costs," Gloria said.

Josie straightened in her chair. She folded her linen napkin neatly and placed it on the table beside her. Her mother and I braced ourselves.

"I am," she said in clipped tones, "making my wedding cake myself."

Mirabelle laughed.

Florence said, "Isn't that maybe taking on too much?"

"I am a professional baker," Josie said. "I've changed my mind, Lucy. I'll be making my cake because I know exactly what I want."

"That's okay then," Florence said softly.

Gloria glared at her.

"I guess," Florence added.

"We're going to have a cupcake tower," Josie said.

"Cupcakes are sooooo passé," Mirabelle said. "That would be okay if you had a retro theme, but you don't. Do you? I hope you aren't thinking of that. It can turn out so tacky. As for the cake, I'm thinking four layers of chocolate with a pistachio cream filling. A beach theme for decorations maybe, sand and water colors. Sea green will be a nice match to the pistachios."

Josie pushed her chair back. "I am having a cupcake tower for my wedding cake and I am making it myself. I am buying my wedding dress in Nags Head and I am not, I repeat not, having purple flowers. Do. You. Understand. Me?"

"No need to get upset, dear," Gloria said. "We only want what's best for you."

"Upset! You and your pack of interfering cousins are ruining my wedding. I'll get upset if I want!"

Josie's voice was rising. Heads of our fellow diners were turning, and the staff stopped what they were doing to stare.

Jake stood up and reached for her hand. "Calm down, babe."

She snatched her hand away. "Calm down! Calm down!"

I'd never seen Josie—practical, down-to-earth Josie—like this. I started to rise, but Aunt Ellen caught my eye. She gave her head a shake and I sank back down.

"Cousin Mirabelle is only trying to be helpful," Gloria said.

"Cousin Mirabelle is trying to steal my fiancé out from under my nose. And he doesn't seem to mind one little bit. You can have your beach-themed cakes and sit-down dinners and purple flowers, but without me. The wedding is off!"

Josie burst into tears and ran out of the dining room. Diners and waiters watched her go. Jake stood frozen in place. I looked at Aunt Ellen. "Leave her be," she mouthed to me.

"I didn't . . ." Jake shook his head. He glanced around the table. "I didn't . . ." He ran after Josie.

Mirabelle giggled. "Don't worry about a thing, Aunt Ellen. Every woman turns into a bridezilla as the big day approaches."

"Bridezilla!" I said. "If there's anyone less like a bridezilla than Josie . . ."

"She'll come around. We only want the best for her wedding, don't we, Aunt Gloria?"

"Of course," the matriarch said.

"You might be taking it too far this time, Mirabelle," Florence said. "It is Josie's wedding. Let her have what she wants. I think . . ."

"I don't much care what you think," Mirabelle snapped. "I'll remind you whose money's keeping your little business afloat. You agreed that we need to make a splash here . . ."

"Enough," Aunt Ellen said. "Until further notice, all talk of wedding plans is canceled."

"I agree with Ellen," Mary Anna said. "I know you mean well, Mama, but Josie knows what she wants."

Gloria bristled. "Weddings are tradition. They are family. They are history. I will see my only granddaughter married in a manner that suits the proud traditions of the O'Malley name."

"Then maybe it should be held on a shrimp boat," Aunt Ellen said. "And we can all wear waders and haul nets."

Gloria's eyes blazed enough fire to match her diamond rings. Mary Anna's eyes opened in shock. Florence laughed.

"Weddings at sea can be great," Mirabelle said. "Definitely great for photographs. But not in February. Are you thinking of delaying the wedding until summer, Aunt Ellen? That would give us time to plan something really great."

Ellen stood up. "Good night, everyone. Gloria, we're leaving."

"That might be an idea," I said. "Mirabelle, why don't you look into that? You could check out the cost of yacht rentals to begin, and start thinking of a wedding dress to match being out at sea. And the food, of course. Fish, shrimp, Outer Banks clam chowder to start."

Mirabelle gave me a huge grin. "Thanks, Lucy. I'm glad you've come around and you're on my side."

Ellen raised one eyebrow at me.

Gloria gripped her cane and rose to her feet in one smooth wave. "I knew we'd all come to an agreement. Yes, a summer wedding will be much nicer. Now, we can be on our way. Excellent dinner. I assume Jake is picking up the check."

She tapped her way across the dining room floor.

"What are you talking about?" Aunt Ellen whispered to me. "We're not having a summer wedding, never mind any other part of that plan."

"Read *The Busman's Honeymoon*," I said, "and all will be revealed."

Jake came back inside. He met Gloria and the others on their way out. His smile was stiff as they exchanged good-nights and brushed cheeks. He stepped out of range when Cousin Mirabelle tried to envelope him in an embrace.

"Call Josie in the morning," Aunt Ellen said to me. "Give her some space tonight. Looks like she got away without making up with Jake."

"Which reminds me," I said. "I need a ride home."

Chapter Five

L ast night, prior to storming out of the restaurant, Josie had declared that she was not going dress shopping with her relatives today. I didn't know if her resolve would last. Mary Anna, Florence, and Mirabelle were staying at the Ocean Side Hotel, but Gloria was at Ellen and Amos's, which gave the family matriarch abundant opportunity to work her will on Ellen and through Ellen on Josie.

Cell phone reception inside the thick stone walls of the lighthouse varies from difficult to impossible, so I have a landline in my apartment. This morning I thought a short text message would be more suitable than a phone call, so I composed my message, pressed send, climbed onto the window bench, cranked open the room's single window, leaned as far between the iron bars as I could get, and stuck my arms out. ARE WE GOING TO RALEIGH?

The message must have gotten through, as the answer was immediate. No!!!!!!!

Now I was faced with a day off and nothing to do. I could

call Ronald and ask to swap again, but he'd rearranged some things on his schedule, so that wouldn't be fair.

Not that having a day with nothing in particular to do was a bad thing.

I put the coffee pot on, got eggs and bread out of the fridge, and made myself a lovely, leisurely breakfast, which I enjoyed while reading the news online. Charles, however, did not have a day off, and so I opened the door and shooed him out.

The phone rang as I was washing up my few dishes.

"Morning, Lucy," said Connor McNeil. "I called the library, and they told me you're having the day off."

"I switched with Ronald so I could do some wedding things with Josie, but something came up and she canceled."

"Does that mean you're free? All day?"

"All day."

"I had an early-morning budget meeting with the police chief, and that never leaves me in a good mood. This afternoon, I have to put a shift in at my practice." Connor was Dr. McNeil, a dentist. While he was serving as mayor, he kept his dental office open part-time so he could still see some of his longtime regular patients and keep his skills up-to-date. "Are you free for lunch?"

"That would be nice."

"Do you want formal or casual?"

"Let's go to Josie's. I need to check on her."

"Why?"

"I'll tell you when I see you. I'll drive myself into town, as I have some errands to do later."

"One o'clock?"

"Perfect."

We hung up. I realized I was smiling. Simply talking to Connor had that effect on me.

*　*　*

I arrived at Josie's Cozy Bakery first and waited on the sidewalk for Connor. He was a couple of minutes late and apologized profusely. A citizen had phoned with a complaint as he was leaving the office and said citizen would not be mollified.

Unlike in the height of summer, today no lunchtime lineup stretched across the bakery floor, out the door, and down the sidewalk.

"You grab a seat," Connor said. "And I'll place the order. What would you like?"

"A sandwich, please. Anything on a baguette." Josie makes what are probably the best baguettes in North Carolina. "And a latte." I found a seat at a table made out of a reclaimed whiskey barrel in a corner. Josie's place was hip urban coffee culture meets traditional Outer Banks. Gleaming steel and chrome at the counter, white subway tiles on the wall behind, hissing espresso machine and glass-fronted display case. The walls of the dining area were whitewashed, accented with paintings of lighthouses and storm-tossed ships; the tables were made of scarred pine or weather-worn barrels, the chairs upholstered blue and white. Everything smelled of warm spices, melting butter, and bread and pastries hot from the oven. I loved this place.

Connor brought our drinks to the table and sat down. Josie came out of the back, wiping her hands on her apron with the

Cozy Bakery logo of a croissant curled around a lighthouse. "Thought I heard your voice, Mr. Mayor," she said, bending into a hug.

"Everything okay?" I asked her.

She tucked a lock of hair into her hairnet. Only Josie could look beautiful in a floury apron and hairnet. "I was worried about how the business would do over the winter, but it's all been good. We've been steady all month."

"You know that's not what I mean," I said.

Connor looked between us.

Josie dropped into a vacant chair with a sigh. "Yeah, I know what you mean. All's good. The wedding's back on."

"That was in doubt?" Connor said.

"No," I said.

"Yes," Josie said. "But not really. Jake and I still want to get married, but my grandmother has arrived and is . . ."

"Full of helpful suggestions," I added.

"To put it mildly," Josie said. "I called Jake last night as soon as I got home, and we talked it out. I apologized for storming out, and he said he understood. He also said he was only trying to be friendly to Mirabelle, but he understands that she might not have taken it that way."

"Who's Mirabelle?" Connor asked.

"Jake and I decided it's important to keep peace in the family, and that means giving Grandma Gloria some of what she wants. As for the morning suit . . ."

"Jake's going to wear a morning suit?" Connor said. "Does that mean I have to wear one too? I don't have such a thing. Not a lot of call for morning suits in Nags Head."

"Fear not, Connor," Josie said. "Jake put his foot down at that. We've agreed to give in on one point and have a sit-down dinner at the restaurant. That means hiring a catering company, because we can't expect our wedding guests who are employees of the restaurant to serve, and I won't have Jake slaving away in the kitchen. Jake hates to do that in his own place, but if it will get Grandma Gloria off our backs . . . I mean, make her happy, so be it."

"What about Mirabelle and Florence?" I said.

"Who's Mirabelle?" Connor asked again. "And who's Florence?"

"They'll have to stay out of it. I can live with purple flowers, if I must, but I don't want their sticky fingers in anything else."

"Florence seems sensible to me," I said. "She pointed out that you can't have the planners arranging something the client doesn't want."

"Florence may be sensible, but Mirabelle isn't. I suspect Mirabelle has her own agenda, and it isn't giving me the wedding of my dreams."

"Who's Mirabelle?" Connor said.

"What sort of agenda?" I asked.

"I don't know. And I don't intend to find out." Josie pushed herself to her feet. "I have to get back at it. I might agree not to make my wedding cake—I only said that in anger—but I intend to supply the desserts for the shower on Sunday."

"I sort of agree with your grandma on that, Josie," I said. "The party's to celebrate you. It's not intended to make more work."

She gave me a grin. "I'd been about to step down from that

and ask you to arrange something with the other bakery, but if I'm not doing my cake, I am doing my shower."

"Don't forget to make some gluten-free things."

"Why would I do that? I know Mom's friends, and they'll eat anything I bake."

"Last night at the restaurant, Gloria asked for crackers rather than bread, and Mirabelle said she was on a gluten-free diet. Didn't you hear?"

Josie let out a puff of air. "Guess I missed that. Probably on purpose. I'm not doing anything special for her."

"It wouldn't hurt to make nice, Josie. You make gluten-free treats all the time."

"Might as well cut up some slices of cardboard and put frosting on them," Connor said. "Gluten-free equals flavor-free."

Josie smiled at him. "Not if I make them."

"If you don't want to, I suppose I could," I said, dragging the words out. "Although I don't have much of a kitchen. Or any equipment. Can I borrow some baking pans?"

"Oh, all right. You win. I'll play nicely and make a plate just for Mirabelle."

"I understand," I said. "About your dress . . ."

"I can't talk about that now, Lucy. Mom won't be able to keep it secret from Grandma that we're going shopping, and Grandma will tell Mirabelle, and . . ."

"Is someone going to tell me who Mirabelle is?" Connor said.

". . . and then Mirabelle and Florence will be all over it. We'll go shopping for the dress when they've gone home. Mom said she's hoping they'll leave on Monday, after the shower."

"You're leaving it pretty late."

"If I have to buy something at the consignment shop, so be it. I won't have Mirabelle . . ."

Connor slapped the table. Then he lifted his hands and made the time-out gesture used in football games. "Why do I feel as though I've suddenly become the invisible man here?"

"Because." I scooped foamy milk off my latte. "When it comes to wedding planning, men are always invisible. Mirabelle is a second cousin, and Florence is Josie's first cousin once removed. Or is it the other way around?"

"I can never sort those things out," Josie said. "You can bet Grandma knows everyone's relationship back to fourth cousins seven times removed."

"Or seventh cousins four times removed," I said. "Anyway, regardless of the relationship, Florence seems nice enough, and well meaning, but Mirabelle . . ."

Josie cut me off. "Mirabelle is a menace. If I'm really lucky, someone will bump her off before she can do any more damage to my wedding and to my relationship with my fiancé. I might even take care of that myself."

"Here you go." The waiter dropped our sandwiches onto the table. "Sorry about the delay. We're, uh"—he glanced at Josie—"kinda backed up." He scurried away.

"Is he new?" I asked. "I don't think I've seen him before."

"That's Blair and he's new, yes. And not working out so well. If he can't deliver a sandwich on time in January, I can't imagine how he'll cope in July. He might have to go before that."

Josie kept her voice down, but Blair must have good ears.

He glanced over his shoulder with a look that wasn't friendly before disappearing into the kitchen.

Josie pushed herself to her feet. "I've got to get back. Talk to you soon." She walked away.

"Just as well I'm the invisible man," Connor said, biting into his sandwich. "I don't think I want to know what all that was about."

"Trust me," I said. "You do not."

* * *

It rained heavily that night. The window of my apartment is set into four-foot-thick stone walls, but all night I could hear thunder crashing overhead and rain pounding on the panes of glass.

Whenever I stirred, I could feel Charles's soft warm body pushed closely up against mine. I'm not afraid of storms, but that night it was nice to know the big cat was near.

I woke to sunlight peeking around the edges of the drapes and Charles digging his claws into my blankets.

"Good morning to you," I said with a yawn. He yawned in return, and I threw the covers off. "Not too frightened, were you?"

He lifted his little chin and leapt off the bed.

"Yes, you were," I said to his retreating tail. "But you're too proud to admit it. Never mind, I won't tell."

First order of business for the day, as every day, I fed the cat. That done, I put the coffee on and jumped into the shower while it brewed. I tried to settle my curls into some sort of order, put on a swipe of blush and lipstick, and got dressed. I had my coffee with a bowl of yogurt and muesli while I checked my email. Replies to the shower invitations were coming in, all of them accepting with pleasure.

I've been living in the Outer Banks only a few months. I'm from Boston, but my mom is an OBX native. She fled for the big city the moment she was old enough, but she brought her kids here for vacation every summer of my childhood, and I grew up close to Aunt Ellen, Uncle Amos, and their three children. Years later, I enjoyed working in the libraries at Harvard very much, but when my long-long-longtime boyfriend finally proposed (egged on by our mothers, not through any desire for commitment on his part), I bolted. I left him, quit my job, loaded all my possessions into my teal Toyota Yaris, and drove to the Outer Banks to throw myself into the loving arms of Aunt Ellen. In a bit of marvelous serendipity, Ellen's good friend Albertina James (whom everyone called Bertie), director of the Bodie Island Lighthouse Library, had been looking for a new assistant librarian. I was lucky enough to get the job, and here I am today.

And very happy to be so.

I studied the guest list for the shower Aunt Ellen had given me. I recognized almost all the names. In Boston, my life was divided into compartments: friends of the family or people from my parents' country club, my sisters-in-law's acquaintances, people from work, girlfriends from college. Few of those people knew each other. Here, as is probably the case in most small communities, the compartments break down and lines of connection tangle all over each other. Most of Aunt Ellen's friends were library volunteers or members of my book club; the mayor played pickup basketball with the groom as well as being my boyfriend; one of my best friends was in a relationship with the groom's brother; clients of Bertie's yoga studio were friends of Ellen's.

And then we had Gloria, Mary Anna, and Florence. And, of course, Mirabelle. I hoped they wouldn't feel too much out of place at Sunday's shower.

I closed the computer. "Time to go," I called to Charles. I opened the door and he dashed out. Charles loves to go to work. I locked the door behind us and took the one hundred stairs that make up my daily commute.

As usual, I was the first to arrive. I switched lights on, powered up the computers, and went to the break room to start the coffee. As I was grinding the beans, Charles strolled in, leaving a trail of muddy paw prints in his wake.

"What have you been into?" I asked.

He didn't answer. I switched the coffee maker on and pulled the mop out of the broom closet. I went out of the break room, down the hall, and into the library proper, wiping the floor as I passed. The wet prints ended beneath the wall in the alcove where we feature seasonal or special displays. I looked at the enormous puddle on the floor in considerable surprise. The pool of water seemed to be growing right before my eyes, but we were nowhere near a window. A small river was pouring down the wall. I reached out and touched it, and my fingers found a crack in the stone beneath the water. I ran for towels and laid them on the floor, but they were soon soaked through. I found a bucket in the back of the closet and set it beneath the crack. When the bucket was about a quarter full, the flow of water began to slow.

Bertie arrived to find me studying the mess. "What's happened here?"

"Looks like a crack in the wall, and a lot of water got in."

"That can't be good," Bertie said.

"No. But it seems to be stopping."

"We should probably have it looked at. Can you call George Grimshaw, Lucy, and ask him to come out? His company does a lot of work on old buildings."

"Sure," I said.

"It probably just needs a patch. No hurry, but we should get that done before the next rain makes it worse." Bertie went into her office. Ronald and Charlene arrived shortly after, and the three of us stood around the damp floor, staring at the crack.

"I don't like the look of that," Ronald said.

"This is an old building," Charlene said. "Bound to get a few cracks now and again."

"Old, but strong," I said.

"True," they chorused. "It'll turn out to be nothing."

"Nothing at all," I agreed. I made the call, and Mr. Grimshaw said he'd be right out to have a look.

Chapter Six

George Grimshaw was a grizzly man in his sixties, all unkempt beard, wild gray hair, bulging eyes, and sheer size. He stood about six foot five and probably weighted three hundred pounds. He came with his son, Zack, a short, skinny, clean-shaven guy who blinked myopically at me through thick glasses. I might have thought Zack was adopted except for the same intelligent hazel eyes and small cleft in the chin as his father.

I called Bertie to say they were here, and she came out of the office. Ronald and Charlene clattered down the stairs, and we, along with every one of our current patrons, stood in a circle watching as George poked the old stone with his fingers and muttered grimly. Zack made notes on an iPad while muttering equally grimly.

Charles had leapt onto the nearest shelf to watch.

Eventually George pushed himself to his feet with a massive grunt. "Outside," he said.

He marched off, followed by Zack, then Bertie, Ronald, Charlene, and all of our patrons. I came last, after firmly shutting the door on Charles. We formed another circle on the lawn next to the wall on the opposite side of the alcove. We could see a large crack running through the stone and disappearing into the earth. George pointed, and Zack handed his father his iPad before dropping to his knees. He pulled a trowel out of his pocket and scraped at the dirt. He dug down about a foot and then leaned back against his heels. As one, the onlookers leaned forward. I had no idea what I was looking at, but it looked okay to me: blocks of stone disappearing into the good North Carolina earth.

Zack stood up. He looked at his father. They shook their heads in unison, the movements identical.

"What!" Bertie said.

"Probably been like this for a while," George said. "Rain came from the northeast last night, which it don't usually do, and got deep enough into the walls so's you noticed it."

"What does that mean?" Bertie asked.

Another jerk of the head and the little expedition trooped back inside.

"Let's go through to my office," Bertie said. "And you can tell me what needs to be done. I'd like to get it fixed before the start of tourist season, if it's going to be a big job."

She led the way down the hallway, followed by George scratching his head, Zack making notes on his iPad, and Charles, determined not to be shut out this time.

The patrons drifted back to what they'd been doing.

"Big job," Ronald said. "I don't like the sound of that."

"Don't worry," Charlene said. "We have money in the contingency fund. Almost five thousand dollars."

Ronald and I nodded. "That'll cover it," I said. "Whatever it is."

My colleagues went back upstairs—Ronald to the children's library on the second floor to prepare for the afternoon preschool story time, Charlene to the research room on the third floor. I sat behind the circulation desk and checked out a stack of books for Mrs. Bradshaw. "I'm so looking forward to the shower on Sunday, Lucy," she said. "Your invitation didn't say anything about gifts. Does Josie have a wedding registry?"

"They don't need much," I said. "If people are so inclined, they can give money toward their businesses."

"I never like giving money. Seems crass somehow."

"I'm sure they'll appreciate anything you'd like to bring to the shower. But remember, it's just a simple party for Ellen's friends."

Her eyes twinkled. "Then I'd better get my thinking cap on." She picked up her books. "See you on Sunday, Lucy."

George and Zack walked past. George gave me a nod, but Zack continued typing. Bertie stood in the hallway, her face frighteningly pale.

"What's the matter?" I said. "Is it going to be expensive?"

Bertie blinked. "George won't know the final sum until he's done a thorough inspection, but he said that crack goes right into the foundation and spreads out from there. Five thousand."

I let out a breath. "Five thousand dollars. We have that much in the contingency fund, right?"

"Five thousand is the cost for the initial estimate, Lucy. He says the job, if it's what he thinks it is, might run in the hundred thousand range."

"Oh my gosh! We don't have that kind of money. Does it have to be done? Maybe we can put it off for a few years."

"George says if the work isn't done immediately, the entire building will be in danger of collapsing. Taking us, your apartment, our library, and everything in it with it."

Charles hissed.

* * *

Bertie went back to her office, saying she had to call an emergency meeting of the library board.

Charles jumped onto the circulation desk. His amber eyes studied my face.

"No library," I said.

Charles shook his head.

"It won't come to that. George is exaggerating for effect, I'm sure. Besides, we're valuable to the town. We attract a lot of tourists. The town will give us what we need."

Charles nodded. I scratched the top of his head, and he rubbed his face against my arm.

No sense in worrying about things I could do nothing about, so I went back to work. Charles headed for the break room to see if food had magically appeared in his bowl.

A few minutes before noon, the door flew open and Mirabelle came in. She wore ankle-length skinny jeans, high heels, a T-shirt with a plunging neckline and a picture of the Eiffel Tower under a denim jacket. Her hair was sprayed within an inch of its life and her makeup freshly plastered on. Uninvited, she bent over the desk and gave me an air kiss, enveloping me in the overpowering scent of hair spray and perfume.

"Good morning," I said, trying not to breathe too deeply. "What brings you here today?" I checked behind her. No sign of anyone else.

She dropped a pile of magazines onto the desk. "I've been thinking over your idea, Lucy, and I love, love, love it. I thought we'd have a little chat on your lunch hour and go over some of my ideas. I brought a few magazines and found some good web pages to get us started."

The magazine on the top was called *Weddings on Water*. The cover picture was of an enormous yacht draped with pink roses and white tulle. Rows of chairs covered in white cloth were laid out on the deck. I flicked through the pile. All wedding magazines, and the cover stories all had something to do with ceremonies and receptions on boats or beaches.

"Isn't this absolutely darling." Mirabelle shoved her iPad under my nose. The screen showed a wooden boat deck strewn with rose petals. Candles mounted on the gunwales threw a soft light, and the background was an empty beach lined with palm trees at dusk.

"That looks expensive," I said.

"Amos is a lawyer, right?" Mirabelle said. "With his own law firm. He's sure to have pots of money. With enough planning, not to mention cash, we can do something that'll be the talk of the east coast for months."

I was about to argue that Amos, never mind Ellen, didn't appear to be involved in this discussion, but remembered that the wedding at sea had been my idea. My idea for getting

Mirabelle out of Josie's plans. As Lord Peter Wimsey would do. "I'd love to go over the ideas with you, Mirabelle, and toss around some suggestions, but I'm working now."

"Don't you get a lunch break?"

"Uh, no. I . . ."

Ronald clattered down the stairs. "You can go now, Lucy, I'll take the desk."

I smiled weakly at Mirabelle.

She picked up her magazines. "Where shall we go?"

"Might as well use my apartment. I can make us a sandwich."

"Do you have gluten-free bread?"

"'fraid not."

"Then I can't eat it. I have to be very careful, Lucy. I feel so much healthier since I started eating gluten-free."

"When was that?" Ronald said. "Nan's been thinking of trying it. She's heard good things."

"One week." Mirabelle put her hand on her hip and threw him a pout. "I've already lost three pounds. Don't you think it looks good on me?"

Ronald blushed to the roots of his hair.

Chapter Seven

"Enthusiasm seems to be growing for that proposed crime writing conference in the summer," Bertie said to me Thursday morning.

"That would be fun. Are we going to get involved? I hope so."

"Possibly. I've invited some of the people on the organizing committee for a casual lunch so they can talk over their plans and what they want from us. Can you go into town for me, please, and pick up some sandwiches?"

"Happy to."

"That's if we still have a library in the summer," Bertie sighed. "I'd just as soon not do any long-range planning right now, not while we're waiting to hear from George about the work, but I scheduled this lunch a couple of weeks ago. How's the wedding planning going?"

"It's . . . uh . . . going okay," I said.

"Glad to hear something's going okay." As proof of how distracted she was over the condition of the library building, Bertie didn't notice the hesitation in my voice or read the doubt on my face. She handed me the library credit card and slipped behind the circulation desk. Charles, who always seems to know when someone he loves needs comfort, jumped into her lap.

As I headed into town on my errand, I tried not to think about the fact that Bertie seemed unusually despondent about the fate of the library if George wasn't able to fix the building at a price we could afford. I was trying so hard not to think about that, I ended up thinking about Mirabelle and her "wedding" plans. My idea for distracting her seemed to be succeeding. Yesterday, I'd made a quick couple of salads and we'd eaten lunch in my apartment while we looked over her magazines and she made copious notes. If I felt a touch of guilt at deliberately making her waste her time, it was soon dispelled when I realized the extent of her ambitions. A yacht would be rented and fully decorated and we'd sail out to sea for the ceremony, followed by a champagne toast and canapés served by circulating waiters. I was about to close up the magazines and say that all sounded good to me when Mirabelle said, "And then . . ." *And then* came the reception, a sit-down dinner for two hundred people, at the yacht club.

"I really think you need to talk to Josie and Uncle Amos and Aunt Ellen about this," I said. "Before we go any further. They might not want to spend this much."

"It's their only daughter's first wedding; of course they want the best for her."

"It's going to be Josie's only wedding," I said.

She laughed. "That's what they all say, honey. I'm thinking

dark blue for the bridesmaids' dresses. That'll look best in the photos with the background of the sea and setting sun."

"The sun doesn't set over the sea in North Carolina. It rises."

"We can move the boat to get the best shots." She made a note on her phone. "I'll talk to my contacts."

"What contacts?"

Mirabelle continued typing. "At the magazine. I met a style editor from *Weddings on Water* at a bridal show last month. She'll know what she wants."

"Why do we care what someone at a magazine wants?"

"Oh, didn't I say?" Her laughter was tinged with embarrassment.

"No, you didn't say. Why do you care what someone at a magazine thinks? I don't. Josie doesn't. You remember Josie, don't you? The bride?"

"Of course I remember Josie, silly. She's so beautiful, lucky thing, that in the right dress and accessories we might even make the cover. Doesn't hurt that Jake's totally hot."

"Oh, right. They have the look of models, but their wedding will be real."

She beamed at me. "Exactly! I'm so glad we're on the same page, Lucy." She leaned closer and lowered her voice. "Just between you and me, Florence is having a terrible time with her little wedding-planning company, which is why she needs my help. She doesn't get it about advertising and marketing. Success is its own advertisement, right? If we get a spread in *Weddings on Water*, we'll be turning customers away. Do you think Jake should wear a business suit, or maybe something more nautical?"

"How about a bathing suit? As though he's about to dive off the boat into the sea?"

For a moment Mirabelle actually looked as though she was taking my suggestion seriously. Then she shook her head. "No. That might imply he's having cold feet. Not a good idea."

I mumbled.

"We'll allow Josie's mother to have her little shower on Sunday because the invitations have already gone out."

"That's kind of you." But I didn't think she even heard me.

"We'll have the *real* shower later." She made another note. "I'll check into availably at the yacht club. We can have the food served on platters decorated to look like boats and hang those colored flags that supposedly mean something to sailors around the room. If it's a nice day, perhaps we can use an outdoor space. Everyone can dress in their best sailing outfits. Won't that be fun?"

"An absolute riot," I said, as all my misgivings about deceiving Mirabelle fled. She wanted to use Josie's wedding, and thus Amos and Ellen's money, for nothing but her own ends.

I texted Ellen and Josie after Mirabelle left: SUMMER WEDDING AT SEA PLANS ARE UNDERWAY. PLAY ALONG.

Josie replied with a line of kisses and hugs.

Aunt Ellen had simply said, THANKS.

I arrived at the bakery and turned my thoughts back to my errand. When it was my turn at the counter, Alison said, "I'll let Josie know you're here."

"Don't bother her if she's busy."

"You're not here to have lunch with her?"

"No. I need to pick up some things to take back for a meeting."

"Oh, sorry. Josie's grandmother's coming in, and I thought you were joining them. We've been told to be on our very best behavior when she's here."

I smiled. "As if you aren't all the time."

At that moment, a loud crash came from the kitchen. Something hard hit the floor, and crockery and glassware smashed. A man swore, loudly. Josie yelled, "Can't you watch where you're going?"

"Chill, will you," the man said. "Accidents happen."

"No, Blair, accidents do not happen in my kitchen," Josie said.

Alison gave me a weak grin.

"New employee not working out so well?" I asked.

"Josie has one nerve left and he's getting on it. He tries, and drops things or gets in everyone's way, so then he doesn't try and he drops things and gets in everyone's way."

"Go and help Alison outside," Josie's voice said. "I'll clean this up."

Blair walked out of the kitchen. "Is she always so bad-tempered?" he said to Alison.

"I don't think you should be saying that in front of the customers," she said.

He shrugged and looked at me. "What can I getcha?"

I asked for six sandwiches in a variety of breads and fillings and a selection of cookies. Alison rang up the bill and I paid before stepping aside to wait for my order.

The front door opened and Aunt Ellen and Gloria came in. My aunt's face was tense as she helped her mother-in-law. When Ellen looked across the room and saw me heading toward them, she broke into a smile of pure relief.

"Hi." I gave Ellen a hug and smiled at Gloria. "How are you today, Mrs. O'Malley?"

"Not getting any younger," she said. "But my knee isn't too dreadfully bad today, so Ellen and I are going to do some shopping at the outlet mall."

"Why don't you take a seat, Gloria," Ellen said. "I'll go to the counter. What would you like?"

Gloria dropped into a chair and hooked her cane over the back of it. She studied the menu on the blackboard behind the counter. "What's good here?" she said.

"Everything," I said. "Absolutely everything."

"It's too early for lunch," she said, "but I wouldn't mind a little sweet treat with my tea."

"Your order's ready, lady," Blair called to me. Alison gave him a sharp look. "What?" he said.

"I have to go," I said. "It was lovely seeing you again, Mrs. O'Malley."

"And you too, dear."

"If you want my advice," I said. "Try the pecan squares. They are the absolute best."

I collected my bag of goodies and left the bakery. As I headed for the door, I head Gloria say, "What are the pecan squares made from, Ellen?"

Aunt Ellen said, "Don't worry about that, Gloria. Why not throw caution to the winds and live a little."

* * *

"What's this I hear about a wedding shower in the library?"

I wasn't at all surprised that Louise Jane McKaughnan knew about Josie's shower. Louise Jane, as she never fails to point out to me, is related to just about everyone descended from Nags Head's original settlers. She makes it her business to keep up-to-date on everything that's going on in town in general, and at the library in particular.

"Ellen O'Malley's having a small shower for Josie on Sunday," I said. "As Ellen's a volunteer here at the library, she's allowed to use our facilities."

"I don't know that that's such a good idea, Lucy honey."

"I don't know that that matters, Louise Jane." Louise Jane and I aren't exactly friends. Her goal in life is to see me heading back to Boston and herself getting my job. "We host plenty of events here. As I recall, you and I met at the party to introduce the Jane Austen exhibit."

"I have nothing against parties in general." She gave me that smile that always puts me in mind of a circling shark. "But this is going to be a wedding shower."

"So?"

She shook her head sadly. "You still don't understand, do you? Any sort of wedding celebration is likely to be awful upsetting to Frances."

"Oh, yes. Frances. Can't have Frances upset."

"I might have mentioned before that some might find your

71

stubborn skepticism admirable. I, however, am beginning to find it tedious in the extreme. The Lady will not take well to being reminded of her own tragic marriage."

I shouldn't have bothered to argue, but I always feel compelled to, thus falling directly into Louise Jane's carefully laid trap. "I'd think that as Frances's marriage was such a disaster, she'd wish any other new bride well."

"She'll attempt to protect Josie by putting a stop to Josie's wedding. And, as you know, the Lady sometimes doesn't realize that her attempts to help don't always leave the other party . . . uh, alive."

I snorted. Frances, also called *the Lady*, is a lighthouse ghost, if you want to look at it that way (and Louise Jane does). As far as I'm concerned, Frances is a lighthouse legend, and that is all. According to Louise Jane, the young woman came to the lighthouse in the years immediately following the Civil War in an arranged marriage to a generations-older lighthouse keeper. She subsequently threw herself from the fourth-floor window in despair. The window that just happens to be the one in my Lighthouse Aerie. Apparently.

A sad story to be sure, and like most legends, this one likely has a grain of truth behind it. But Louise Jane has embellished the tale further, claiming Frances haunts the fourth floor, wanting to help any woman she believes is trapped in the building as she once was.

Helping means throwing them out the fourth-floor window.

Louise Jane is a well-known and popular storyteller in this area. She, like her grandmother and great-grandmother before her, has collected tales and legends of the Outer Banks. This lighthouse has seen a lot of things over the years, but the Lady is Louise Jane's favorite story.

I'd never seen the slightest trace of any haunting, Frances or otherwise, in my time here. Except, I remembered, last Halloween, when . . . But I'd managed to convince myself all that (whatever *that* had been) had been the product of an overactive imagination stimulated by Halloween festivities and talk of the night on which the spirits wander and the veil between the worlds is thin.

According to Louise Jane, never to be discouraged, that I'd never seen anything only meant the ghostly residents were biding their time before revealing themselves to me.

"If Frances does show up at the shower, I'm sure she'll enjoy a pecan square," I said. "Josie's doing the desserts herself."

"I see I won't convince you. No point in trying to warn Josie either. She's even more pigheaded than you are. I'll be on high alert, to make sure nothing happens. It would seem as though my invitation got misplaced. Very careless of you, Lucy. Never mind; you can consider this a verbal acceptance. I hope we're not going to have silly games at this shower, but you'll need some sort of entertainment. I hear Josie's grandmother and other relations will be here. They'd love to hear genuine stories of the real Outer Banks, I'm sure. Bye now. See you Sunday." And, with a wiggle of her fingers and a self-satisfied smirk, she left.

Chapter Eight

T he guests were due to arrive for the bridal shower at one. Grace and Steph would be here at eleven to help me make the sandwiches and decorate the room, and Aunt Ellen would come at noon.

I enjoyed a Sunday lie-in and a leisurely morning. After making myself a treat of scrambled eggs, bacon, and toast for breakfast, I got ready for the party. Charles and I were downstairs at five to eleven to greet our friends. I'd debated tying a red ribbon around his neck, but one look at the expression on his little face as I held it up and asked him what he thought dissuaded me.

"Josie called me last night," Grace said, "asking what time we were getting here. I told her five to one."

I took the heavy box containing sandwich and canapé ingredients from her so she could bend to greet Charles.

"Naughty, naughty," Steph said. "You lied."

"Had to. This is supposed to be a party for her. She shouldn't be making sandwiches and hanging decorations. I shouldn't have bothered. When I drove past the bakery, her car was parked outside, meaning she'd gone to work."

"She's making the dessert trays," I said.

"That's our Josie," Grace said with a laugh. "She simply doesn't know how to let her friends do things for her. You're in charge; tell us what to do, Lucy."

I hadn't wanted to go too overboard with silly shower things, but we decorated the main room in pink, red, and white bunting. I cleared off the circulation desk and the public computer stations, and Grace and I covered them in ironed white tablecloths and dark-red runners while Steph hung a big welcome sign she'd made on the front door. We cleared off the magazine nook table to hold gifts and set a chair up next to it. We covered the chair in bunting and draped it in white cloth and stuck a sign on it saying, RESERVED FOR THE BRIDE.

Aunt Ellen arrived at noon with the flowers—pink and red roses and white baby's breath—and matching balloons. Then we all trooped into the staff room to make the sandwiches.

"Who's bringing Gloria?" I asked Ellen as I spread a thin layer of butter onto sliced white bread. We were working assembly-line style. I buttered the bread and passed it to Aunt Ellen, who put on the filling and passed it on to Grace, who applied the top layer of bread and sliced it, before Steph arranged the final product on a tray.

"Florence, Mary Anna, and Mirabelle are picking her up at the house and bringing her here," Ellen said.

"How's the visit going?"

My aunt groaned. "They're leaving tomorrow and I simply cannot wait. Fortunately, they're not all staying in the house; Gloria herself is more than enough to deal with. If I ask her what she wants for dinner, she says whatever I feel like making is good enough for her. As soon as I start cooking, she tells me she's on a special diet. So I put away the pasta and go back to the market for fish. Then she says she doesn't care for fish. The next night, I tried a beef stew with eggplant and tomatoes. She doesn't like eggplant and is allergic to cooked tomatoes." Ellen rolled her eyes to the sky. "She'll eat anything for breakfast, she says. Anything turns out to be one egg boiled for three and a half minutes, not three, and a serving of zero-fat plain Greek yogurt with fresh berries. No blackberries."

We clucked in sympathy. "I haven't heard from Mirabelle for a few days," I said. "What's she been up to?"

"Wedding planning, what else? It's exhausting keeping her away from Josie. Mirabelle wants to talk about all her marvelous ideas, and needless to say, Josie doesn't. Mirabelle went to the bakery yesterday carrying her stack of ever-present bridal magazines, and I heard Josie refused to come out of the kitchen, so Mirabelle went in after her."

"That was dangerous," Grace said. "Josie has knives. I think I'll cut the salmon sandwiches into fingers rather than squares; would that be okay?"

"Variety is good," Steph said.

"Dangerous, yes," Aunt Ellen said. "But I'm beginning to think Mirabelle likes to live dangerously." She sighed. "Josie was furious and yelled at Mirabelle to get out of her kitchen, and Mirabelle yelled back that she was only trying to help and what was the matter with Josie anyway. Josie threw her out of the kitchen."

"That sounds awful," Grace said. "Were you there, Ellen?"

"No, but you can be sure I heard about it. Several times. It hit the Nags Head grapevine in minutes."

"Josie doesn't need that," I said.

"Josie doesn't care about gossip," Grace said. "Do you think this tray looks okay?"

"It looks perfect," I said. And it did.

"Mirabelle and Florence have been spending much of their time visiting yacht clubs all over the Outer Banks," Ellen said.

I grimaced. "Maybe sending them on a wild-goose chase wasn't such a good idea. I hope she's not putting a deposit down anywhere."

"Why would she do that?" Steph asked, and I explained my plan.

Steph and Grace roared with laughter. Aunt Ellen chuckled.

"In *The Busman's Honeymoon* there weren't any repercussions," I said. "Helen, Lord Peter Wimsey's sister-in-law, didn't seem to mind that they tricked her."

"Let's get this shower over with," Aunt Ellen said, "and worry about Mirabelle later. She hasn't made any down payments or deposits, as we haven't given her any money, and you can be sure she won't be spending her own. She told me she's using the trip, including the stay at the Ocean Side, as a tax write-off because she's generating ideas for her business. Which is supposed to be Florence's business, but I get the feeling poor Florence isn't being consulted much, if at all."

"Mirabelle must love being feted by event managers at the yacht clubs," Grace said.

I still felt a frisson of guilt at my deception, but at that moment the bell at the front door rang, and I washed my hands quickly before hurrying to answer.

It was Josie, laden with her bakery box. She stopped in the doorway and studied the room. "Lucy, this looks marvelous. You shouldn't have gone to so much trouble."

"Of course we should have," I said. "You're worth it."

She would have wrapped me in a hug if not for the giant white box between us. Instead she gave me a radiant smile.

"Is that all?" I nodded toward the box.

"There's a smaller one in the car. I made some gluten-free treats, as you asked, for Mirabelle. She came into the bakery yesterday wanting to talk wedding plans, and I'm afraid I over-reacted and threw her out. I feel bad about that."

"Don't," I said. "I get the feeling Mirabelle doesn't know anything about boundaries. Is the car unlocked? I'll get the rest."

"Thanks, sweetie. I marked it clearly so as to not get them mixed up. There's a small sign inside the box as well."

I ran outside. A small bakery box sat on the back seat of Josie's car with GF written in thick black marker across the top. I took it inside. The sandwiches were made and covered in cling wrap, the cheese and crackers laid out. Josie was putting the finishing touches on her arrangement of coconut cupcakes, shortbread, and nutty chocolate brownies. I arranged the gluten-free treats—banana cupcakes and slices of cornmeal cake with a light coating of pale-yellow glaze—on a small platter. The color of the cake was accented by a sprinkling of purple flower petals. Nice of Josie to make the extra effort for something she didn't want to do in the first place. She'd printed a sign on a tiny blackboard and I propped it against the tray.

The doorbell rang.

"Group hug time," Grace said. We fell into the circle, and then we went to greet our guests.

Chapter Nine

Josie's bridal shower was a huge success, but it did not end well.

Grandma Gloria sat in the biggest chair in the center of the room, a gnarled ring-encrusted hand gripping her falcon-topped cane, and held court. She told anyone interested, and many who were not, about the illustrious history of the O'Malley family in Louisiana. Mary Anna fetched her mother drinks and delivered orders to me about the proper arrangement of the food trays or the conduct of the games. Mirabelle cornered any young, or youngish, women present, including Grace and Steph and me, and asked us, not at all subtly, if we had wedding plans, and stuffed her business card into our hands. Florence just looked embarrassed. She spent a lot of time in a chair in the corner, fussing over Charles, who always enjoyed being fussed over.

Josie seemed to be having a genuinely good time, and Ellen was clearly pleased as she greeted her guests and chatted to old friends.

We served champagne or sparkling water plus hot tea and played a few silly games, and then Josie sat on the bridal throne to open her presents while Charles attempted to help her with the brightly colored paper and streaming ribbons. She received a beautiful assortment of gifts and at times seemed almost to choke up in very un-Josie-like displays of emotion at the outpouring of affection from her friends and her mother's friends. Several times I thought Aunt Ellen was on the verge of tears.

Presents opened and games finished, we brought out the food. The sandwiches and main selection of baked goods went on the center table, and I put the smaller plate of gluten-free baking on a side table. Everyone helped themselves and then found a place to sit and chat.

Charles went from one person to another, hoping for a handout. He was not disappointed.

I filled my plate and snagged a seat next to Bertie. This wasn't an occasion to talk about library business, but I couldn't help myself. "Is George Grimshaw's crew still planning on coming on Wednesday?"

"I haven't heard otherwise," Bertie said. "Fingers crossed he's going to be able to do a quick fix."

"Things seem to be going all right, Lucy." Louise Jane took the seat on the other side of me.

I almost said, "Why wouldn't they?" but I remembered the Lady in time and nibbled daintily on my coconut cupcake. I'd earlier noticed Louise Jane peeking around corners and checking the shadows beneath the spiral iron staircase. "I hope you're not too disappointed she didn't put in an appearance."

Louise Jane sniffed. "I am never disappointed when Frances is content. I sometimes feel as though she and I share a powerful bond, Lucy."

"I'm not even going to ask who you're talking about," Bertie said. "I see Ava Franks is momentarily sitting alone. She's always been a loyal patron and a generous donor. Excuse me."

"Does the fact that Bertie is chatting to library supporters have anything to do with Grimshaw Contracting being scheduled to be here on Wednesday, Lucy?" Louise Jane asked me.

"It might." I popped the last of my cupcake into my mouth and stood up. "But then again, it might not. Bertie is always friendly to our patrons. Time to get back to work."

Eventually Grace, Steph, and I brought out coffee and poured the last of the champagne. Women began getting to their feet, hugging Josie and Ellen, and making their way to their cars.

Soon only Josie, Steph, Grace, Aunt Ellen, and the Louisiana Mafia were left to start the cleaning up. Josie began to help. We told her to sit down, and she told us not to be silly.

Mirabelle fell into the chair next to Gloria. "I don't feel too well," she said.

"Nonsense. You're only saying that because you're needed in the kitchen."

"My stomach's upset."

"Then you shouldn't have eaten so much," Florence said.

Mirabelle gave her a filthy look. I had to admit, Mirabelle didn't look too good. Beneath her makeup her face was pale, and beads of sweat were appearing on her upper lip.

Florence carried a stack of coffee mugs into the kitchen.

"Did you drive here?" I said. "Do you need a lift back to the hotel?"

Mirabelle nodded, but Gloria said, "No need to put yourself out, Lucy. She'll be fine in a minute. A glass of water maybe."

"I'll get it," I said.

I was soon back, and I passed the glass to Mirabelle. Her hand shook as she accepted it. She closed her eyes and took a sip. "I really don't feel too good."

Gloria gripped her cane. "Very well. We'll go back with Florence. Someone will have to pick the other car up later. Most inconvenient, I'm sure, but I'm certainly not driving it."

"You didn't come together?" I asked.

"Mirabelle collected me at Amos's house because Ellen wanted to get here early to help with the preparations," Gloria said. "Florence came with Mary Anna. Why they rented two cars is beyond me. Young people today have no sense of managing money."

"We rented two cars because we're here on business as well as for family, and we have different places to be," Mirabelle said. Her voice was so low it came out almost as a whisper.

"Playing at being on business, I'd say," Gloria said. "Now, where are Florence and Mary Anna?"

"Florence is helping put chairs away," I said. "And Mary Anna is washing glasses."

"Tell them I'm ready to leave." Gloria stood up. "Come along, Mirabelle."

Mirabelle gripped the arms of her chair and pushed herself to her feet. I was about to go in search of the rest of their party but was stopped by a low moan.

I turned to see Mirabelle swaying. Her eyes rolled back in her head and the last of the blood drained from her face. I leaped forward, but before I could grab her arm, her legs gave way and she fell to the floor in a tumbled heap.

Chapter Ten

"Dead! That can't possibly be right."

"I'm sorry, Lucy, but it's true." Ellen's voice broke. "Mirabelle was pronounced dead soon after arriving at the hospital."

"Thanks for letting me know." I put down the phone and turned to my friends. Three faces stared at me in shock.

"Mirabelle died?" Steph said. "That's awful."

We were having a post-shower get-together upstairs in my apartment. Steph, Grace, and I had been working all afternoon at the party, so we wanted some time to relax and talk it over. And, not at all incidentally, to finish off the remaining treats, of which there weren't many. Josie'd come with us, saying she needed some downtime to relax and continue to enjoy the rare time off from the bakery.

Mirabelle had regained consciousness immediately after collapsing, but she was unable to walk or even to stand up. Aunt Ellen called an ambulance and it arrived quickly. Ellen accompanied Mirabelle to the hospital, while Gloria, Florence, and Mary Anna went to the beach house or the hotel to wait for news.

Mirabelle had obviously taken ill, but I'd had no idea it was so serious.

"She seemed fine when she arrived," Steph said. "She cornered me to ask if I had wedding plans and was perfectly lucid. When I said my boyfriend and I were slowly getting to know each other, she said that at my age I shouldn't wait too long. Men's eyes wander. Whatever happened, it came on awful fast."

"Do you suppose it was something she ate?" Grace asked.

I put the sandwich in my hand back onto my plate.

As one we glanced at the platters containing the leftovers. A handful of sandwiches, some of the cheese and crackers, and most of the gluten-free desserts were all that remained. "Maybe the salmon was off," Steph said.

"I had one of those." I mentally checked myself over. "I feel fine."

"No one else complained of feeling unwell," Steph said. "And several elderly ladies were present, including Gloria."

"Gloria might be tiny," Grace said, "But she sure can vacuum up the groceries. She practically dove into those coconut cupcakes and chocolate brownies headfirst."

"It wasn't anything Mirabelle ate," Josie said. "She must have been sick already and it showed itself this afternoon. Poor Mirabelle. I didn't like her much, but she certainly didn't deserve to die. Not so young."

"I'm sure it wasn't the food." I opened the cupboard under

the sink and took out the trash can. "But just in case . . ." I dumped the last of the leftovers into it.

"I'd better go," Josie said. "Grandma Gloria will be devastated and Mom needs my support."

"Let us know if we can do anything to help," Grace said.

I walked my friends downstairs, and we helped Josie carry her presents to her car.

"Thanks for this." Josie stuffed the last gift-wrapped box into the trunk. "Despite the way it ended, it was a lovely shower."

"Most of the guests had left before Mirabelle collapsed," Steph said. "So it didn't ruin their afternoon."

Steph and Grace had come together. They gave us hugs and drove away. Josie stood beside me, watching them go. When she turned to me, her eyes were wet.

"You take care," I said. "And tell your mom and your grandmother I'm thinking of them."

* * *

I was woken the next morning by the simultaneous ringing of my phone and the bell at the front door. I fumbled for the phone on the night table and said, "Hold on, please. I'll be right back."

So I don't have to run downstairs every time someone rings the bell to ask if the library is open (which it wouldn't be if the door is locked, now, would it?), a camera and buzzer have been installed in my apartment to show what's happening at the front door. I leapt out of bed and crossed the room to switch on the camera. The stern face of Detective Sam Watson stared back at me. I pressed the buzzer. "Good morning, Detective."

"Let me in, Lucy," he said.

"I'm still in bed. Is it important? The library opens at nine." I must have been half asleep. Watson was obviously not here to check out a book.

"I have a warrant to search the premises," he said. "You'd better call Bertie and tell her to get down here."

"I'll be right there." I was half out the door, preceded by Charles, when I remembered the phone. I ran back into my room and snatched up the receiver. "What is it? Sorry, but I haven't got time to talk."

"Lucy, it's Alison at the bakery. Josie told me to call you. The police are here. They've ordered us closed and are searching the premises."

"What? Is Josie okay?"

"She's fine, but she's got a heck of a big burr in her saddle. They have a warrant, but I don't know what it says. I didn't see it."

"The police are here too," I said. "At the library. I'll try to find out what's happening. Tell Josie to stay calm." I hung up and dashed downstairs.

It was much easier to say stay calm than to do it. My heart was pounding and my head spinning. This had to have something to do with Mirabelle, but I couldn't imagine what. She hadn't died here. That had happened at the hospital.

I threw open the door and police officers streamed in, led by Detective Sam Watson. He slapped a piece of paper into my hand. I read quickly although I barely took in a word. It was a warrant authorizing them to search the premises.

"I don't understand," I said.

"You had a party here yesterday," Watson said.

"Yes. A bridal shower for Josie O'Malley. One of the guests took ill and an ambulance was called. I later heard she died. That's dreadful, but I don't see what it has to do with us."

Watson's gray eyes studied me. His wife, CeeCee, was one of my book club members, and he and I had met on several occasions. Sometimes, I'm sorry to say, those meetings had been when he was working. "Call Bertie, Lucy." I saw a spark of what might have been kindness in the depths of his eyes. "She needs to get down here. Was the party in this room?"

"Yes. We only used the ground floor."

"Then we shouldn't need to search upstairs. How many guests do you think you had?"

"I drew up the guest list myself, so I know for sure. Twenty-five people, not a lot, all of them friends of Josie's mom. Oh, twenty-six guests, as Louise Jane came uninvited. Counting Josie and Ellen and me, there were twenty-nine people."

"Did you prepare all the food and drink on site?"

"We made sandwiches and laid out cheese and crackers. And yes, we did all the work here ourselves with things we bought at the supermarket."

"Is that all the food you served?"

I studied his face. No point in lying. If the police were already at Josie's, they knew. "The desserts were catered."

"Catered by?"

"Josie's Cozy Bakery."

He nodded. "Go upstairs, please. Call Bertie and get yourself dressed."

Only then did I realize I was still in my pajamas. Cute shorty things festooned with yellow cartoon characters. My feet were bare and I must have had a serious case of bedhead.

"Take the cat with you," Watson said.

While we talked, a woman in plainclothes with coverings on her shoes had come into the room. She crouched on the carpet underneath the center table and used a tiny brush and pan to sweep at it. Charles, always an inquisitive fellow, was keenly observing what she was doing. She pushed him away; he came back. She pushed again; he came back again. "I assume," the woman said, "I'm going to find cat hair on everything."

"Pretty much." I scooped Charles up, and he gave me a dirty look. He hissed at Watson. The police detective and the Himalayan had also met before.

"Get dressed," Watson repeated. "And then either stay upstairs until I tell you you can come down or leave the premises. Don't touch anything, and don't take anything with you. Except the cat."

"What happened to Mirabelle? What are you looking for? Maybe I can help." Charles struggled to get out of my arms. I held on tight.

"You can help," the woman said, "by moving your feet."

I did so.

I called Bertie from my apartment, and she said she'd heard what was happening and was on her way. I jumped into the shower, tried to do something with my hair, and dressed quickly in jeans, T-shirt, and sweater. Watson had said nothing about not opening the library today, but that was almost certainly going to be the case.

My window faces east, across the marsh and the beach out to sea, not over the parking lot. I climbed the spiral iron stairs to the next landing, where the window looks to the west. Bertie's car was in the lot, alongside Watson's, a patrol car, and several white vans. I went back to my apartment, checked to make sure Charles had sufficient food and water for the day in case I couldn't get home, grabbed my keys and purse, and headed out. After engaging in an invigorating round of keep-the-cat-inside.

I walked slowly down the twisting iron stairs, trying not to make a sound. I stood on the bottom step and listened. At the moment no one was in the main room, but I heard voices and the sound of moving furniture coming from the break room. The voices weren't those of Bertie or Sam Watson, so I jumped off the step and ran across the room, trying not to leave any prints behind me. I threw open the door.

A uniformed officer stood there, notebook at the ready, taking down details of everyone who came in or out. "Who are you?" he said to me.

"I live here," I said.

"Oh, yeah," he said. "They told me about you."

I momentarily wondered what "they" had had to say about me, but I spotted Watson and Bertie standing together on the lawn. Bertie stood straight, her arms stiffly at her side. She turned her head when she heard me, and I could see the anger in her eyes. I gave the uniformed officer a weak smile and hurried toward them.

"Most ridiculous thing I've ever heard." Bertie waved the warrant in the air. "Good morning, Lucy."

Watson shrugged.

"What's happening?" I asked.

No one answered me.

"Need I remind you, Detective," Bertie said. "We have a public library to run here. We have patrons to serve and a full lineup of children's programming scheduled for today."

"We'll do our best to be out of your way soon," he said. "But you won't be opening the library today. Maybe not tomorrow either."

Bertie harrumphed.

"What's going on over there?" Watson pointed to the disturbed earth at the base of the lighthouse tower, where George and his gang had started digging last week.

"We're not burying any bodies, if you must know," Bertie said. "We're not quite so foolish as to forget to cover it back up, if that were the case."

I put my hand on her arm. Watson was only doing his job. No need to antagonize him. She turned to me with a weak smile and said, "Sorry, Sam. I know this is no laughing matter. In answer to your question, George Grimshaw has discovered a problem with the foundations of the building."

"I hope it's not too serious," he said. "I'll give you a call when we're finished here."

"What have you found?" I said.

Never one to offer information, Watson turned and walked away. The officer held the door open to let him in.

"What's happening?" I said to Bertie. "I don't understand

what any of this has to do with us. We had a nice party here yesterday. One of the guests took ill and died at the hospital, and that's a tragedy, but surely it doesn't need to involve the police." Only then did I remember the phone call from Alison. "Josie! The police are at the bakery too. I'd better go over there and see if she needs support."

"I'll drive you," Bertie said. "There's nothing I can do here and I can tell you what little I know in the car."

"I have to assume," I said, as soon as I had my seat belt fastened, "the hospital found something to indicate Mirabelle was poisoned. They can't have done the autopsy already, can they?"

Bertie took the corner onto the highway on two wheels. I clung to my seat belt. "The regular pathologist is on vacation, Sam told me. His temporary replacement is very young and very keen. This is his first position out of medical school. So young and keen, he likes to get to work at a time that others refer to as the middle of the night. Ellen told me the ER doctor who examined Mirabelle when they came in said he suspected she'd consumed a toxic substance, and thus the autopsy was done quickly. Sam asked a lot of questions about what food was served at the shower and where Mirabelle might have eaten earlier. Call Ronald and Charlene. Tell them what's happening and not to come in to work until I give them the all-clear."

She roared around a family sedan going the speed limit. Sea grasses and sand dunes and occasional glimpses of the blue ocean sped past my window, the wild spaces turning into a neat line of houses as we approached town. Bertie is a part-time yoga instructor, and she has a *Namaste* approach to life.

Meaning she is easygoing and laid-back. Unless something threatens her beloved library or her friends or staff, and then she turns into a tiger in front of your eyes.

She was turning now, as we sped through Whalebone Junction at an alarming speed, onto the Croatan Highway that led into Nags Head proper. It was a good thing, I thought, that the Nags Head police were all at the library or the bakery; otherwise we'd have had flashing lights shining in our mirrors. I called Ronald first. Nan told me he was in the shower and took my message. Charlene asked what was going on and I told her what I knew.

That didn't take long.

"So they did the autopsy already," I said to Bertie as I put my phone away. "What did it find?"

"Nothing conclusive."

"Why all the fuss then?"

"They found enough to make the pathologist suspect Mirabelle had consumed a high concentration of what Sam called an illicit substance, as the ER doctor suspected."

"An illicit substance? You mean poison? Maybe it was drugs or prescription medication and she misjudged the dose. If Mirabelle was a regular user, then it doesn't have anything to do with us, does it?" I thought about my interactions with Mirabelle. I'd seen nothing to indicate she was a druggie, but then again, I don't know what a druggie looks like.

"Sam didn't say anything more than that, but there has to be some reason the police are so interested in what she ate."

I let out a long breath. That was what I'd suspected, with Watson's questions about the food we'd served and the searching of the bakery, but it still came as a shock. "No one else seems to have become ill."

"And that, I suspect," Bertie said, "is the point. Samples have been sent away for toxicology testing. That will take another few days, but in the meanwhile the police need to get 'places of interest,' and I quote, locked down before evidence can be destroyed."

"If I had evidence to destroy, I'd have destroyed it last night."

"Traces remain," Bertie said dryly. "Don't you ever watch TV?"

"Apparently not enough. I prefer to read."

"If Mirabelle consumed an illicit substance, they believe it was at the shower."

"They think she was deliberately poisoned, then? It couldn't have been an accident?"

"That's what Sam said."

"I don't see how anything like that could have happened. If someone had poisoned the food we served at the party, other people would have taken sick. I didn't. What about you?"

"I'm feeling perfectly normal," Bertie said. "I ate just about everything that was put out. I haven't heard of anyone else needing to go to the ER yesterday."

"I made the sandwiches with store-bought bread and fillings. The cheese and crackers were bought at the supermarket by Grace and Stephanie." I hated the very thought that food I'd prepared might have killed a woman.

"Watson's taken the library trash. As I recall, not much food was left over. They'll be ordering those brands of cheese and cold cuts off the shelves until they can get them analyzed."

"Everything was served on trays and platters, from which the guests helped themselves," I said. "Nothing was plated and served separately. The drinks came from bottles. We served sparkling water and champagne, along with tea and coffee. I suppose something could have been in the water and it didn't boil sufficiently."

"Except that," Bertie said, "once again, several people had tea or coffee. I know I did. Two cups of coffee with a generous helping of cream from the pitcher provided. I saw Eunice Fitzgerald adding two heaping spoons of sugar to her tea."

"There was one thing," I said slowly. I scarcely wanted to think it, much less say it out loud, but I had to.

"What?" Bertie caught the tone in my voice and turned to face me. Fortunately we were stopped at a red light at the time.

"A tray of food was prepared specifically for Mirabelle. Josie didn't want to, but I convinced her to do it."

The light changed and Bertie took off like a race horse at the starting gate. "What sort of special food?"

"Gluten-free desserts. Mirabelle was apparently on a gluten-free diet. Josie, to whom flour and sugar are two of the main food groups, agreed to prepare some extra treats for her. They were put on a separate plate and had a sign telling everyone what they were."

"I saw them," Bertie said. "I didn't have any."

"Neither did I." I thought back. "Not many people did. I don't remember exactly, but at a guess I'd say there might have been six cupcakes and maybe six slices of cake. They weren't very popular. The other food was almost all eaten, but some of those things remained. I took the leftovers upstairs after everyone left, and Josie, Steph, Grace, and I had another glass of champagne. We didn't eat the gluten-free things then either. I'd had more than enough at the party, and eating those would be a waste of precious calories."

We took another corner at a hair-raising angle and screeched to a halt in the parking lot of the strip mall that houses Josie's Cozy Bakery. Police cars and more of the ubiquitous white vans were parked outside the bakery. The shops on either side weren't open yet, but people had gathered on the sidewalk to gape.

Bertie turned to me, shock written across her face. "You're saying Mirabelle did potentially eat food no one else did? Where are those desserts now?"

"In the trash in my apartment." With a burst of horror, I remembered Charles. Charles, left upstairs this morning to keep him out of the way of the investigators. Charles, who loved nothing more than to snack on party food. Charles, a notorious food thief. With a rush of relief, I realized he was in no danger. Because Charles tries to steal bits of human food, I'm careful about the disposal of my garbage. I'd scraped the last of the party food into the trash can. The can has a lid, which fastens securely, and it's kept inside a cabinet under the sink. A cabinet with a door. I'd fed Charles hastily this morning, but the cat food was kept in the cabinet next to the one with cleaning liquids and trash. If that door had been open, I would have noticed.

"I potentially have a murder weapon in my apartment," I said.

"You didn't tell Sam?"

"He didn't ask, and I didn't think about it until now."

"You're going to have to."

"Let's try to find out what's going on first." I got out of the car.

Officer Franklin, whom I knew, guarded the door. "Sorry, Lucy," she said. "The bakery's closed today."

"That's okay," I said. "I'm here to see Josie. Is she inside?"

"Yes."

"Can I go in?"

"No."

"Can you tell her I'm here?"

"I guess I can do that. Hold on." She spoke into the radio at her shoulder. "Ms. O'Malley's cousin's here. Wants to speak to Ms. O'Malley." A burst of static came in reply. "She'll be right out."

Josie burst through the doors and practically fell into my arms. She wore jeans under a bakery apron. Tendrils of long glossy hair had escaped their net. Her face was covered in red blotches, her eyes were red, and her cheeks were streaked with tears. "Oh, Lucy. Thanks for coming. This is all just so awful."

A man had followed her out of the bakery. He was about five foot nine, shorter than Josie, with a stomach that indicated he enjoyed more than the occasional glass of beer. What bit of hair he had left was arranged across the top of his head in a failed attempt to make it look as though he wasn't going bald. Small black eyes stared at me. "Who are you?" he asked.

"Lucy Richardson. Josie's cousin. Who are you?"

"Detective Yarmouth. North Carolina State Police." He glared at Bertie. "And you?"

"Albertina James. Citizen." I could see instant dislike written across Bertie's face.

"Let's go someplace and talk," I said to Josie.

"I'd prefer if you didn't leave," Yarmouth said.

"Is Ms. O'Malley under arrest?" Bertie asked.

"Not at this time." I didn't like that answer. He could have just said no.

"Then we'll talk where we want," Bertie said. "Let's go."

"I need to stay here," Josie said, "and keep an eye on my place."

"We can talk in the car," I said.

In the summertime, Josie's Cozy Bakery sets tables outside for customers to enjoy their food and drink in the fresh sea air and hot North Carolina sun, but at this time of year the sidewalk was empty and unadorned. Not even a potted plant or hanging basket of flowers lightened the mood. Bertie flicked the fob on her key chain. "You two sit in the car. I'll wait out here so you can have a private chat."

I threw her a smile. Josie and I got into the back seat. My cousin put her head in her hands and groaned.

"First things first," I said. "Have you called Jake?"

She shook her head, as I'd expected her to. "I don't want to worry him."

"He'll want to know, Josie. It's his job as your fiancé and soon-to-be-husband to worry when you're in trouble. As it's your job to worry over him. Give him a call, but first, what the heck is going on?"

"I don't really know. The police came in at seven thirty. They ordered all my customers to leave and locked the doors. They were polite enough about it, but it was still frightening. They have a warrant to search the premises, looking for potentially poisonous or illicit substances." Josie threw up her hands. "Poison! That word will be all over town in no time. No one will ever want to eat here again."

"Did they say why?" I asked.

She lifted her head. "Mirabelle died. The pathologist thinks it was something she ate. I did the baking. I don't like that Detective Yarmouth. I suspect he's already got me tried and convicted."

"Don't even think that. Why isn't Sam Watson here?" He'd been at the library, but if the police thought the food that killed Mirabelle had been prepared here and only consumed at the library, then I'd have thought the bakery would be the primary place for the initial investigation.

"I asked Yarmouth that. He said Watson and I are friends, so he's been called in to run the investigation, and Watson will be secondary on this case."

I didn't like the sound of that. Sam Watson and I had clashed before in cases that involved the library community, but I'd always thought he was a good, and fair, cop.

"Detective Watson's at the library," I said. "He has a warrant to search us too."

A car pulled up and two people got out, a man and a woman. They both carried cameras. I recognized the woman as a reporter for the local newspaper, but I didn't know the man with her. They walked up to Officer Franklin. The woman spoke and Franklin shook her head. The man stepped past her and tried to peer into the bakery windows. Franklin ordered him to step away. He shrugged, took a few steps down the sidewalk, and looked around.

Josie called, "Duck!" and scooted down in her seat. I bent double and wrapped my arms around my knees. "I do not want my picture in the newspaper," she said. "That's Judy Jensen, and she's a good sort, but I don't know the man with her. He looks sneaky."

I ventured a peek. The sneaky-looking fellow was taking pictures of the front of the bakery and the police cars and officers. Judy was talking to Bertie, who waved her arms and pointed north, toward the center of town.

Josie still had her head down, wrapped in her arms. I decided not to tell her that pictures were being taken of the police preventing anyone from entering her place.

"Watson's at the library?" she said. "That's good, right? It means the poison, if it was poison, was added to the food after it was brought out. Not done by me. Here."

I wasn't so sure, but I said nothing.

"Can you see what's happening out there?" she asked.

I lifted my head again and peeked out. Judy thanked Bertie and called to her companion. He lowered his camera and followed her to her car. "Bertie got rid of them."

"They won't stay rid of for long."

"Probably not. You can't stay here. More reporters will be arriving soon, and those two might come back. Let's go to your parents' house."

Josie straightened up. "I went to Mom and Dad's last night

after we got the news. Mary Anna was quiet, stunned I thought, Florence was weeping and wailing something awful, and Grandma was telling her not to be such a drama queen."

"Did your mom call your dad?"

"Yes, and he's on his way home. He booked an early flight this morning. Should be home soon. She also called Uncle Warren, Mirabelle's dad, and gave him the news. He wants to have the"—Josie swallowed heavily—"body sent home to New Orleans. My dad said he'd make the arrangements at this end."

"You call Jake. I suggest we meet at the beach house. We need to talk things over. All of us."

"You think I'm in trouble, don't you, Lucy?"

"It doesn't hurt to be prepared," I said.

Chapter Eleven

I've always been a winter person. I love the snow, as long as I don't have to shovel it, and I love the cold, as long as I'm well wrapped up or sitting inside in front of a roaring fire with a thick sweater and a mug of creamy, marshmallow-topped hot chocolate. There's nothing I love more than a long walk through the woods after a fresh snowfall when the sun turns it to scattered diamonds. Back in New England, I skied regularly, and I didn't mind not being very good at it because I enjoyed the day and the exercise so much.

My mom was born and raised in the Outer Banks, daughter of a longtime fishing family. She met my dad when he was here on vacation and they married young, her straight out of high school, him still in law school. He comes from a prominent old-money Boston family, and that's where they settled and raised their four children, three boys and me, the youngest. Every year of my childhood into my teenage years, we spent a large part of our summers on the Outer Banks, visiting Aunt Ellen and Uncle Amos. I fell in love with the long beaches, the wild, open ocean, the quirky weathered-gray or pastel-colored houses on stilts.

But I'd never before been to the Outer Banks in winter. I hadn't thought I'd like it: the snow, when they get it, is wet and doesn't stay on the ground for long, and the temperatures hover around freezing, too cold for the beach, too hot for winter sports. But there's something about the stark winter beauty of the coast that appeals to me. The quiet of the long beach, once the vacationing crowds have left, the roaring surf, the beam of the lighthouse reflecting off falling snow, the marsh and the sky teeming with birds spending the season here.

I appreciated none of it today as the family gathered around the kitchen table in Ellen and Amos's beach house. The sun was shining, the air cool and crisp, and the surf high. A few surfers, dressed in full wet suits, braved the cold waves, while people well wrapped in coats and scarves strolled on the sand. Two brightly colored kites danced in the wind further down the beach.

Before we left the bakery, I'd gotten out of the car to give Josie some privacy to phone Jake, and then I waited while she went inside to tell the police she was leaving and they could call her if they needed anything more. Yarmouth followed her out and stood in the center of the parking lot, arms crossed, strands of loose hair blowing in the wind, and watched us drive away. I felt the hairs on the back of my neck rise under his steady, unfriendly stare. Bertie dropped us at the beach house and then headed back to the library to check on what was happening there.

Ellen met us at the door. She hugged Josie hard, and when they separated, both women's eyes were wet. Then my aunt wrapped me in her arms. "Come through," she said. "Amos just got home."

My uncle's suitcase was in the hallway.

Amos rose from the table when we came into the kitchen and gave his daughter a hug and me a tight smile. Mary Anna nodded in greeting. She twisted a tattered tissue between her fingers. Gloria was seated at the table, her hand resting on the top of her cane. "Stuff and nonsense," she proclaimed.

"It may be, Mama," Amos said, "but we have to take it seriously."

"Where's Florence?" Josie asked.

"At the hotel," Mary Anna said. "She's extremely upset and wants to be alone."

"We're all upset," Gloria said, "but we aren't all cowering under the covers."

"That's a bit harsh, Mama," Amos said. "Florence and Mirabelle were close."

Gloria snorted.

Amos and Ellen exchanged a look, and then Ellen said, "You must be tired, Gloria. Why don't you lie down for a brief rest?"

"Because it's ten o'clock in the morning, and I'm not a feeble old lady, despite what some might think."

"I thought Amos might want to talk to Josie privately," Ellen said.

"I know you did, but that is not a good idea. We keep no secrets in this family. Besides, I might have ideas to contribute." She leaned back in her chair. "I will have a glass of tea, though. And another one of those delicious oatmeal cookies." She looked at me. "They're from Josie's bakery, best I've ever had."

Josie was so lost in thought, she didn't even say thank you.

Ellen got to her feet with a sigh. The doorbell rang, and I said, "I'll get it."

It was Jake. For him, it was early in the day, and he must have left his house in a rush. He hadn't shaved and his hair stood out in all directions. He'd pulled on a pair of jeans and a sweater and stuffed bare feet into unlaced sneakers. He put his hand on my arm as I turned to go back to the kitchen. "What the heck's going on, Lucy?" he said in a low voice.

"What did Josie tell you?"

"Nothing. Just that she'd like it if I came around to her parents' place." He lifted his hands. "I can't imagine she's going to tell me the wedding's off in front of half her family."

"It's nothing like that. Mirabelle died last night."

Jake's mouth dropped open. "That's awful. What happened?"

"That's why you're here. There's some suggestion the food she ate at our shower killed her. Come on in."

Back in the kitchen, no one was talking. Josie leapt to her feet when we came in, and Jake wrapped her in his arms.

Gloria sipped her tea. "Welcome, young man. I'm glad to see you're here. I trust all this won't delay the wedding plans."

Mary Anna gasped. "Mother! You can't possibly be thinking of that. Not at a time like this."

"Why ever not? The wedding date is less than a month away." She gave me a look. "You didn't think you could fool me with a wild-goose chase such as you sent Mirabelle on, did you?"

"No," I said.

"I'm glad we understand each other. Now, if you want to delay the wedding, Josie dear, for appearances' sake, that would give me time to send invitations to a few more of the relatives. They'll all accept, naturally, and then we'd need to find a larger venue. Ellen can work with Florence to arrange that."

"I don't . . ." Aunt Ellen began.

"This isn't the time . . ." Josie said.

"We're not here to talk about weddings," Uncle Amos said. "Jake, have a seat, and let's find out what we are here to talk about."

The first time I saw the movie version of *To Kill a Mockingbird*, I thought Gregory Peck was portraying my Uncle Amos. The slow southern accent, the tall lanky frame, the penetrating eyes, the relentless pursuit of justice. Now, Amos put his elbows on the table and steepled his fingers. His thick gray eyebrows drew closer together and his eyes narrowed. In his day, my uncle was one of the top defense attorneys in the state. These days he is semiretired and takes the more mundane cases that come into his office. The serious cases he hands over to his new law partner: my friend Stephanie Stanton. "You two tell me exactly what happened yesterday. Lucy, you start. Tell me everything you remember."

"I don't need to hear it all again," Gloria said. "I think I'll go to my room after all. Ellen, you seem to have forgotten the cookies to go with my tea. Mary Anna will bring them."

Ellen leapt to her feet and laid cookies out on a plate.

"But . . ." Mary Anna said.

"How many times have I told you—no buts," Gloria said.

Amos stood up, assisted his mother, and handed her the

cane. Mary Anna sighed heavily, but she stood. Ellen handed her the plate with the cookies, and Mary Anna followed as her mother slowly tapped her way out of the kitchen.

When the door shut behind them, Josie said, "Grandma seems to be handling a sudden death in the family well."

"Don't be fooled, honey," Amos said. "Your grandmother is of the generation that doesn't display their emotions in public."

"Our kitchen is hardly in public," Josie said. "I think it's mighty poor taste to want to talk about using Mirabelle's death to reschedule my wedding so she can invite more of the blasted extended family."

"Your grandmother," Amos said, "is also perfectly capable of separating two events in her mind. She'll mourn Mirabelle when she thinks about Mirabelle and plan your wedding when she thinks about that."

Josie shook her head.

"Do you think it would be okay if I dropped in on Florence later?" I asked. "I'd like to check on how she's doing." Mary Anna had said Florence wanted to be alone. That was understandable, and if she didn't want my company, I'd leave. But I thought it likely to be more a case of not wanting Gloria's company. "I don't have to go to work today, for obvious reasons."

"She'd love to see you, Lucy." Ellen glanced toward the closed kitchen door. "Gloria can be particularly hard on Florence sometimes."

"Grandma can be hard on everyone who doesn't rise to her so-called standards," Josie said. "And that means everyone except the men in the family. Sorry, Dad, but that's the way it is, and I don't think this is the time to beat about the bush."

"My mother isn't always an easy woman to get on with," he said. "But I've never doubted she loves you all. As for the men in the family, she never had much time for her brothers, Clive and Oliver. Oliver in particular. *Ne'er-do-well* is the phrase she uses constantly. Oliver is Florence's father. But all of that is neither here nor there. Lucy, what happened at the shower?"

The kitchen door opened, and Mary Anna's head popped back in. "Sorry, Ellen, but now she wants to have a bath, and I can't find those nice bath salts that were out yesterday."

"You mean, my favorite bath treat my friend Barbara bought for me in Paris? The ones I'm using sparingly because I like them so much?"

"That would be the ones," Mary Anna said. "Sorry. I can say they're finished."

Ellen stood up. "No, I'll get them."

When they'd left, I told Uncle Amos about the shower. I gave him all the details I could remember, up to the point of throwing the leftover gluten-free desserts, the ones prepared specifically for Mirabelle, in the trash. Uncle Amos sat back in his chair and peered at me through his thick glasses. No one said anything for a long time, and then he turned to Josie.

"We're going to hope the toxicology reports turn up negative. Nothing found. An ER doctor with a suspicious mind and an overzealous new pathologist. If, however, that is not the case, we need to try to understand what might have happened. I'd prefer to keep the presence of unconsumed desserts to ourselves, but I don't think that would be wise. Lucy, you'll have to hand them over to Detective Watson."

"But . . ." Josie said.

"You don't run a careless kitchen," Amos said. "And you didn't deliberately poison your cousin. Therefore, if something is found in the lab that points to Mirabelle being poisoned or drugged, someone killed her. The police need all the evidence that's available in order to determine who did that."

"Rumors alone will be enough to kill my business," Josie said. "By now everyone in town knows the police are sifting through my flour and analyzing the sugar. They'll hear my cousin died at my bridal shower and put two and two together mighty fast. The bakery might never recover."

Jake is what they called the strong, silent type. Up until now, he'd sat silently, watching the family drama play out, his face getting darker and darker as we talked about death and poison. He spoke now. "It will recover because everyone in town knows you, Josie. They love you, and they love your place. The tourists won't hear about it because this'll all be long over by the start of the season."

Josie gave him a weak smile. "Thanks, sweetheart, but . . ."

"That's not your biggest problem right now," Amos said. "I don't suppose you heard anything about what's happening from Butch, Jake?"

Jake shook his head. "He won't tell me if he does know anything, and he's unlikely to. He'll be kept well away from this case because of possible conflict of interest."

"I don't trust that Detective Yarmouth," Josie said.

"Who's that?" Amos asked.

"The state police sent someone to take control of the investigation because Sam Watson and I know each other too well."

"I'll look into him," Amos said. "Tell me about the special plate for Mirabelle. Did you leave it alone at any time?"

Josie began to shake her head. Then her pretty face paled. "I totally forgot until now. I put all the things for the shower on the back seat of my car as soon as I finished making them. It's January and the temperature yesterday was in the midthirties, so it was easier for me to put them in the car than find room in the kitchen or the fridge."

"What time was that?" Amos asked.

"Eleven or shortly after. I then helped with lunch until it was time to leave at quarter to one."

"Did you lock your car?"

Josie's face crunched in thought, and then she said, "I can't remember. I might not have. I often don't when it's parked at work." She laughed without humor. "No one's likely to steal my old car, and I keep nothing of value in it."

"What about allergies?" I asked. "Is it possible Mirabelle was allergic to something in the food? It didn't have to be the baking. We made salmon sandwiches. Some people are deathly allergic to fish, aren't they?"

"The sandwiches were all on regular bread," Josie said. "If she was gluten-free, she wouldn't have eaten them."

"She wouldn't be the first person to break her diet," I said.

"Tell me about it," Josie said. "My grandmother has an ever-changing diet. Whatever's the latest fad, that's the one she's on. But whether Mirabelle ate a salmon sandwich or not, allergies that severe don't appear overnight, not to an adult. Mirabelle lives in New Orleans; if she was allergic to any sort of fish or seafood she would have known it, and told us."

"Y'all ate at my place the other night," Jake said. "And she didn't mention any allergies. At a seafood restaurant we've got to be super careful of that sort of thing."

"The gluten-free diet she was on wasn't for health reasons," I said. "Just a weight-loss attempt. She bragged about how much weight she'd lost on it."

"No point in speculating," Amos said. "We'll find out soon enough. The autopsy and toxicology reports should tell us exactly what killed her."

We sat in silence for a long time. From where I was sitting, I could see outside, to the path leading down to the beach. Mary Anna appeared, wrapped in a warm sweater, a scarf around her head. She walked slowly, her hands in her pockets, kicking sand as she went.

Ellen came into the kitchen and dropped into a chair. "I brought her her book, and she's comfortable in the bath. Now that she *accidentally* poured an excessive amount of my special bath salts into the tub."

"I need to get back," Josie said.

"There's nothing you can do there, honey," Amos said.

"No, but it's my place. I have to be there."

"I'll come with you." Jake pushed back his chair.

"You don't have to do that," she said. "You have to get ready to open the restaurant."

"The restaurant can stay closed today."

She gave him a smile, and the one he returned was almost dazzling in its intensity.

Uncle Amos coughed lightly and turned away. The corners of Aunt Ellen's mouth turned up. I leapt to my feet and wrapped

Josie and Jake in a spontaneous hug. "Everything's going to be okay. Lucy is on the case! I'll go to the library now and tell Detective Watson about the leftover desserts. Then I'm going to pay a call on Florence. She and Mirabelle worked together, so she might know about health problems Mirabelle kept, for some reason, to herself. I'll let you know what I find out." I marched out of the kitchen focused on my errand.

Josie was in trouble, and I intended to do what I could to help her.

Only when I had my hand on the doorknob did I remember. I didn't have a car. I slunk back to the kitchen. "Uh, sorry, but I need a lift."

Chapter Twelve

Aunt Ellen drove me to the library. Only three vehicles remained in the parking lot: my teal Yaris, Bertie's car, and one unmarked police car.

Bertie and Sam Watson were standing on the front steps, and they both looked over at us as we drove up. Aunt Ellen switched off the engine and opened her door.

"Why don't I talk to Watson alone," I said.

"I suppose that would be better." She slammed the car door. "You'll tell me what he says?"

"Of course."

She drove away as I trotted up the path.

"We're finished here, Lucy," Watson said. "For now. I've told Bertie she can't open the library today, in case we need to return later, but you can both go in."

"That's what I'm here about," I said. "I've been to Josie's and they're searching the bakery."

"That's right. I can't tell you if they found anything, because I don't know."

"I assume you're doing that because you suspect Mirabelle

113

was deliberately poisoned by something that was served at the shower."

"I don't know how she died," he said. "But if it might have been caused by something she ate, deliberately administered or not, that's something we're going to look into."

"I'm assuming you searched our garbage and took away what food was left for analysis."

"Must have been a good party," he said. "About all we found were crumbs, and yes, we've sent those to the lab along with the packets the bread and cheese came in and the tins of salmon."

"What are you getting at, Lucy?" Bertie said.

"I took some leftovers to my apartment once everyone had left."

Watson's face tightened in anger. For a moment I thought he was mad at me, but then he said, "I must be getting sloppy in my old age. I should have asked you that straight up."

"Stephanie Stanton, Grace Sullivan, and Josie came upstairs with me after everyone left. We had another glass of wine, but didn't eat much. We were all stuffed. I threw the leftovers in the trash. They'll still be there." I glanced at Bertie. She gave me a slight nod. Watson, of course, noticed.

"What else, Lucy?" he said.

"Mirabelle was on a gluten-free diet. A plate of gluten-free desserts was prepared for her. It had a sign on it saying so."

"Did you see her eating from that plate?" Watson asked.

"No. I can't say I noticed what anyone ate. I was the hostess and kept busy the entire time."

"Where," Watson asked, as I feared he would, "did these gluten-free desserts come from?"

"Josie's Cozy Bakery," I said.

"Anyone could have tampered with them," Bertie said quickly. "They weren't kept under lock and key."

"Did anyone else try them? Other than Mirabelle?"

"Again, I can't say I noticed, but most of them were left after everyone had gone. No one who's not committed to gluten-free is going to eat them when Josie's pecan squares are on offer."

Watson nodded. He'd eaten his share of Josie's baking in his time.

I tried to remember what I'd noticed about them. "I took the gluten-free baked goods out of the box they'd come in and arranged them on a tray in the break room with the sign saying what they were. They were brought out along with the other food when we served. At a guess, two pieces of cake and one cupcake were taken."

"Let's get them," Watson said. "Bertie, I'll call you later and let you know if you can open the library tomorrow. Lucy, I'll come with you."

We walked through the empty library and up the spiral stairs in silence. I unlocked my door and Charles hurried to greet me. He narrowed his eyes and hissed when he saw Detective Watson behind me. Charles and Watson had never gotten on. Perhaps it was because whenever the good detective was here, Charles ended up locked in a closet.

I opened the cabinet under the sink and took out the trash can. Charles jumped onto the counter to watch. "I didn't have anything for dinner last night," I said. "I wasn't hungry after the shower. I didn't have breakfast this morning either, come to think of it." Watson took the can from me and opened the lid. The three of us, Detective Watson, me, and Charles peered in. I'd taken my garbage downstairs Sunday morning, so the only things in the can were the unwanted cupcakes and slices of cake along with a few crumpled napkins and the last of the sandwiches.

"Thank you for telling me about this, Lucy," Watson said. "Is there anything else I should know?"

"Nothing I can think of."

"Tell me about Mirabelle. Your personal impressions."

"I didn't know her," I said. "I met her for the first time the other day. She's Josie's cousin, second cousin, I think. She came with Josie's grandmother to . . . uh . . . to help with the wedding preparations." He gave me *that* look.

"Although," I reluctantly admitted, "Josie didn't want their help."

"Was there tension between them because of that?"

Mirabelle had left a couple of her wedding magazines for me to read. I tried hard not to glance at the table where I'd tossed them. I guess I failed, because Watson saw them, but he said nothing. I suppose, to a man, a wedding is just a wedding. Not something requiring deception to a degree that would make a James Bond villain proud.

"Josie's grandmother can be the imperious type," I said, deflecting the question about any tension between Josie and Mirabelle.

"I'll take this," he said. "I'll let you know when you can have your trash can back." He headed for the door. He paused on the landing and then turned around. "I don't suppose there's any point in me telling you not to interfere in this, is there?"

I smiled innocently at him.

"I'm not going to be the lead detective on the case. The state police have brought someone in because I'm acquainted with many of the people who were at the shower. I'll do what I can to advise him, but he doesn't have to listen to me. I've found that sometimes it helps when an investigator knows the people involved. CeeCee's reading that book for your book club, the one about the old-time English detective. She's enjoying it, she says. I might give it a try. I can see myself out, thanks."

He clattered down the stairs, gripping my garbage to his chest. When he was gone, I turned to Charles. "Did you hear that? Did Detective Watson actually ask me to interfere in imitation of Lord Peter Wimsey and Harriet Vane?"

In the past, I'd always been told, sometimes politely, sometimes not-so-politely, to mind my own business and leave the detecting to the detectives.

That this time Watson seemed to have almost invited me to ask questions made me feel rather good.

Until I realized that if such was the case, it had to be because he thought things looked mighty bad for Josie.

*   *   *

I hadn't had dinner last night and not so much as a cup of coffee this morning. Any hunger I might have had fled at the sight of the contents of my trash. If I'd eaten some of those desserts last night, they might have killed me.

I checked my watch. It was coming up to eleven. A good time for a social visit.

"Won't be long," I said to Charles.

He rolled his eyes.

I decided not to call ahead. If Florence was out, I didn't have her cell phone number, and if she was at the hotel, I'd find her there.

I ran downstairs, got my car, and drove into town. The Ocean Side is one of the nicest hotels on the Outer Banks south of the causeway to the mainland at Kitty Hawk. It's where my mother always stays when she visits, and I know it's not cheap. A few months ago it had been looking as though the hotel was going into decline, tattered and worn around the edges, but the owners had poured money into it since and everything had been modernized and spruced up over the fall.

I walked up to the reception desk. The woman behind it gave me a professional smile. "I wonder if you can put me through to . . ." And I realized I didn't know Florence's last name.

Some detective I am.

I didn't know Mirabelle's surname either. Florence and Mirabelle were a daughter and a granddaughter of Amos's mother's brothers, so assuming O'Malley was Amos's mother's married name, their names wouldn't ever have been O'Malley, never mind that Mirabelle had been married twice. "I'm so sorry, but I don't know the last name of the person I'm looking for. Florence?"

"I can't check the guest register without a last name."

"Give me a sec." I pulled out my phone and called Aunt Ellen. She answered immediately. "What's Florence's surname?"

"Offhand, I don't remember. I don't know if she's ever been

married. Hold on, Gloria's here. I'll ask. We're having lunch." I heard muttering voices and then Ellen was back. "She says it's Fanshaw, which is her maiden name and thus the name of her brothers, and Florence still has it because she never married, although it's getting long past time and if she doesn't hurry up she's going to be left on the shelf, and why do you want to know anyway?" Now I remembered: Festivities by Fanshaw was the name of Florence's event-planning business.

I didn't answer Aunt Ellen's question. "What about Mirabelle?"

"Hold on again."

"Sorry, won't be a minute more," I said to the receptionist.

Aunt Ellen came back on the line. "Henkel, the name of her second husband. In contrast to Florence, in danger of being left on the shelf, Mirabelle has had two husbands already, which is one too many for a woman not yet out of her thirties. Or so Gloria tells me. Hold on, she's waving at me. She wants me to hand over the phone." Ellen's voice was muffled as she took the mouthpiece away. "Lucy's busy, Gloria. She doesn't have time to talk. All right, I'll tell her." She spoke to me. "Speaking of women in their thirties, Gloria is wondering if you have prospects."

"Tell her I've taken a vow of chastity. Thanks." I hung up and turned back to the receptionist. "Florence Fanshaw. I'm Lucy."

"Why would you do that?" the clerk said.

"Do what?"

"Take a vow of chastity." She studied me—jeans, T-shirt, earrings. "Are you wanting to become a nun? You don't look like one."

"Just making a joke. My call?"

"One minute. I'll check her room." She picked up a phone and pressed buttons. "There's a lady here to see you, Ms. Fanshaw. A Lucy? Yes, thank you." She hung up. "She'll be down in a few minutes."

"Thanks."

I took a seat in a comfortable wingback chair upholstered in red damask. An enormous bowl of peach roses and trailing vines sat on the table in front of me. A few hotel guests walked across the lobby, many dressed in waterproof jackets and heavy boots with binoculars around their necks. The Outer Banks in January is a great destination for birdwatchers, and we get a lot of them coming to explore the marshes around the lighthouse.

I didn't have long to wait before the elevator button pinged, and Florence emerged. She looked, I thought, dreadful. Her face was blotchy, her eyes and nose red, her hair mussed and unwashed. I got to my feet to greet her, and to my surprise, she threw herself into my arms and burst into tears. "Oh, Lucy. It's so nice of you to come. This is dreadful. Absolutely dreadful."

I patted her back and mumbled something sympathetic. Finally, she pulled herself away from me and forced out a tight smile. "I haven't spoken to Aunt Gloria today. Mary Anna went to Amos's house this morning when she heard he'd arrived home, but I didn't want to go. I don't think I can bear it right now. Is Gloria okay?"

"She's fine. Handling her grief in her own way."

"As she does everything."

"Would you like a coffee or something? I haven't had

breakfast yet." I still didn't feel like eating, but as I sat in the comfortable chair waiting for Florence, my body reminded me I was seriously undercaffeinated.

"That would be nice, thanks."

"How about right here in the hotel?"

"Sounds good to me."

It was lunchtime, but this being the off-season, we had our choice of seats in the restaurant. I led the way to a table for two by the window overlooking the spacious veranda. The pool was closed and covered, the umbrellas and lounge chairs put away for the season. In the summer this hotel has beautiful gardens, but even in the winter they managed to make the outdoors attractive with a variety of colored grasses in giant terra-cotta pots. A wooden boardwalk led from the pool deck, across the dunes, and through the long waving sea oats to the wide beach. Today being a Monday in January, the grounds were empty.

"Except for the pool," Florence said, "this must be the same view they had from this spot two hundred years ago."

"I never tire of it," I said. The waitress took our orders. Two coffees.

"Weren't you planning to go home today?" I said. "I suppose your plans have changed."

"Mary Anna and Gloria are staying, so I might as well."

"Can you afford to be away from your business much longer?"

"Andrew, that's my assistant, can handle anything that comes in. If anything comes in, and there's no guarantee that's going to happen. He can call me if he needs to. Mary Anna and I are checking out of this hotel and going to stay at Amos's.

I can't afford to stay here any longer and Mary Anna doesn't want to, so we'll share the second guest room. I'll just have to put up with Mary Anna's snoring. A freight train coming through the bedroom would be quieter. Mirabelle's dad asked Gloria to travel with her remains when she goes home. Do you know anything about when that can happen?"

"Sorry, no. Were you and Mirabelle close?"

"We're similar in age, so we grew up together, but we hadn't seen much of each other over the years until recently. We didn't . . . well, we didn't always get along. I . . . I mean we, have an event-planning company. Weddings, bar and bat mitzvahs, anniversary celebrations. That sort of thing. It's a small company, only me and Andrew."

"And Mirabelle?"

"Oh, yes. And Mirabelle. About a year ago, we got talking at Aunt Gloria's birthday party, and Mirabelle seemed interested in my business. She'd recently gotten divorced, again, and was looking for something interesting to do, so I agreed to take her on as a partner. Mirabelle didn't want us to remain small. She had big plans."

I read the look on her face. "And you didn't like that?"

"I liked her plans just fine. Until I realized she had no idea of what she was doing to make those plans a reality. All this nonsense about getting a cover spread in *Weddings on Water*." Florence snorted. "Running up and down the coast visiting yacht clubs and the like. It was all for show. She loved being treated by the event managers at those places as though she had hundreds of thousands to spend."

"You didn't agree?"

"Even if Festivities by Fanshaw did manage to snag the contract for the wedding of the season, we couldn't pull it off. We're not big enough and we have no contacts in North Carolina."

This, I thought, *is more interesting than I expected.* A falling out of business partners. I leaned back to allow the waitress to put a pot of coffee on the table. "Surely Mirabelle would have come to realize that, soon enough."

"Sure she would. After she'd ruined Festivities by Fanshaw's reputation. The only good thing about it is that we don't have a reputation in North Carolina to ruin, and I could hope no one back home would hear about it."

"Why did you keep her on as your partner then?"

"It wasn't a matter of keeping her on, Lucy." Florence studied me over the rim of her coffee cup. "Mirabelle got a lot of money in her latest divorce settlement. She wanted to invest a good chunk of it in my company. I wasn't too sure that was a good idea right from the beginning, but to be honest, we weren't doing so well. It's a highly competitive business and we weren't getting enough contracts to keep afloat. Andrew's constantly out on the street, pounding the pavement, trying to drum up work, but we're simply not getting enough. I was in danger of having to lay off Andrew, close the company, and get"—she shuddered—"a job. Whereupon Aunt Gloria would tell me she always knew I was a failure. I went to my dad and asked him to help me out, but he's temporarily embarrassed, as we say in the South. Much politer than saying he's broke. Again."

"You're being very forthright," I said. "Telling me this. You hardly know me."

"Maybe that's why I'm telling you. Because I hardly know you. I'm not going to tell anyone in my family I'm about to be tossed out onto the street, now, am I? No secrets in the Fanshaw and O'Malley families are kept from Gloria, not for long. Besides," she added, "I got the feeling you were no fonder of dear cousin Mirabelle than I was. She didn't exactly endear herself to Josie either, flirting with her boyfriend and rearranging her wedding plans."

I sipped my coffee, said nothing, and tried to look sympathetic. In the meantime, I was planning on making a call to Sam Watson before I'd even left the hotel.

Mirabelle had invested in Festivities by Fanshaw, Florence's failing company. Mirabelle had been causing problems that threatened to destroy Florence's business. Mirabelle had died.

Cui bono? is what they ask in the mystery novels I read.

Who benefits?

I smiled at Florence sitting across from me. Sometimes this detecting stuff is pretty easy.

"I thought things couldn't get any worse," she said. "But they have."

"Why?"

"Now I'm truly up the creek. I wanted to take out partnership insurance for Mirabelle and me. I made appointments at the insurance company; she'd fail to show up. I'd ask her to suggest another time; she'd say she was too busy. She always said we'd have time later." Florence sighed. "So I have no insurance. Mirabelle decided our offices needed to be upgraded to reflect the modern, forward-thinking, hip young company we are. We spent fifty thousand, out of the company account, on an interior decorator, and I haven't even made the final payments yet. Never mind that I can't stand what she and Mirabelle did with the place, so I'd like to rip it all out. We were supposed to be doing a big sixtieth-wedding-anniversary party, but just last week the customer pulled out." Tears welled up in her eyes, and she wiped angrily at them with the back of her hand.

"Why'd they do that?"

"They couldn't get on with Mirabelle. The family wanted their party to be homespun and casual. Mirabelle didn't think homespun and casual suits our image and kept nagging at them to upgrade. Words were said and the customer walked. Mirabelle had paid the deposit on the hall without waiting for the client's check to clear. They contacted the bank and canceled it."

"Didn't you say Mirabelle put money into your business?"

"Sure. But not up front." Florence fumbled in her purse for a tissue. "She's supposed to pay monthly. She hasn't given me anything in the last two months. I wasn't too worried about it, not yet. She always was an airhead with her money. And now she's left me with all those debts and I'll never see another cent from her. Look at this place." She threw her arms out to indicate the hotel. "I can't afford to stay here. I wanted to share a room at least, but Mirabelle doesn't share, and Mary Anna snores dreadfully. Mirabelle said it would be okay, we could charge the stay to the company, as we're here on business. She put all three rooms on the company credit card." Florence burst into tears. "The only thing worse than having Mirabelle as a partner is not having Mirabelle as a partner."

I drank my coffee and let her cry. My theory lay in ruins. Mirabelle's death did not *bono* Florence.

Finally she blew her nose and wiped her eyes. "I'm sorry, Lucy, you don't need to hear all my problems."

"It's okay. You needed to talk."

"Maybe you have a sympathetic face."

I cracked a smile. "Did Mirabelle have any allergies or a heart condition or anything?"

"No. She complained about catching everything going, but that was nothing but the usual attention-seeking histrionics. She didn't like going to the doctor, which was part of the reason she dragged her feet at taking out the partners' insurance. It would have required a full checkup. 'Doctors don't know what they're doing,' she always said. When Ellen called Mary Anna and me from the hospital with the news, she said the ER doctor was asking a lot of questions about what Mirabelle had eaten recently. The police came and talked to us last night. They asked about what we'd had to eat. Mary Anna and Mirabelle had lunch here at the hotel. I didn't join them, because I knew there'd be food at the shower and I'm sorta trying to lose some weight." She picked up a teaspoon and stirred her coffee. "I told the cops a little white lie. I didn't have lunch with them because I couldn't bear to spend more time than I had to in Mirabelle's company. All she ever does is talk about herself or all the great plans she has for my company—which she soon started calling her company. She wanted to change the name to Mirabelle and Florence Presents. Aside from the fact that anyone seeing that in writing would think we were a gift-shopping service, her name would come first. I tuned her out most of the time.

Sounds mean, doesn't it, saying I didn't like her now that she's dead?" She shook her head with such force her heavy bangs moved. "I still can't believe it."

"Your feelings toward her are real," I said. "You don't have to pretend."

"Doesn't everyone say you're not supposed to speak ill of the dead?" She stared off into space and I sipped my coffee, giving her time.

"I came back to the hotel to get ready to go to the shower. I drove Mary Anna, while Mirabelle went to get Gloria." Florence lifted her head and looked directly at me through her thick glasses. "You and your friends made the sandwiches, didn't you?"

"Yes, we did, but there can't have been anything wrong with them. No one else got sick."

She lowered her eyes again. "I don't suppose your cousin made anything especially for Mirabelle, did she?"

"I don't know," I lied. If Florence was suggesting something Josie made had killed Mirabelle, I didn't want to do anything to encourage that thought.

"Mirabelle and Jake seemed to get on real well the other night. Josie didn't like that, did she?"

"Hey! What are you implying?"

"I'm just wondering. I'm sure it'll turn out to have been an accident, but we all know how women can turn into Bridezilla over their wedding, don't we?"

"No, we do not. Josie's the furthest thing from . . ."

"And Mirabelle had plans for her wedding Josie didn't like."

I was about to tell Florence that Mirabelle was being led on a wild-goose chase to keep her from bothering Josie and that Jake was only showing good manners, but I didn't get the chance. A man came into the restaurant. He spoke to the hostess, and she pointed directly at our table. He thanked her and crossed the room in a few quick strides.

Detective Yarmouth.

I smothered a groan. I couldn't risk Florence talking to him, not immediately after the idea had popped into her head that Josie might have had reason to kill Mirabelle.

Yarmouth loomed over our table. "Good day, ladies. I believe we met earlier. Ms. Richardson, isn't it?"

"Yes."

He turned to Florence. "Are you Florence Fanshaw?"

"Yes."

"I'm Detective Yarmouth. North Carolina State Police. You spoke to one of my colleagues yesterday, but I'd like to talk to you myself about the death of Mirabelle Henkel."

More tears began to flow. Florence wiped her eyes.

"Ms. Henkel was your cousin, I understand. You traveled here together from New Orleans for the wedding shower of your other cousin, Josephine O'Malley."

"We came to help plan the wedding at the invitation of Josie's grandmother," Florence said. "We didn't hear about the shower until we got here. Josie didn't want Mirabelle coming to her shower."

"Hey!" I said. "That's not right. The shower was for Aunt Ellen's friends. Her local friends. A small get-together. Not a big deal."

"Mirabelle wanted to make Josie's wedding into a big deal," Florence said. "Josie didn't like that."

"If you're finished here"—Yarmouth eyed the two empty coffee cups and unused plates—"I'd like to go someplace we can talk."

I threw money on the table. "Good idea. I was at the shower also, so I was one of the last people to see Mirabelle. You'll want to talk to me as well. You can do us both at the same time."

His small dark eyes studied me. "I'll interview you privately, Ms. Richardson."

"I don't mind," I said. "It'll save you wasting time."

"It's my time to waste," he said. "You live at the lighthouse, I've been told. Where this party took place. I intend to check it out next."

"That's true, but I'm not going there now. I'm going . . . out of town. For a few days. To Boston. My father's ill." Realizing I was babbling, I forced myself to shut my mouth.

"Sorry to hear that, but you'll have to change your plans. I need to see this library, and I can talk to you then. Or—" He glanced toward the door. I ventured a peek and saw a uniformed officer watching us. "I can ask my colleague to take you down to the police station, where you can wait until I've finished what I have to do. Which might be around midnight."

Florence had stopped crying. She watched us carefully.

"I guess I'll go home then," I said.

"Good idea," Yarmouth said. "If you're not there when I arrive, I won't be happy. The restaurant seems empty enough.

We should be able to talk here in some privacy. Would you like more coffee, Ms. Fanshaw?"

Florence shook her head. I hesitated.

Yarmouth looked at me. "Would you like to wait for me at the station, Ms. Richardson?"

"No." I fled.

Chapter Thirteen

D etective Yarmouth's interrogation of me was somewhat anticlimactic.

I'd waited for him in the main room of the library, pacing up and down, taking books off the shelves, opening them, reading one line, and then reshelving them, while Charles swished his tail, back and forth, back and forth, and watched me through narrow amber eyes. Yarmouth arrived about an hour after me. Charles made no effort to greet the visitor. He sat on a high shelf, tail moving. Yarmouth examined the room while I watched nervously. He muttered something under his breath when he caught sight of Charles, and his gaze moved on. He then went into the staff break room.

When he came out, he and Charles eyed each other for a moment, then the detective asked me to take a seat. The uniformed officer stood by the door, his feet apart, staring straight ahead, not smiling, as though he expected me to bolt for freedom any minute.

Yarmouth had obviously spoken to other party guests as well as Florence, because he knew most of what I had to tell him. He knew about the food we'd served and about the gluten-free plate prepared for Mirabelle and that Watson had taken the remains to be tested. He asked me if I'd seen anyone tampering with the food, and I said I hadn't.

"Thank you for your time," he said at last. He hadn't bothered to take off his coat.

"This is all moving very quickly," I said. "You're not even sure she was killed by something she ate."

"Would you like me to wait until that's confirmed, Ms. Richardson? While potentially hundreds of people risk exposure to the same thing?"

"Uh, no."

He headed for the door. The cop stood aside. I let out a long breath. Yarmouth turned. "Oh, one more thing," he said. I'd seen the old TV show *Columbo* many times. It was one of my dad's favorites. The move was still darn intimidating though. "Your cousin, Josephine O'Malley, are you close?"

"Yes, we are."

"Fond of her?"

"Very. I mean, yeah, sort of."

"Is she known to have a temper?"

"No. Absolutely not."

"You were a witness to an incident last week in which she threatened to kill Mirabelle Henkel."

I let out a burst of strained laughter. That was about the last thing I'd expected him to say. "I have no idea what you're talking about. Nothing like that ever happened."

"That's not what I've been told. Oh, if you have to rush to your father's bedside, let the people at the Nags Head police station know where you can be contacted, will you. Have a nice day, Ms. Richardson."

I stood in the doorway and watched him drive away.

What the heck?

Josie had never threatened Mirabelle. She was annoyed; she might even have been downright angry, but she'd never threatened to kill her cousin.

I'd begun to turn to go back inside, thinking I'd better call Uncle Amos right away and let him know Yarmouth was making unfounded accusations, when my attention was caught by a rusty van bouncing down the lane.

I groaned. Louise Jane. Aside from Detective Yarmouth, this was the last person I wanted to see. I considered running inside and bolting the door, but she'd spotted me. Louise Jane never gives up.

"This isn't a good time," I said, once she'd parked her car and walked up the path. "The library's closed."

"So I heard. It's all anyone's talking about in town. Another murder at the Lighthouse Library." She shook her head. "You've stirred things up again, Lucy."

"Me? This has nothing to do with me. None of it ever has."

"Your innocent protests are so endearing, Lucy honey. But it's time you faced facts. The spirits who live here don't like you."

I sputtered.

Louise Jane pushed past me and went inside. She stood in the center of the floor, hands firmly planted on her bony hips. She closed her eyes and took a deep breath. Charles leapt off the shelf and settled into the wingback chair for an afternoon nap.

"What are you doing?" I said.

"Shush," Louise Jane said.

More deep breaths. I was about to go in search of something to read when she opened her eyes again. "All is quiet."

"It was quiet until you arrived."

"I mean, Lucy honey, on a spiritual level. I warned you, didn't I? I warned you not to have a wedding shower here."

"Please, Louise Jane, I can't handle this now. A woman died yesterday. The police will soon determine the cause, and it will not be because one of your invisible friends put a curse on her."

Her eyes narrowed. "Don't mock what you don't understand."

"Sorry," I muttered. Yes, Louise Jane wanted to see me heading back to Boston. She wanted me out of my Lighthouse Aerie and she wanted my job. And yes, for those reasons she didn't like me, but I'd never thought she actively disliked me. Her efforts to frighten me were clumsy at best.

None of her so-called ghosts had ever bothered me or left any evidence of their presence. What's more, Charles didn't appear to sense anything either, and animals are supposedly highly sensitive to the supernatural.

Only once, around the time of Halloween, had I thought I'd seen something unexplained and unexplainable, moving outside in the marsh. At the same time, strange things had been happening here, inside the library, when the sailors on a model ship Louise Jane had lent us to be part of the seasonal display appeared to move all by themselves. I hadn't mentioned what I'd seen to Louise Jane, and she seemed to know nothing about it.

Louise Jane's great-grandmother was an Outer Banks legend, and being her heir and attempting to keep alive the history and legends of this stretch of the coast was a responsibility Louise Jane took seriously.

She had the respect, I reminded myself, of many people.

"What I've heard," she said, "is that Mirabelle was on a diet and Josie prepared a special tray of low-fat desserts for the shower."

"Where did you hear that?"

She waved her hand. "Everyone's talking about it, Lucy."

So much for hoping rumors wouldn't spread. "Everyone shouldn't be talking about it. The police haven't said anything about her being killed by something she ate." *Not publicly*, I added under my breath.

"Forensic vans are parked outside Josie's Cozy Bakery. No one's being allowed in. Josie's been seen pacing up and down outside. Valerie Manning was having her morning coffee when the state police charged into the bakery and ordered everyone out. You don't have to be a genius to know what they're thinking." Louise Jane narrowed her eyes and peered at me. "Or some sort of hotshot private detective."

"I've never claimed to be a hotshot anything. I'm just a librarian."

"It's even on Twitter."

"What's on Twitter?"

"The news about Mirabelle's death and about Josie's being closed while the police search it."

"Well then, if it's on Twitter, it must be true." I tried to sound unconcerned, but my stomach dropped to the approximate vicinity of my toes. Josie had been worried about the hit the reputation of her bakery would take if gossip started spreading. Looked as though it had. Twitter had a national reach. Plenty of people who vacationed in the Outer Banks would see it, and if, I mean when, Josie was found to have had nothing to do with Mirabelle's death, that news wouldn't spread nearly as far or as fast.

"You haven't had anything to do with these vicious rumors going on Twitter, have you, Louise Jane?"

She looked genuinely hurt. "Other than my parents and my grandmothers, I care about nothing in this world more than the Outer Banks in general and this library in particular. And Josie O'Malley is very much a vital part of both of those things."

"Sorry," I said. And I was. Louise Jane's loyalty has never been in doubt.

"Apology accepted. You know I only want to help." She smiled at me in the way that always makes me fear a sudden attack is imminent. "Now, if we're going to remove the cloud of suspicion from Josie, we have to understand what did happen here. Don't take what I'm saying the wrong way, but I can't help but notice you've put on a few pounds lately."

"What!"

"Must be that being-in-love stuff." She winked. "You'd better be careful; a few pounds here and there can lead to a few more. Or so I've heard." Louise Jane herself is as thin as a needlefish. And, at times, her teeth can be as sharp.

"I have not put on weight, and I don't see what that has to do with anything."

"That's what I'm trying to explain to you. Please try to follow along, Lucy honey. I fear you're in danger. As I've told you many times, the Lady bears no ill will toward anyone, not even you, but other spirits are at work here. Spirits who might not have been happy to have crowds of people in the building on what should have been a quiet Sunday and you coming and going at all hours of the night. Logical enough for them to have a look at your weight gain . . ."

"I have not . . ."

"And assume the fat-free treats were made for you."

"That's the most ridiculous thing I've ever heard." Every time I start to like Louise Jane, she hits me with another crazy idea that somehow manages to make me look like the foolish one.

"Is it? Mirabelle wasn't from around here, and she should have been going home the next day. There was absolutely no reason for any of the lighthouse residents to want to do her harm. You have to agree."

"Well, yes, that's true, but it seems like an indirect way to get to me."

"I'm trying to learn all I can about the inhabitants of the spirit world, Lucy, but sometimes they can be beyond our understanding."

"Those particular baked goods weren't fat-free anyway. They were gluten-free. A sign was posted next to them saying so."

Louise Jane lifted one eyebrow. "Yes, I saw that, but do you think a Civil War–era soldier or an uneducated laborer who'd been part of the crew that built the original lighthouse would know what gluten-free means?"

"No, I guess not. Hey! Why am I agreeing with you anyway? This will all turn out to have perfectly natural causes."

"I hope so, Lucy, but in the meantime, you have to consider that the poisoned food was meant for you, and poor Mirabelle got in the way. How time flies; I have to be off. Have you heard anything more from George?"

"Who?"

"George Grimshaw. About the work to secure the building?" Louise Jane pointed to the crack in the alcove wall. "I'm positive that's bigger than the last time I saw it."

I couldn't help but look. The crack did seem to have grown longer and wider. "He's supposed to be coming Wednesday to do the inspection. I don't know if that's going to happen now."

"Nice chatting to you. You'll let me know if you want me to put some spells down in front of your door, won't you? Although, if someone, or something, is after you in the rest of the building, that might not help much."

Louise Jane let herself out. When the door had shut behind her, I gave my head a shake. From the comfort of the chair, Charles called me to come and pat him, and I obliged.

Mind games. Louise Jane and her silly, childish mind games.

Before calling Uncle Amos to let him know what Yarmouth had told me, I ran upstairs and dug into the back of the closet in search of the bathroom scale. I hadn't been on it for a long time. I kicked off my shoes, took off my sweater, ensured Charles wasn't standing behind me pressing the scale with his paw, and with great trepidation stepped onto it.

Two pounds down from the last time I'd looked.

More mind games.

Which, I had to admit, worked every time.

Chapter Fourteen

I called Uncle Amos and told him Detective Yarmouth was saying Josie had been heard to threaten Mirabelle.

"I suspect he was trying to draw you out, Lucy. Make you say something you shouldn't. Ellen's waving her arms. She says come to dinner. Josie and Jake will be here and we can discuss any new developments."

"Can I bring Connor?"

He chuckled. "Of course."

"One other thing I think you should know."

"Go ahead."

"Florence is implying that Josie was angry enough at Mirabelle to kill her."

An icy silence came down the line. "Is that so," Uncle Amos said at last.

"She said as much to me, and unfortunately Detective Yarmouth arrived to interview her almost immediately after that. So she might have told him too."

"I'll have Ellen remove one person from our guest list for dinner." He hung up.

I hadn't bothered to tell my uncle that, according to Louise Jane, the lighthouse spirits had intended to kill me rather than Mirabelle.

I then sent a text to Connor, who I knew was in meetings all day. OKAY IF WE CHANGE PLANS? DINNER AT E & A?

They must have been on a break (or he was excessively bored and checking his phone under the table), because he replied almost immediately: SURE.

*   *   *

I hadn't told Uncle Amos what Louise Jane had reported about Twitter either. If it was true, I was hoping the news wouldn't get to Josie.

Unfortunately, it was true.

Not what they were saying, of course, but that it was being said.

I hunted for mention of Josie's name or her bakery and found nothing more recent than a couple of days ago when someone raved about the lemon cake they'd enjoyed there. I then searched for Mirabelle. The heading picture on her page was of her standing on a yacht club veranda pointing to an enormous yacht decked out for a party. The impression she had evidently hoped to give was that this was her yacht or her party. Posts on the page were mostly about work she'd done for her and Florence's event-planning company. Florence, notably, was never mentioned. A squealing tweet from Saturday saying she was excited to be involved in organizing a mega-wedding on the ocean was the most recent post.

Next I looked up the Nags Head Police official page, which

said only that a suspicious death was under investigation. No names, no location or other identifying characteristics.

A broad search for Nags Head brought up nothing but vacation and fishing photos.

I was about to close my iPad when I did one more search. And there it was under #OUTBANKX. Someone with the handle @roguejourno222 had posted:

HAS POPULAR #OUTBANKX COFFEE SPOT JCB KILLED A CUSTOMER?

The tweet showed a picture of the exterior of Josie's Cozy Bakery, the sign over the door highly visible, being guarded by a scowling Officer Franklin.

I groaned. Charles jumped onto the table to have a look. He swatted at the screen of the iPad. "You're right," I said, "it couldn't be much worse." Whoever @roguejourno222 was hadn't named the bakery outright, but the sign spoke for itself. It didn't so much speak as shout in great big black capital letters. He'd used the hashtag popular with our tourist industry to ensure people thinking of coming here for their vacation would see it.

Several comments followed, most of them, I was glad to see, supportive of Josie: NOTHING HAS BEEN PROVEN. MUCKRAKING JOURNALISM AT ITS WORST. BEST BREAD IN NORTH CAROLINA.

Someone said Mirabelle had been on drugs and it was her own fault she'd died. I didn't think comments like that would be terribly helpful.

I studied the picture. Judging by the angle of the sun, it

had been taken early in the morning. About the time Bertie and I had arrived at the bakery in answer to Alison's call.

About the time Judy Jensen and her nosy friend had been poking around, searching for a story.

I followed the links to @roguejourno222's page. The picture was of a man holding a black Nikon with a long lens to his face. Most of his face was concealed by the camera, but I was pretty sure it was the guy I'd seen this morning. His bio said he was a freelance journalist and photographer. I quickly read through his Twitter feed. Plenty of celebrity gossip, pictures of second-rate movie stars and reality TV personalities coming out of restaurants or walking down the street. The pictures were mostly grainy, many of them out of focus, probably taken from behind dumpsters or out the windows of speeding cabs. One photo showed a disgraced politician yelling directly into the camera. The picture was not flattering.

Muck-raking journalist was right. Of the worst sort.

I wondered how he'd gotten word of what was happening at Josie's so quickly and why he'd care. Josie wasn't famous. She was very pretty, which might have some appeal to him, but she wasn't in any of the pictures.

I didn't want to, but I had to tell her what was happening. She'd ducked when a reporter she recognized arrived at the bakery, but she might not have had a good look at Judy's companion. I placed the call.

"Heads up," I said when she answered. "That guy who was at the bakery this morning with Judy Jensen thinks he's some sort of a journalist, but he's not affiliated with any of the respectable media outlets."

"Meaning?"

"Meaning, he's put a picture on Twitter."

"A picture? Of me?"

"No, but it shows the bakery and the police outside. It was taken this morning. I debated telling you about it, but I decided you need to be warned. You don't want him snapping a picture of you."

"A picture of me, I don't mind. I do mind one of my place, though. What else are people saying? Is anyone seriously thinking I caused Mirabelle's death?"

"The good news is that, so far at least, his post didn't get many replies and those that did were on your side."

"I can't bear to look."

"Don't. Leave it up to me. I'll keep an eye on this, and if there's anything you need to know, I'll tell you."

"Thanks, sweetie. Don't say anything to Jake, please."

"Why not?"

"I don't need Jake getting into a confrontation with anyone over this."

"Understood. Do you know Judy Jensen? Personally, I mean?"

"Not really. I've seen her around. She did a feature on us when the bakery first opened."

"Is she the muck-raking sort?"

"I don't think so. She covers high school basketball games, store openings, town council meetings, storm damage. All the standard local events. I'll ask Dad about her. He'll know if she tries to make court cases sound more serious than they are."

"What are you up to for the rest of today?" I asked.

"Right now, I'm sitting on a stool in my own place watching the police tear my livelihood apart. As I don't have a business to run or customers to feed, I'm going to go to Jake's later and help with dinner prep before we go to the folks' for dinner. You?"

"We're closed too. I might dig into Mirabelle's past, see if I can find any reason someone might want to do her harm. Is that okay?"

"Sure it is. I can't help you with that. I hadn't seen her for a long time and haven't kept up on her news. I went to her first wedding but not to the second. My mom and dad didn't go to that one either. Despite all the claptrap about the importance of family weddings, no one from our side did. Her second husband is from Ecuador, and the wedding was held there although they lived in New Orleans. Even Grandma didn't attend."

"Were her divorces bitter affairs? Strongly contested?"

"I don't think so. I never heard about anything like that. Both men were quite a bit older than Mirabelle and had a fair amount of money. Not super rich but well enough off."

"I'll see what I can find. Unlike Lord Peter Wimsey, I have the Internet at my disposal and a world of information at my fingertips."

"Speaking of Lord Peter, is the book club still on for next week?"

"Do you want it to be? I can cancel."

"No, don't do that. I need to keep my mind on other things, and that book presents quite a puzzle. Imagine, the murder victim died twice, and got up and walked around in between. I'll see you tonight at dinner?"

"I'll be there. Bye for now," I said.

I went back to my iPad and spent a good part of my unexpected day off work finding out what I could about Mirabelle and those around her. I went to the website for Florence's event-planning business and saw lots of pictures of beautiful settings and read pages of glowing testimonials. I was invited to send an email or drop in to their office to chat about my "event-planning needs." I was also promised "the wedding of your dreams at a cost perfect for your budget."

The web page was professional and well done. If I'd been in the market for an event-planning company, I'd have had no reason not to consider using them.

I next searched for information on Mirabelle herself. She was mentioned a few times in what passes for the social pages in New Orleans, at parties or fund-raising events, but she was never more than one of a crowd. One picture showed her with her then-husband Andres Henkel, who was considerably older than her and was referred to as a "financier." Whatever that meant. He'd married again recently, to a woman even younger than Mirabelle, and they'd moved to Tampa, Florida. I studied the picture of Andres and his new wife carefully, looking for something familiar about them, but I was positive I'd never seen either of them before. Certainly not lurking outside Josie's Cozy Bakery, waiting for an opportunity to poison the baked goods.

Eventually, I put the iPad away and pulled on my hiking shoes. A good walk along the beach would go a long way toward clearing my head. I'd have liked to think it would allow me to sort out my thoughts, but I had no thoughts that needed to be sorted out.

I had not the slightest idea who might have wanted to kill Mirabelle. Florence might have *wanted* to, but she would have secured her financial future first and insisted on partnership insurance. As it was, according to what Florence had told me, Mirabelle's death had left her pretty badly off.

I supposed it was possible she'd decided things were only going to get worse and she had to put a stop to Mirabelle now, but Florence appeared to be genuinely distraught at the death of her cousin and partner.

Gloria and Mary Anna hadn't gotten on well with Mirabelle or even appeared to have been fond of her, but well-bred southern ladies rarely bumped off relatives just because they found them annoying.

*   *   *

The weather was cool but sunny, and a handful of walkers were on the beach enjoying the day. The temperatures were expected to drop dramatically tonight, bringing in a winter storm. The surf pounded the shore and seagulls circled overhead, screeching and diving. Sandpipers darted in and out of the waves, and tiny crabs buried themselves in the soft sand. I lifted my face to the sun and soaked up its warmth. I walked for a long time as my mind went around and around in circles. Eventually I turned back and headed for the car. The footprints I'd laid down only moments before were already fading as the sea washed over them.

It was entirely possible I'd never met whoever'd killed Mirabelle. Maybe they'd slipped into town, heard about the shower, poisoned the baking, and left again.

That seemed like a heck of a stretch. Josie was a professional pastry chef. She regularly provided baked goods for hotels and functions all over Nags Head. That tray could have been intended for literally almost anyone.

I stopped dead.

Was it possible the killer hadn't cared who ate the poisoned food?

Is someone out to destroy Josie, and was Mirabelle's death merely a means to that end?

Had the poisoner not known they were tampering with the tray of gluten-free desserts, intended for a specific individual? Few people not on gluten-free diets would eat those treats when Josie's justifiably famous pecan squares or coconut cupcakes were available. If the main tray of desserts had been poisoned, more people would have taken ill or died. At the minimum, Josie would be forced out of business. Jake's restaurant would suffer by association and might have to close. At worst, Josie would go to prison.

Who on earth would want to do that to Josie? She was one of the nicest people I knew. Everyone loved her.

No. Not everyone.

Josie was a businesswoman. That meant she had rivals and disgruntled employees. I couldn't see a Nags Head bakery going to such extremes, and Josie's place wasn't new. In the summer, she'd fired an employee for coming to work drunk more than once. It had been hard on her, but she'd had to do it. Norm Kivas was his name. He'd been furious and made threats against her, but last I'd heard he was going to AA and helping to take care of his grandchildren. He brought them to the library sometimes for the children's programs. I'd check with Ronald to see if anything had changed in Norm's life. Maybe he was back on the bottle and now out for revenge.

And then there was Jake's ex-girlfriend, the one who'd followed him from New York. He'd told me the night we dined at his restaurant that she'd showed up in Nags Head wanting them to get back together. He was worried she'd start bothering Josie.

Had she? And if so, how far had this bothering gone?

Yes, it was possible that even Josie had enemies, enemies angry, or disturbed, enough they wanted to destroy her.

Slowly I became aware that my feet were cold. I looked down. The tide was coming in and the winter sea washed over the tops of my boots.

Chapter Fifteen

I first met Connor McNeil at a beach party the summer I was fourteen and he was fifteen, when I was spending my vacation with Aunt Ellen and Uncle Amos. We'd had the briefest, and most innocent, of summer romances. He'd been gone the next year, spending the season working on a charter fishing boat, and I hadn't thought much about him since then. But, to my surprise and increasing delight, the feelings we'd had for each other as teens had been rekindled when I moved to the Outer Banks a few months ago.

He picked me up at the library, and we arrived at the beach house at six o'clock. Connor took my hand and gave it an encouraging squeeze as we walked up the path together. Aunt Ellen, wearing a white-and-pink apron with a bib and sash, opened the door. She greeted us with a big welcoming smile, but I could see the tension lurking behind her eyes.

"Something smells great." Connor handed her the bouquet of colorful mixed flowers he'd brought.

She accepted the gift with thanks and said, "Come on in. We're having drinks in the living room before dinner."

A small crowd had gathered in the cheerful room. A log fire was burning in the big fireplace that was the centerpiece of the room, and candles in glass candlesticks flickered on side tables. The room was cheerful, but the people were anything but. Faces were long and serious. Jake and Josie sat close together on the couch. Gloria was seated in the big leather chair next to the fireplace that I knew was Uncle Amos's favorite chair. Stephanie sat next to Amos, who looked highly uncomfortable perched on the edge of the love seat trying not to glance wistfully at "his" chair.

"Come in," Gloria said to Connor, "and let me have a look at you. We haven't met, but I hear you are Lucy's young man. Lucy is now an honorary niece of mine, and I want nothing but the best for her. You're the mayor, I understand."

"Yes, ma'am, I am," Connor said.

"Don't care for politicians," she said. "Slimy bunch, the lot of them. Still, you're young and handsome enough."

Ellen sucked in a breath. Amos smothered a laugh. Conner looked momentarily confused, and then decided to take Gloria in stride. "Thank you, ma'am."

"What do you do when you're not mayoring? And I hope you're not going to tell me you have ambitions at the state or federal level."

"I'm a dentist and I have a practice here in town. When my term is up, I intend to go back to it full-time."

Gloria beamed. "A doctor! Excellent. You'll do. Lucy, when you begin to plan the wedding, call on Florence for help. Now that Mirabelle's not around, she needs the business."

"That's a bit blunt, isn't it, Grandma?" Josie said.

"It's true," Gloria said. "I can always be counted on to speak my mind."

"No kidding," Ellen muttered.

"What was that, dear?"

"Nothing."

"I do believe I smell something burning. Not coming from your kitchen, I hope."

Ellen gasped and hurried away. Amos got to his feet and said, "How about a drink?"

"Where's Florence and Mary Anna?" I asked, accepting a glass of wine from Amos.

"Not invited," Gloria snorted. "I do believe I've never heard anything so foolish in all my years. Imagine, not inviting visiting family to dinner. I raised you better than that, Amos."

"I think you'll enjoy this wine, Connor," my uncle said. "It's from a winery in Oregon I've recently come across."

"I always agree with your taste," Connor said.

Connor and I found seats. Amos gave us a slight shake of his head. We nodded, having received the silent message not to talk about the one thing that was foremost on all our minds.

Conversation was difficult. As if trying to ignore a shark thrashing around in the bottom of a fishing boat, we didn't discuss the death of Mirabelle. Gloria wanted to talk about Josie and Jake's wedding, and Josie tried to sound upbeat, but she couldn't quite pull it off. Stephanie and Amos talked about business for a few minutes, boring the rest of us.

Soon, Ellen was back, calling us to dinner, and we gratefully trooped into the dining room. She'd made a roast chicken and served it with thick gravy, fluffy mashed potatoes, and roasted root vegetables. The food was delicious but the conversation strained. After dinner, I helped clear the table, and then Ellen served an apple pie and put the coffee pot on. It seemed to me that we were lingering a long time over our pie and coffee, as though we were waiting for something.

Eventually, once the plates were scraped clean and seconds declined, Amos said, "Anyone care for an after-dinner drink? Mother, can I pour you a brandy?"

"You may." Gloria pushed her chair back. Jake, Connor, and Amos leapt to their feet. Conner, who was nearest, helped her to rise. Amos got the bottle out of the liquor cabinet, and Jake brought his prospective grandmother-in-law her cane.

"Good night," she said. "Lovely meeting you, Mr. Mayor. Ellen, next time put more butter in the mashed potatoes. They were too dry." Josie took a heavy lead glass, containing a good couple of inches of dark liquid, from her father and followed her grandmother down the hall.

"My mother," Amos said, resuming his seat, "likes to retire after dinner with a small drink to watch television before turning in. In light of what Lucy told me Florence is thinking, I thought it best not to discuss possible developments in front of Mother."

"She isn't known"—Ellen dropped into her chair with a sigh of relief—"for her discretion."

"What's Florence thinking?" Connor asked.

"Let's wait until we're all here," Amos said. "So we don't have to repeat things."

We waited for Josie to return. When she did, she said, "The TV in Grandma's room's turned up nice and loud."

"More coffee, anyone?" Ellen got up and fetched the pot.

"What did Florence say to Lucy?" Jake asked.

I studied the circle of faces, all of which I loved so very much, watching me expectantly, took a deep breath, and then said, "She implied that Josie had reason to kill Mirabelle."

Jake sucked in a breath. Josie groaned.

"Unfortunately, only seconds after saying that to me, Detective Yarmouth arrived to talk to her. I did my best to convince him to let me stay, but he was having none of that, and I was unceremoniously kicked out."

Jake groaned. "Great. That's all we need."

"There's something else you need to hear," Amos said. "About threats. Lucy?"

I turned to my cousin. "Detective Yarmouth told me someone overheard you threatening to kill Mirabelle."

Josie's face twisted, and Jake muttered.

"At first, I thought he was lying," I said, "trying to trick me into saying I'd heard you talk like that myself. But then I remembered." I didn't want to say it, but I had to. "Yarmouth specifically told me I'd been present when that threat had been made."

"Preposterous!" Aunt Ellen was going around the table refilling coffee cups. She almost poured the entire pot onto her husband's lap. Amos leapt to his feet, and Stephanie handed him her napkin. He dabbed at his pants. Fortunately, Ellen's pot was almost empty; she hadn't even noticed what had happened. "He can't go around making accusations like that."

"Unfortunately," Amos said, "he can say anything he wants."

Ellen dropped into her chair with a groan. "We all say

things we don't mean. 'I'm going to kill him' is such a common statement, no one pays it any attention." She couldn't help but glance toward the door through which her mother-in-law had recently passed.

"Unless the object of the threat dies immediately after," Steph said. "Then state of mind comes into play."

"Precisely," Amos said. "Go on, Lucy. Please tell us exactly what you heard."

"Connor and I went to the bakery last Tuesday for lunch. You sat with us for a few minutes, Josie, and we were talking about Mirabelle and her plans for the wedding. And you said . . ."

"That I wished someone would bump her off." Josie's voice was very low.

"Unfortunately, you said more," Connor said. "I remember now. You said you might take care of that yourself."

"What of it?" Jake shouted. "I've wanted to kill more than a few people in my time. And every one of them is still breathing."

"Blair," Josie said.

"Yes," I said.

"Who's Blair?" Aunt Ellen asked.

"A new employee," Josie said. "He's not working out at all. He spent some time in jail for minor theft and a bar brawl that got out of hand and is out on parole. I wanted to give him a chance. He tries, he really does, but he simply doesn't get it. He says inappropriate things to the customers, thinking he's being funny, and bosses around the other employees, who've been with me longer. Alison's threatened to quit if I don't get rid of him. I can't lose Alison. I was planning on telling him he had to go this morning. Then the police arrived and I had more important things on my mind."

"If Blair overheard you making that comment about Mirabelle to Connor and me," I said, "it's possible he also heard you tell us you were considering firing him."

Josie shook her head. Jake put his hand on hers. "Obviously I can't do that now, can I?" she said.

"No, you can't." Steph said. "It would look as though you were firing him for talking to the police. I'd call that solid job security." She turned to Jake. "Whatever you do, do not have any contact with this Blair. It won't do Josie any good if he tells the police you threatened him."

"I wasn't . . ." Jake said.

"Yes, you were," she said. "I can read your mind. Like your brother, your face is an open book."

Jake sat up straighter in his chair and tried hard to close the book.

"Blair blabbed to the police," I said. "He was clever enough to mention that I'd overheard the comment as well, not to mention our illustrious mayor. We'll have to admit it if we're asked directly."

"You haven't been?" Amos said.

"Not yet."

"You will."

"Yarmouth is still not convinced this was a murder," Steph said. I realized now why she'd been invited to dinner. Not as a friend of Josie but as a lawyer. Amos and Steph could never represent Josie, if it came to that, but they could give her good advice and keep their ears to the ground in an attempt to find out what was going on. "He's gathering ammunition for when the toxicology reports come back."

"If they show something," Jake said, "which they won't."

"That's what we all hope," Amos said. "In the meantime, we need to keep our powder dry."

"When all this is over and we're back to business," Josie said, "I am going to get rid of that Blair so fast his head'll spin. Imagine taking advantage of a woman's death to save his own job."

"Is it possible," I said, "that he did more than that? Might he have tampered with your baking himself, as a way of getting back at you? He might not have intended to kill anyone. Maybe he wanted everyone at the party to get sick and he misjudged the dose."

"Good thinking, Lucy," Amos said. "You're getting good at this."

I groaned. "I'd rather I wasn't."

"I'll dig around in his records," Steph said. "See if he's been in any other trouble, anything more serious than what Josie mentioned."

"And I'll dig around in the Nags Head grapevine," Ellen said. "Far more reliable than any legal records."

Jake shifted uncomfortably in his seat. He looked at me and I nodded, telling him to go ahead. "There is one other possibility," he said. "I hadn't given it a thought until Lucy mentioned that this might be an attack on Josie herself."

"You don't think . . ." Josie said.

"We have to consider it." He went on to tell the table about his ex-girlfriend Toni.

"You think she'd do something this extreme?" Amos asked.

"It's happened before," Steph said. "What better way to get Jake back than to have Josie slapped in prison and poor Jake in need of consoling? Even if it never comes to that but Jake *thinks* Josie killed someone . . ."

"This is a nightmare," Josie said. "Do I have enemies everywhere?"

"No," we chorused.

"We're only tossing around ideas, honeybunch," Amos said.

"Because you have friends everywhere," Steph said. "And we're with you."

Tears welled up in Josie's eyes. Jake took her hand.

"What's this woman's name?" Steph asked Jake. "I can find out if she's attracted police attention before."

"Toni, with an *i*, Ambrose. Toni is short for Antonia, I think."

"Does anyone know anything about this Detective Yarmouth?" Connor asked. "It's unfortunate Sam isn't in charge of the case, but I understand them bringing someone in from outside."

"I ran a check earlier," Steph said. "He's had a totally undistinguished career. No highs, but no lows either. No blots on his record that I can see."

Josie stood up. "Time to go. I'm beat. It's been a heck of a hard day, and I fear tomorrow won't be much better. I've stopped taking calls from anyone but my close friends."

Jake, Connor, Steph, and I got to our feet and mumbled that it was time for us to go too.

Josie turned to Jake. "I guess the wedding's off. For now, anyway."

"Absolutely not," he said. "We wanted something small and intimate, and that's what we're going to have. First Saturday in February as arranged. We're in this together, and we'll face it together, whatever happens. As a married couple."

I glanced at Amos and Ellen. He had his arm over her shoulders and they were both smiling.

Chapter Sixteen

"Hang on a sec," Josie whispered to me. She pulled me aside as Amos asked Connor how plans were going for repairs to the pilings under the pier and Jake told Steph he was considering enlarging the restaurant's deck. Last summer they'd been full most weekend evenings, meaning customers had been turned away.

"What is it?" I asked my cousin.

"I didn't want to say anything in front of Jake, but that ex-girlfriend of his was hanging around the bakery today."

"What do you mean, hanging around? You're closed."

"Precisely. We might be closed, but I have invoices to send out and bills to pay." She sighed. "I still have expenses, rent and such, although at the moment, no income. But that's beside the point. Detective Yarmouth said I can work in the office but not do any baking, so I spent some time in there today. My car was parked outside. Anyone could have known I was there. It wasn't long after you and I talked on the phone. When I finished what I had to do and came outside, there she was. She was standing on the sidewalk on the other side of the parking lot, holding a shopping bag from the accessories store a couple of doors down from me."

"Maybe she was genuinely shopping."

"I might have thought that except for the way she stared at me. She didn't move, she didn't say anything. She just stared. It creeped me out, badly."

"What did you do?"

"I decided to confront her."

"That wasn't wise."

"Doesn't matter. Soon as I took a step toward her, she gave me one last look and jumped into her car and drove away."

"You're not going to tell Jake?"

"The last thing I need is him deciding he has to have it out with her and the police being called. Nothing happened. I needed to tell someone, that's all."

"What's her name again?"

"Toni Ambrose."

"Jake said she found a job in town. Do you know where?"

"At the Blue Lagoon, waitressing. He told me so I'd be sure to stay far away. Why do you—" Josie was cut off when Jake said, "Ready, babe?"

"Coming." She wrapped me in a tight hug, and then we went out into the night. The winter storm had arrived and an icy cold wind hit us full in our faces. A perfect match to our moods.

* * *

Bertie had called an emergency meeting of the board of the Bodie Island Lighthouse Library for Tuesday at noon to discuss work needed on the lighthouse building. As the board was going to meet in the staff break room at the library, Bertie had been unsure if it could go ahead. Sam Watson called her Monday evening and said the library could open the following morning. Bertie let us know, and then she contacted the members of the board to tell them the meeting would proceed as scheduled.

At eleven o'clock Tuesday morning, she said she'd watch the desk for me while I went into town to pick up food for the meeting.

"Is everyone coming?" I asked.

"Yes. I had to offer lunch to get those who have jobs to agree to attend."

"You mean Curtis wouldn't come if there wasn't free food on offer."

The twinkle in her eyes took some of the heaviness out of her face. "That might be the case."

Bertie looked, to put it mildly, dreadful. I wondered if she'd slept much the last few nights. The bad news about potentially expensive building repairs followed by the murder placed a great deal of worry on her shoulders. Thick circles lay under her eyes and her color wasn't good. "It'll all be okay," I said.

She smiled at me. "I'm sure it will. Somehow, at the Lighthouse Library, things always work out."

"Did you tell them what the meeting's about?"

"I had to give a few brief details."

"Why do you even want Curtis here? You know he and Diane are no friends of the library. They won't agree to spend the money."

"We can't make a decision of this magnitude without the input of all the members. If we did, Curtis would have grounds to lay a complaint. Even to go ahead and release money from our contingency fund requires a vote by the full board. I didn't sleep much last night, thinking it over. I've decided to lay it all out before the board and suggest we have to plan for the worst-case scenario. George will be here tomorrow to make a more detailed inspection of the work. And then we'll know. No point in worrying about it until then, but we can be prepared. Is Josie and Jake's wedding still on? I hope so. I'm looking forward to it."

"Yes, it is, as planned. I can only hope the cloud of suspicion's no longer hanging over Josie's head by then."

"They don't seriously think Josie killed her cousin? The very idea is preposterous."

"I don't know, Bertie. I really don't know."

Bertie handed me the library credit card and I headed out. I went the long way to the sandwich shop, not wanting to see Josie's place closed and police cars parked outside.

Back at the library, Bertie was helping a young man at one of the public computers, so I took the sandwiches and cookies to the break room, where the meeting would be held. I found Charlene arranging napkins, glasses, and printouts of the library budget by each place.

"Important meeting," I said.

Charlene let out a long breath. "Oh yeah." She held up her right hand, showing me crossed fingers.

We went into the main room in time to greet the first of the board members. No one was smiling. Mrs. Fitzgerald, chair of the board, kissed Bertie lightly on the cheek and mumbled, "Try not to worry, dear."

"So this is the problem, is it?" Curtis bent to examine the crack in the wall. The rest of the board gathered around, peering over his shoulder. Curtis mumbled something about structural integrity and dangerous tilting. Everyone stood back to check if the wall was visibly sloping to one side. It wasn't, at least not to the unaided eye, but Diane cocked her head and said, "Looks awful bad." As one, most of the board leaned to the left.

Mrs. Fitzgerald did not. Instead she asked, "Where did you get your engineering degree, Mr. Gardner?"

"Don't have a degree ma'am," Curtis said. "Don't need one. I've been around building sites all my life. It's in the blood, you might say. My father built our house with his bare hands."

"Oh, yes. I remember that. Fell down in a light breeze, as I recall. Of course, it wasn't too serious, was it? Not quite a home for people to live in, more a garden shed. Come along everyone, let's not keep Bertie waiting." She walked away, leaving Curtis glaring at her back and a couple of the older board members chuckling.

Diane patted Curtis's arm. "Anyone can see this entire wall is about to fall down on itself." She turned to Charlene and me, malice shining happily in her eyes. "I wonder you two girls aren't scared to death to be in this building all day. I know I would be. One more strong wind like we had the other night . . ." Her voice trailed away, and she and Curtis trotted after the others.

Charles followed, but he was soon back, having been evicted from the meeting.

Charlene went upstairs and the man working at the computer called me over. I showed him how to print out the job application he was looking at and he thanked me profusely. He was dreadfully shy but polite and presentable, and I hoped he'd get the job.

I kept one ear open, trying to get wind of what was happening in the break room, but they seemed to be keeping their voices down. No one was shouting, at least not yet.

Louise Jane McKaughnan came in as I was checking out a stack of historical mysteries. Once the patron had gathered up her books and left, Louise Jane leaned closer to me and whispered, "What's this about the library having to close?"

"Where did you hear that?"

"It's what the rumor mill's saying. The building foundations are crumbling and the whole thing's in danger of falling on your heads. Is it true?"

"Some work's required, but it can be fixed."

She let out a puff of breath. "That's good, then. I was worried there for a while."

"Were you?" I said.

She eyed me. "This library, this lighthouse, is awful important to me, Lucy. You, being an outsider, might not understand the strength of attachment we locals have to . . ."

"I understand, Louise Jane."

"Where's the damage?"

I pointed. "That crack in the wall."

She wandered over to have a look and was soon back.

"Heavens, Lucy. I've seen bigger cracks in half the old houses on the Outer Banks. Joan McKnight once lost a pair of boots in her walls. The ground is soft around here, and it settles. Some people are getting excited over nothing. Gives them something to fuss over. Makes them feel important."

At that moment, the board members—including *some people*—begin filing through the main room, heading for the front door. They did not look happy and several didn't even bother to say goodbye, shaking their heads and muttering darkly. Diane Uppiton and Curtis Gardner pretended to be dismayed. Mrs. Fitzgerald, board chair, came last, walking with Bertie. "I wish I could tell you, dear, that George was being pessimistic, but I've known him for many years, man and boy, and his father before him, and they've always said exactly what they mean. Nothing more and nothing less."

She left.

Ronald and Charlene came down the stairs so soon, they must have been listening from the landing. We, including Louise Jane, who always seems to appear when important library matters are being discussed, gathered in a circle around Bertie, and she kept her voice low. "The board's approved an expenditure of up to five thousand dollars for evaluation of the work and minor repairs if necessary. If it comes to more than that, which it almost certainly will, we'll go to the town for funding. I called George and he said he can have his crew here tomorrow first thing to do the initial inspection and prepare our estimate."

I glanced at Louise Jane. A narrow line had formed above her eyebrows. Even she wasn't as optimistic as she was trying to pretend.

"Do you think the town will give us what we need?" Charlene asked.

"They'd be fools not to," Ronald said. "This library is vitally important to the entire area."

"Not to mention the wealth of history contained within the walls," Louise Jane added.

"I agree," Bertie said, "but times are tight and budgets are too. There are those on the board of commissioners who think the lighthouse could be better used as a revenue-generating attraction." From his vantage point on the shelf above my left shoulder, Charles hissed.

"Louise Jane, I trust you'll keep this conversation to yourself," Bertie said.

"Goes without saying. No one in this room cares about this building more than me."

We were standing on the far side of the room from the alcove. But somehow, none of us could stop continually glancing in that direction. Had that crack widened since I'd last looked at it? Was it growing before my eyes, like some sort of demented sea monster?

"Perhaps," Charlene said, "Lucy could use the . . . uh, personal approach on the mayor."

"Absolutely not," Bertie said. "It might be necessary for Connor to recluse himself from the vote. Which would be highly unfortunate, as he's always been a strong supporter of the library."

"That's one of the reasons he was reelected with such a landslide," Ronald said.

"There cannot be even the whisper of a suggestion," Bertie

said, "that he wants to use town funds to save his girlfriend's job."

And didn't that make me feel absolutely awful.

* * *

"Ronald," I said, once Louise Jane had left and Bertie and Charlene had returned to their offices. "Can I have a minute?"

"Sure. What's up?"

"Nice tie, by the way. Is it new?" The object in question featured Sherlock Holmes: silhouette of a hawk-nosed man with a pipe clenched in his teeth, deerstalker hat perched on his head.

"A gift from one of my sisters, who's a devotee of the Great Detective. She bought it at a quirky little store on Cape Cod dedicated to all things Holmes."

"I haven't seen Norm Kivas here in a while," I said. "Has he been around?" Norm was the man Josie'd had to fire over the summer for showing up to work late and/or drunk one time too many.

Ronald ran his hand through his mane of curly gray hair. "His grandchildren are Jasmine and Savannah. Super kids. Their mom usually brings them to Friday story time. I haven't seen Norm in a while. The mom's work schedule changed, so she's free on Fridays to take care of the kids, and she doesn't need Norm to help with that anymore."

"Did she say anything about how he's doing?"

Ronald studied my face. "Shall I assume this has nothing to do with you being a gossip?"

"You can. Norm was angry at Josie over the summer. Norm was angry at the world, but he eventually came to realize that his daughter and his grandchildren needed him, so he made an effort to sober up. I'm hoping he didn't fall off the wagon and decide Josie was the cause of all his problems."

"I see what you're getting at," Ronald said. "I'll give his daughter a call today. I can say I'm checking with the parents as to a possible change to the Friday program, and then try to ever so subtly check up on Norm."

"Thanks, Ronald." As a children's librarian, Ronald is party to a heck of a lot of family secrets. He knows how to be subtle and discreet.

*　*　*

Speaking of subtle and discreet, the next people to visit the library were anything but.

I was standing at the mystery shelves, helping Glenda Covington, a regular patron, locate the latest in Daryl Wood Gerber's French bistro mysteries, when the door opened. "It should be right here." I ran my index finger down the line of books. "It's not been checked out."

"Things get misplaced," Glenda said. "If we can't find it today, can I put a hold on it?"

"Of course."

A head popped around the shelf. "Hi. Got a minute?" Judy Jensen, the reporter.

"I do," I said. "If you're looking for a book or wanting to consult with a librarian."

"Just a minute of your time," she said.

Charles leapt onto the shelf behind me. He hissed at the newcomer. Judy forced out a smile. "What a lovely cat."

Charles hissed again.

"Small, but mighty," I said.

"And totally adorable," Glenda said. She stroked the long, thick fur. "Go ahead and help this lady, Lucy. I'll keep searching."

I followed Judy out from between the shelves to find the man who called himself @roguejourno222 examining the papers on top of the circulation desk. "What do you want?"

He grinned at me. "A moment of your time."

I turned to Judy. "I'd like you both to leave, please."

"Come on," she said. "A murder was committed here a couple of days ago. The police are investigating. The public has the right to know . . ."

"A woman fell ill here and the public has the right to respect her privacy. The police have not concluded foul play was involved."

"Something she ate, I heard," @roguejourno222 said.

"That has not been determined. I have nothing to say. If you're not here for a book, I'm asking you to leave. Do you have a name, by the way?"

"Calhoon. Roger Calhoon. At your service."

"I am not at yours."

He grinned at me, no offence taken. His face was craggy, his eyebrows bushy, his stomach pronounced, his hair badly cut. He wore jeans that were torn and worn, not because that was the fashion, and a shirt with a permanent stain over the pocket.

"Roger," I said. "Roguejourno222."

He spread his arms and flashed me another grin. "My fame spreads."

"Not favorably. I saw what you put on Twitter." I'd checked his page again this morning. He'd said nothing new, because there was nothing new to say, but he'd put up more pictures of Josie's bakery, police coming and going, the bakery sign prominent in the background. One picture had shown my cousin making a dash for her car. Fortunately, anyone who didn't know Josie well wouldn't have recognized her. She wore a winter coat with the hood pulled down to her eyes and a scarf wrapped up to her chin. Good thing this had happened in the winter. It's hard to make yourself anonymous when everyone is in sundresses and tank tops.

Judy didn't look entirely comfortable at the exchange between Roger and me. "You're a local," I said to her. "You know if you want a statement from the library, you need to talk to Bertie James. Not to me."

"We're not here for a formal statement," she said, "just checking things out, maybe have an off-the-record chat. Roger wanted to have a look around."

"I won't be having any chat, off the record or otherwise. If you want to look, the view from the top of the lighthouse tower is magnificent. I can open the gate if you want me to and let you climb up. Two hundred and seventeen steps. The last two hundred and ten are the hardest."

"Sounds like too much exercise for me." Roger patted his round belly. "Sorry, I didn't get your full name. Lucy?"

I tightened my lips and said nothing.

He cleared his throat. "Okay, you don't want to be mentioned. I get that. Were you here for the fatal bridal shower?"

"No." I lied without the slightest twinge of guilt.

His face fell. "That's too bad. Anyone around who can tell us what happened that day?"

"No."

"Why don't I poke around myself for a couple minutes? Check things out. I won't touch anything. Not much, anyway."

"No."

"This was a mistake," Judy said. "Let's go, Roger."

"Give me a break here," he said. "I can do us both a favor. You tell me what happened at this fatal shower, and I can put your library in a good light. I hear you're in need of funds. Something about the building falling down."

I fought to control my temper. "That sounds like blackmail to me."

"Does it? I didn't mean it that way." He gave me a slow, insolent wink. "We can help each other out, is all I'm saying. It would be a shame if this nice place had to close down because visitors were afraid of coming."

"Careful, Roger," Judy said.

"Found it!" Glenda emerged from the shelves. She held the desired book in her left hand and had Charles tucked into the crook of her right arm. "Or rather, Charles found it. It was under the shelf. Must have fallen to the floor and gotten kicked under. Aren't you the clever cat?"

For once, Charles didn't bask in the praise. Instead, he took one look at our visitors and launched himself out of Glenda's arms. He flew through the air, a ball of tan-and-white fur, teeth bared and claws flashing.

Judy yelped. Glenda gasped. Charles landed square in the center of @roguejourno222's ample stomach and clung on.

Roger screamed and flailed at the cat, trying to swat him away. "Get it off me! Get it off me!"

Before I could move, Charles let go, performed a backflip, twisted himself in midair, flew forward, landed nimbly on the returns cart, and whirled around. He spat once, in Roger's direction, jumped off the cart, and stalked away, tail high, hips swinging.

Roger's mouth hung open. Judy's yell turned into a bark of laughter. "Wow! He sure showed you what he thought of you."

I said nothing. I could think of nothing to say. I could only hope Roger wouldn't sue the library for keeping a vicious animal on the premises.

"No harm done," Glenda said. "Can I check out my book now?"

"One minute of your time, please." Roger tried to sound as though he hadn't been frightened almost half to death only moments before. "Were you here on Sunday, when a woman took sick and died?"

"Me? Never been in this place before. A woman died? How sad." Glenda turned away from him and put her book on the desk. She gave me a wink, and I gave her a smile of thanks. Glenda is a member of the Friends of the Library group and comes to the library several times a week to take out the latest cozy mysteries. She is a good friend of Ellen's and had been at the shower. Her gift to Josie had been a certificate for a massage therapist.

When the door shut behind Glenda, I turned to Roger and Judy. "If there's nothing else I can help you with . . ."

"Okay," he said. "Keep your secrets. For now. Let's go, Judy. There's nothing to see here. As for you"—he pointed his finger at me—"you'd better keep that cat under control. If he scratched me, I'd sue you for all you're worth." He walked out.

Judy started to follow, and then she hesitated and turned back to me. "I'm sorry. Roger's my cousin. He's always drifted from one gig to another, and last month he got fired from his job at a newspaper in the Midwest. He doesn't have much hope of finding another, so he came here, hoping I could put something his way. When he heard what happened here at the library, he jumped all over it. He asked me if I'd help him poke around; maybe we could dig up something to report on that would help him get a new job. I'm sorry," she repeated. "I thought he was a crime reporter, not a sleazy gossip columnist."

"Can you keep him away from Josie? She did nothing wrong, and she and her bakery don't deserve any bad press. Even if it's only on Twitter."

"I'll try. But Roger can be mighty stubborn when he gets an idea in his head." She grinned. "Nice job with the cat."

* * *

"How about a girls' night out?" I said to Grace.

"I'm hardly in the mood, Lucy, and I can't see Josie being so either. I drove past the bakery earlier, and it's still closed, with a police car parked outside. They might as well fly a skull and crossbones from the roof, warning people away."

"I'm not planning to invite Josie," I said. "And I'm not exactly in the mood to kick up my heels either, but I do have an ulterior motive and I need backup."

"In that case, you can count on me."

"I'll pick you up at eight. Dress appropriately." I put down the phone.

Next, I called Stephanie and asked her the same. I got the same response. When I explained what I wanted, she said, "I'm in. I went to that chain coffee shop down the road on my way back from court this morning to grab something for breakfast, and what's happening at Josie's was all anyone's talking about."

"What are they saying?"

"The consensus seems to be that Josie's been unfairly targeted because someone got sick and died after an event she catered. My mom tells me she's hearing lots of grumbling about overzealous police and health inspectors with nothing better to do."

"No one's saying she did it deliberately?"

"Not that I heard or that Mom told me, and she would have. No one who knows Josie thinks she's an idiot. If she wanted to kill someone, she'd scarcely point a big red arrow at herself, now, would she?"

I'd considered that myself, and that was part of the reason I was sorry Sam Watson wasn't leading the investigation. He knew Josie, and like Steph said, he'd know she was not that stupid. "I'll pick you up at ten after eight."

"I suppose I can get off work early for a good cause."

I shuddered to think of someone who was at court before breakfast and thought leaving work at eight was early.

* * *

I studied the contents of my closet. It was January, so I didn't want to wear anything too skimpy. Not that I owned anything skimpy in any event. Charles sat on the bed, washing his face and watching me.

"How's this?" I held up a plain black dress.

He licked his paw.

"Too librarian, is it?" I put the dress back and chose another. He yawned.

"You're right. Boring. Oh, for heaven's sake, what am I thinking? It doesn't matter. I'm not trying to impress anyone."

I dressed in jeans, a white shirt, and a red faux-leather jacket, and tied a red scarf around my neck. I studied myself in the mirror. I would do. Charles jumped off the bed and went to inspect his food bowl.

I told him to guard the lighthouse and left. I picked Grace up first and then Stephanie. They'd dressed for a girls' night on the town, and they both looked as though, like me, they weren't quite sure what that meant.

"Those are some killer heels," Grace said when Steph got into the car.

"You think so? They're what I wore to court this morning, and I didn't bother to change because they match this dress."

The black dress was low cut and close fitting, and the red patent leather pumps had sky-high heels. Steph stood at five

175

foot two in her bare feet. She needed to work at looking inti-
mating when she faced opposing attorneys or hostile witnesses
in court.

I backed out of her driveway as she said, "Okay. We're here
as ordered. Ready for a fun-filled night on the town. What's
up?"

"We're going to the Blue Lagoon. It's a bar near the pier."

"I've seen it," Steph said. "It's supposed to be a popular
pickup spot. I hope this isn't your way of telling us things aren't
going well with Connor."

"Ha ha," I said.

"We'll be the oldest people there," Grace said.

"We're three friends enjoying a night out, because one of
them—that'll be you, Grace—has been dumped by your
cheating boyfriend."

"That's a part I don't have go to a lot of trouble to act."

"But you've forgiven him, and you want him back."

"As if."

"Jake's ex-girlfriend followed him from New York. She's
been hanging around, trying to get him to come back to her.
She was at the bakery yesterday, watching Josie. Nothing happened, and she drove away when Josie spotted her, but it rattled
Josie."

"I'm sure it did," Steph said.

"That's not good," Grace said. "Some women don't know
when to give up. Some men, too."

"You're thinking this woman might have murdered Mirabelle?" Steph asked.

I pulled into the parking lot of the Blue Lagoon. Colored

lights shone in the windows and spilled out the doors. They hadn't taken down their Christmas decorations yet, and they looked limp and tacky. On a Tuesday night in January, the place wasn't busy. I'd been counting on it being a quiet evening.

"Perhaps not with the intention of killing anyone," I said, "but to damage Josie's reputation."

"Makes sense," Steph said.

"It does?" Grace said.

"Not to me, or to you, but to some people, yeah. What's this woman's name?"

"Toni," I said. "With an *i*."

"Let me at 'er," Grace said.

"How do you know she's working tonight?" Steph asked.

"I don't. I could hardly phone and ask, could I? If she isn't here, we'll have to come back another night."

The Blue Lagoon tried hard to look modern and hip. Glass, chrome, concrete, exposed ceiling pipes. A soft blue glow hung over everything, which clashed badly with the leftover Christmas decorations. A man stood behind the long bar, wiping glasses, looking totally bored. The mirror on the wall reflected rows and rows of colorful glass bottles and the bartender's heavy man-bun. A few tables were taken by mixed groups or couples. Most of the people, both patrons and staff, were in their early to mid-twenties, younger than us. The dance floor was small, very small, and currently empty. A sign on the door advertised the forthcoming weekend's live music, but tonight's recorded dance music played too loudly through the speakers.

A woman in a short black skirt and tight T-shirt with blue

trim smiled at us. "Hi. Welcome to the Blue Lagoon." Her accent was pure New York City. I recognized the spiked black hair and multi-pierced ears from the photo Jake had shown me.

"Thanks," I said.

Grace was wearing flats, but she'd wobbled slightly as we crossed the threshold, and Steph had taken her arm. "Steady there." Steph grinned sheepishly at the waitress. "Our friend's had a bad breakup."

Adele was spreading rumors from the sound system. "Love that song." Grace swayed to the music. "She really knew how to get back at him. Maybe I should do that to Eric."

The waitress grinned. She was pretty enough but not exceptionally so. Something about the twist to her mouth and the heaviness in her eyes ruined, I thought, her looks. Then again, maybe I was only seeing what I wanted to see. She wore too much makeup, and paler roots showed at the base of her spiked midnight-black hair. In case there was any doubt this was our quarry, her name tag said TONI.

"Where would you like to sit?" she asked.

"Near the bar would be fine." I thought Toni would be more likely to chat with us if she didn't have to walk across the room. She led us to a table for four, and we sat down. My friends took the seats on either side of me.

Toni placed menus on the table. "Nothing to eat, thanks," I said. "We had dinner earlier."

"It was yum . . . yummy." Grace slurred her words.

Toni shrugged and collected the menus. "What can I get you to drink, then?"

We each ordered a glass of wine. I had a bottle of water

concealed in the depths of my purse to top up the drinks in case we had to look as though we were drinking more than we wanted to.

"You've had a lot tonight, hon," Steph said to Grace. "You should probably have a small glass."

"Don't want the small one," Grace said. "I'm going to drink that man right out of my hair. I'll have a large, please."

Steph shrugged.

Toni left to get our drinks. I leaned over the table. "Don't lay it on too thick."

"That's not too thick," Grace said. "You should have seen my cousin Janice when her boyfriend dumped her."

"You should see some of the things I see in court," Steph added.

Toni came back with three glasses balanced on a tray. She handed the drinks around. Silver rings were on most of her fingers, and I particularly noticed a large one made up of several intertwining triangles on the thumb of her right hand.

We sipped our wine and tried to chat, although conversation was difficult without mentioning Josie and what was foremost on all our minds.

"When you see her heading our way," I whispered to Grace when my glass was almost empty, "go to the restroom."

"Got it. Looks like that's now." Grace stood up, fell against Steph, hiccupped, and staggered away.

"Get you another?" Toni asked.

"Not for me," I said. "I'm driving. You have one if you want."

"Sure," Steph said.

"Don't ask our friend if she wants another, okay?" I said. "She's in a bad way, and I'm getting worried."

"She doesn't look drunk enough for us to cut her off," Toni said. "Long as she's not driving. I don't want any trouble if she asks for one."

"I'm worried if she has too much to drink, she's going to go around to Eric's place and try to get him to come back to her." I shook my head sadly. "Which would be the worst possible thing she could do, showing up drunk like that and making a scene."

"Yeah," Steph said. "Particularly if that new girlfriend of his is there."

I smiled at Toni. I waited. It didn't seem as though she was going to take the bait. The table of six in the far corner got up and left. Toni glanced around the nearly empty room. "We've all been there," she said.

"Some worse than others," Steph said.

"It's bad enough when you break up," I said, "'cause things aren't working out between you, but when another woman steals him from you, that's not right."

"You can say that again," Toni said. "Some women get downright desperate once they hit thirty."

I shifted uncomfortably in my seat. I was thirty-two. I didn't think I was *that* old.

"Your friend's taking a long time," Toni said. "Maybe you should go and see if she's all right."

"She's fine," Steph said.

"If you say so," Toni said.

"Are you from New York?" I asked.

"Yeah, Brooklyn."

"You have the accent," I said. "Been here long?"

"About a month."

"Do you like it?"

"Not particularly. They say it gets busier in the summer, but right now things are mighty slow." She gestured to the nearly empty bar. "Hard to live on the tips I'm getting."

"What brings you down here?" Steph asked.

"A man. What else." She walked away.

"This is getting us nowhere," Steph said. "We can hardly ask the name of this man and if she wants to see his girlfriend in jail."

"I have to agree. Dumb plan anyway. Like she was going to confess to us that she'll go to extremes to get Jake back."

Grace returned to the table, wobbling slightly. Her face was wet and she wiped her mouth. She was a better actor than I'd expected. She dropped into her chair with a grunt.

"I've asked for another drink," Steph said. "Might as well join me if you want and then we can leave."

Toni brought Steph's wine and a glass of water for me. She put the drinks down and then glanced behind her. No one was paying us any attention. She kept her voice low. "My boyfriend and I had something good, but he was tired of New York and wanted to come here, to his hometown. When he told me he was leaving, I said I'd come too, but he said we were finished. I figured he'd be back soon enough, and I waited. I waited long enough, and when I didn't hear from him, I came down to see what's what." She shook her head. "I could tell he was happy to see me, but he said he wasn't. He said I had to go back to New

York, that we were finished and he'd moved on. Then he told me he'd gone and gotten himself engaged."

"No!" Steph said. "What a rat."

"What are you going to do about it?" I asked.

"I quit my job in Brooklyn, so I figure I'll hang around here and pretty soon he'll get tired of her and remember that I'm the one for him. Me. Not her. He needs the right moment, that's all."

"Has that moment happened yet?" Steph asked.

"It will. Soon." Toni leaned over the table and spoke to Grace in a low, serious voice. "You sober yourself up, girl, and get yourself strong. Men can be downright stupid sometimes. You need to remind him you're the one for him."

Grace blinked.

"Get his new girl into a mess of trouble, and you'll see how fast he comes back to you. Now, get you another drink?"

"Oh yeah," Grace said.

Chapter Seventeen

B ertie regularly leads a yoga class at the seniors' center on Wednesday mornings, so she asked me to be on hand when Grimshaw Contracting arrived at seven o'clock to let them into the building.

It was a beautiful sunny day, but cold. At the appointed time, I heard vehicles coming down the road. I pulled on track pants and a heavy sweater, poured my coffee into a traveling mug, and went outside to watch George and his crew work. They unloaded a backhoe from the bed of the truck, but much of the work was up close. Inside the lighthouse, Zack carefully measured the size of the crack in the wall and various distances, made notes, and snapped pictures, while outside George and his men dug away at the foundations, peeling back the earth and exposing the old stones that had been laid to form the base of the magnificent building more than a hundred and fifty years ago.

I stood back, trying to keep myself well out of the way but occasionally stepping forward to get a closer look when I dared. I didn't know what I was looking at other than dirt and stone and mortar, but it all looked okay to me. Except for the long, ragged crack running down the walls and into the earth like an arrow pointing to our doom.

George and his men dug and took measurements and huddled together, making notes on their iPads or in binders. Zack finally emerged from the library, shaking his head mournfully.

"What took you so danged long?" George growled.

"A cat," Zack said with a shrug. "Wanted to play."

George rolled his eyes, but I smiled at the younger Grimshaw. Charles, I believed, had a great instinct for people. If Charles liked Zack, then I liked Zack too.

The men closed their iPads. George shut his binder with a loud snap. They picked up their shovels and measuring instruments and loaded the small digging machine onto the back of the truck. Then they muttered some sort of goodbyes and headed for their vehicles.

"Wait," I called to George and Zack. "What have you learned? What can you tell me? It's not nearly as bad as it first appeared, is it?"

"I'll be making my report to Ms. James." George climbed into the passenger seat of the truck. "Have a nice day."

"Sorry," Zack said, ducking his head and avoiding my eyes.

They drove away.

They did not leave me with warm and fuzzy feelings.

* * *

"I'd like to leave for an hour or two once Charlene gets here, if that's okay," I said to Bertie after George and his crew had left and she'd arrived. "It's library business. Well, sort of."

"You mean murder-in-the-library business?"

"Unfortunately, yes."

"Take all the time you need," she said.

I drove into town. Automatically, I turned toward Josie's Cozy Bakery before I remembered it was still closed. I drove slowly past. A police car was parked outside, a notice stuck to the door. I kept going and went into the chain coffee shop further up the highway. I bought two large takeout coffees and a selection of muffins and then continued on my way.

I've found that, when paying a call on the police, it helps to bring an offering.

I was climbing the steps to the police station when the door opened and Butch Greenblatt came out. He saw me and smiled. His smile grew wider when he saw what I was carrying. "Planning to bribe anyone in particular, Lucy?"

"I was hungry and thought I'd share my bounty with my favorite detective. Is he in?"

"Watson? Yes."

"I'm hoping Detective Yarmouth is not?"

"Haven't seen him." He lowered his voice. "I feel bad about not being in touch, Lucy, but I don't know what to do. Jake's my brother, and you know how much I love Josie."

"I do."

"Jake tells me the wedding's still on."

"Absolutely. Nothing has changed in the feelings they have

for each other, so they have no intention of postponing it. I only hope I can drag the bride to a dress shop in time."

"Steph and I went for a walk on the beach this morning," he said.

I smiled at the thought. Butch and I had flirted when I first arrived in the Outer Banks. We'd been at the point of starting a tentative relationship when Steph arrived in town and knocked the big guy off his feet. At the same time I'd realized the depths of my feelings for Connor. During that brief time, I'd often walked with Butch first thing in the morning. He said it was his way of getting his head in a good place before going on shift.

"She told me you had an interesting evening last night," he said.

"We did."

"Watson will tell you not to interfere in a police case, Lucy."

"As he always does."

"Don't listen to him this time. Steph asked me if I'd ever met Toni. I hadn't. I'd never even heard of her until Jake told me she showed up here wanting to pick things up again. They dated a few times when he was working in New York, but it was never anything serious and he had no idea she was hearing wedding bells. They'd broken up by the time he decided to return to Nags Head and open his own place here. She showed up out of the blue a couple weeks ago, all tears and anger, begging him to come back to her. I'm not happy to hear she's still hanging around town."

"She's not inclined to let things go," I said.

"I can't do anything about it," Butch said, "not as long as she behaves herself."

"I understand."

"One thing before you go in. Toxicology reports can take a long time because they're highly complex, but a simple analysis of something like a food sample is a lot faster. That report came in this morning. I don't know what it says."

"Thanks," I said.

Butch continued on his way and I went inside the station. I told the man behind the desk I was here to see Detective Watson, and he placed the call.

Watson came out almost immediately. "Good morning, Lucy. What can I do for you?"

I held up my bribe . . . I mean, my treat. "I thought you might enjoy a snack."

"In exchange for?"

"A few minutes of your time."

"Doesn't sound like too high a price to pay." He nodded to the desk officer, and I was buzzed through.

Sam Watson's office wasn't really an office, more a slightly cleared space in the corner of a busy room. A few people, officers and civilian clerks, glanced at me but went back to their own business. Watson sat behind his desk and I took the visitor's chair. I handed him a cup of coffee and laid the muffins next to the computer. Two pictures were on his desk, and as he shifted them aside to make room, I could see them. One had been taken on his wedding day, CeeCee young and beautiful, Sam young and handsome, both of them glowing with happiness. The second was of CeeCee at the beach, taken recently, still radiantly happy.

"Nice wedding photo," I said. "How long have you been married?"

"Twenty-four years in June, and I'm not handling the Mirabelle Henkel case, if that's why you're here. The state police are in charge of that." Not one for small talk, our Detective Watson.

"I have some thoughts, and I'd rather share them with you. If you want me to then talk to Detective Yarmouth, I will."

He took the lid off his cup and took a sip. "Go ahead."

The busy office swirled around us. Phones rang, people shouted, a woman swore at the printer as she ripped out a torn piece of paper, and a man laughed. No one paid us any attention.

"You know Josie," I said.

"Yes, I do. Which is why I'm not running this investigation."

"Then you know she isn't stupid, and she isn't impulsive. If she wanted to kill Mirabelle, which I'm not saying she did, she would hardly have gone about it in a way pretty much guaranteed to throw suspicion on herself."

"I raised the point with Yarmouth. He says maybe she's too clever and did precisely that, to throw us off."

"He's been watching too many spy movies. Double agents and triple crosses."

"Thank you for the coffee, Lucy. Have a nice day." He studied the muffin assortment before selecting a blueberry one. I couldn't help but think that Josie used far more berries in her muffins.

"So, if Josie didn't do it, then we have to ask who did. If anyone did. I don't suppose you got any forensic results back yet?"

He looked at me for a long time. I tried to appear firm and

imposing. Watson tapped the paper on the desk in front of him. "You didn't hear it from me, but it won't be kept quiet for much longer. The yellow cake which had been made with corn-meal, pieces of which I took from your garbage, had a substantial amount of GHB in it."

I sucked in a breath. Up until now, I'd been hoping it was all a misunderstanding and Mirabelle had died of natural causes. "So she was murdered."

"No doubt about it," Watson said. "I'm sorry."

"I don't know what GHB is," I admitted. "But I assume it shouldn't be found in a cake. Is it difficult to get?"

"Not at all. It's a street drug. Commonly called liquid ecstasy. Not uncommon and not hard to find, if one knows where to look. It's particularly notorious because it has no taste, so can be added to drinks without the victim realizing they're consuming it."

"Maybe she took the drug willingly. Added it to her own food for some reason. Have you considered that?"

"According to the autopsy report, Mirabelle showed no signs of ever being a drug user. Highly unlikely she'd decide to start, and then go about it in such an odd way."

"But if it's a street drug, why did it kill her? Was an excessive amount used? Enough to kill?"

"In the average dose, GHB reacts negatively on someone with a heart condition. Mirabelle had a very iffy heart."

"I didn't know that."

"It seems no one else did either. We spoke to her father, and he didn't know about it. He gave us the name of their family doctor, who said he hadn't seen Mirabelle in ten years or more.

If she didn't visit the doctor, she might not have been aware of her heart problem."

"So it's possible this drug wasn't intended to kill her?"

"Doesn't matter what the intent was." Watson took a bite of his muffin. "If the end result is that someone died."

"Was this stuff baked in," I asked, "or added on?"

"It was spread across the top. In its liquid form, it's clear, odorless, and colorless."

"Meaning it was added later, after the cake was cooked." I suppressed a shudder as I remembered admiring the cake, particularly the pretty pale-yellow glaze, the color accented by tiny purple flowers.

"Apparently."

"Josie left the goods she'd made for the shower in her car for several hours. It was a cool day, so they were fine there. She doesn't remember if she locked her car or not. That means anyone could have had access to the food. I assume the police know all this?"

He nodded and chewed.

"She shouldn't even be a suspect."

"The dead woman was flirting with Josie's fiancé. He appeared, according to witnesses, not to be entirely averse to her attentions."

"What witnesses?"

"Lucy, I'm not going to tell you that."

As far as I knew, the only time Jake and Mirabelle had been together was at the family dinner at his restaurant. Meaning this witness had to be either one of Jake's waitstaff or one of the family.

Florence was my guess. "He was trying to be polite."

"The dead woman was interfering with Josie's wedding plans, and they had a public spat about that."

"It was being taken care of."

"How?"

"By me. I had a plan to distract Mirabelle by having her make separate plans that would never come to fruition."

"For you to go to all that trouble, Lucy, means even you thought Mirabelle was a problem."

"A problem, yes. I've never denied that. No one has ever denied that, but I'm trying to tell you no one murdered her because of it."

"Josie was heard to make threats against Mirabelle."

I started to throw up my hands, but I remembered in time that I was holding my own coffee cup. "We all say things like that. 'I'm going to kill him.' You don't take comments like that seriously or everyone in town would be in jail. Probably including you."

"When the person in question turns up dead a short while later, then we do take verbal threats seriously, Lucy."

"You have to take into account the reputation of the so-called witness to this threat."

"Tell me about that."

"I assume you're talking about Blair Someone. I don't know his last name. He works for Josie, and she was about to fire him. She can't do that now, not without giving him cause to lay a complaint for unfair dismissal."

Watson's nod was so slight as to be almost unnoticeable. I was pleased he seemed to be taking me seriously. At least he was nodding in the right places and looking not entirely skeptical. "I'm not going to reveal the name of this witness," he said, "but that might be a significant piece of information. When did Josie tell you about this idea for a staffing change?"

"At the same time Blair overheard us talking about Mirabelle. If he overheard that, then he might have also heard Josie telling me he wasn't working out and would probably have to be terminated." I suddenly realized what I'd said. Too late to swallow the word. "I don't mean terminated as in . . . uh . . . terminated permanently. I mean Josie was planning to tell him his services would no longer be required. His employment services, I mean . . ."

"I know what you mean, Lucy. I'm not in charge of the investigation, as I told you, but I can pass pertinent information on."

"If this Blair Someone has a police record, then maybe he's been involved in drugs in the past. Meaning, he'd know how to find GBH."

"GHB."

"Whatever. It's something to consider, isn't it?"

"Got a sec, Sam?" A woman in civilian clothes had come up to his desk. She held a sheaf of papers in her hands. "I need your signature."

"We're done here," he said. "Thanks for coming in, Lucy."

I refused to take the hint. "When can Josie reopen her business?"

"I can tell you, unofficially, that should be not too much longer. The public health department had, naturally enough, concerns. No evidence of anything untoward has so far been found in the bakery itself or any food ingredients."

"Which it won't be. Thanks for listening to me, Detective."

"I can't eat all these muffins by myself." He eyed the selection. "Actually, I can, but I shouldn't."

"Share them around if you like." I started to stand. "Oh, one more thing." I can do *Columbo* myself. "You might want to look into a woman by the name of Toni—with an *i*—Ambrose. Probably short for Antonia. Recently of Brooklyn, New York, currently of Nags Head, North Carolina, specifically the Blue Lagoon Restaurant and Bar. She's Jake Greenblatt's ex-girlfriend, and she's out for revenge. Isn't ecstasy sometimes added to unwitting women's drinks in bars?"

I walked away. No one paid me any attention, but I could feel Watson's eyes following me.

That had gone well, I thought. Not only had I laid out my thought process in front of Detective Watson, but it had helped me to clarify my thoughts.

I hadn't said anything about Norm Kivas. I hadn't needed to. First thing this morning, Ronald had told me he'd spoken to Norm's daughter last night, and she'd said Norm hadn't been bringing the kids to the library because he had a new job. He was attending his AA meetings regularly and was enjoying his job and spending his free time with the family. Things were good, she was pleased to report. I was glad to hear it. If he'd slipped enough that he'd be wanting revenge on Josie, his daughter would have known about it.

* * *

I headed out of town on Highway 12, toward the lighthouse. The road leads deeper into the Cape Hatteras National Seashore to a collection of tiny villages including Rodanthe and Buxton, winding through sand dunes that edge onto the road, running close to the open ocean, ending at the ferry to Ocracoke. Wild, remote, and beautiful, it doesn't get much traffic in winter.

A car pulled out of the police station behind me. It stayed close, but not too close, keeping pace. I turned on my indicators to make the right-hand turn onto the library grounds, and it did so as well.

Just another library patron, I thought.

A good number of cars were in the parking lot, people visiting the library, here to see the lighthouse or explore the marsh. I found a spot and got out of my car. The car that had been behind me pulled in next to me and the driver also got out.

I sucked in a breath.

Blair Someone. He was a big guy, well over six feet and hard muscled. His dark hair was cut to the scalp and his head formed an almost perfect square. He wore jeans, a black leather jacket, and black gloves. He looked at me through surprisingly warm hazel eyes rimmed with thick lashes. His jacket was open, and he wore a white V-necked T-shirt beneath. A tattoo of the handle of a knife was drawn into his breastbone, the blade plunging beneath the shirt.

I glanced quickly around me. At the moment, no one was coming or going from the library or the boardwalk. I clutched my keys tightly in my hand.

"Hi," he said.

"Uh, hi."

"I've been wanting to talk to you."

"I'm sorry, but I don't have time now. I have to get to work."
I half ran toward the building. I fumbled in my purse for my
phone. I had it here somewhere. I always put it in the front
pocket, where I could locate it immediately.

It didn't seem to be there. My searching fingers found pens,
a packet of tissues, a granola bar, a lipstick, a handful of mints.

Blair fell into step beside me.

All I could think of was that I'd been right. He'd killed
Mirabelle, accidentally or otherwise, to get at Josie, and now he
was after me because I was getting too close.

The parking lot was crowded with vehicles, but not a single
person could be seen.

I walked faster.

Blair walked faster. He had no trouble keeping pace with
me. "What are you looking for?"

"My phone. It's in here somewhere."

"You've been asking questions about the death of Josie's
cousin."

"Yes, I have, and if you've been following me, you'll know
I just left the police station. I told the detectives everything I
know."

"I haven't been following you. It's a condition of my parole
that I check in with the police once a week. I did that, and I
was leaving when I saw you get into your car. I wanted to talk
to you, but you drove away before I got the chance."

"You want to talk to me? What about?"

The library door opened and two women came out. They

carried bulging Friends of the Library canvas book bags and chatted cheerfully.

"Good morning, Lucy," the first one said.

"Lovely day," the second one said. "Blair. How nice to see you. It's been a while. How's your mother?"

"She struggles on, Mrs. Singer. It's not easy for her with that arthritis, but she manages to keep her spirits up."

"Give her my love."

"I will, thanks."

The women carried on their way. All the tension flooded out of my body. I took my hand out of my purse. If Blair was planning to kill me and hide my body in the marsh, unlikely he'd exchange his mother's health news with a library patron before doing so.

"What do you want to talk to me about?" I asked.

"I want your advice. I've seen you around the bakery, and Alison tells me you and Josie are close."

"My advice? What about?"

"Look, I feel bad, real bad, that I told the cops about Josie threatening to kill her cousin. She didn't make a threat, not really; she just muttered something we all say all the time. But that cop, the one from the state police . . ."

"Yarmouth?"

"Yeah, him. The fat one." Blair studied the ground beneath his feet. "I tried to tell him it didn't mean anything, but that wasn't what he wanted to hear. He said if I didn't tell him what I'd really heard, he'd tell my parole officer I'd been obstructing the police investigation. So I made it sound like Josie was making real threats, and you and the mayor heard. I . . . I'm sorry, but he scared me and he didn't give me time to think. Look, I made a mistake, a bad one, and I paid for it. I want to put that all behind me, but if I get on the wrong side of someone like Yarmouth, that won't happen."

"Why are you telling me?"

"'Cause I'm sorry. I like Josie. She's tough but fair, really fair, and she's given me a chance. I know I make mistakes sometimes. Yeah, I can be a bumbling clod. She gets mad at me, but she's under a lot of pressure running that place. I like that job." He stirred the dirt with his toe. "I need that job."

"You want me to tell Josie what you're telling me?"

"I'm asking you if you think I should tell her what happened. Tell her I'm sorry about it. I'd like her to give me another chance." He lifted his head and looked at me.

Maybe I'm a fool, but I liked his warm hazel eyes, his awkward manner when he talked to me. I believed him.

"Yes, I think you should. I can talk to her for you, if you want. I can tell her what you said to me, but I think it would be better coming from you."

He smiled for the first time. The smile matched his eyes, not his square head, intimidating bulk, or aggressive tattoo. "Okay, I'll do that. I feel better just talking to you, Lucy. It's been bothering me, a lot, that I might have stitched up Josie."

"Great," I said. "Have you ever been to our library?"

He shook his head.

"You should visit sometime. You'd be very welcome."

"I might do that. But not now. I'm going to call Josie." He turned to walk away.

"Let me ask you a question," I asked. "Don't take what I'm

about to say out of context; I'm only trying to understand. If I wanted to buy some liquid ecstasy, how would I go about that?"

"Once upon a time, I'd have told you to ask me, but that's in my past. It's not hard to get that stuff. Go into a bar and say what you're looking for. They'll find you. Doesn't have to be a seedy bar either; some of the nice ones do a good trade. Catch you later, Lucy."

*　*　*

I stayed in that evening, wanting a quiet night of reading and early to bed. After a light supper of chicken salad, I curled up on the window seat to finish *The Busman's Honeymoon* while Charles stretched out on the bed. I hadn't read for long when my phone rang.

"Hi, sweetie," Josie said. "Hope I haven't disturbed anything."

"I'm finishing the book for book club. What's up?" I could hear dishes clanging and the murmur of conversation. I guessed she was at Jake's restaurant.

"I had a phone call from Blair."

"Is that so?"

The background noises died away as she moved to a spot with more privacy. "He told me he'd spoken to you. He was apologetic, and said Detective Yarmouth pretty strongly hinted that he wanted Blair to point the finger of suspicion at me."

"Did you believe him?"

"Yeah, I did. Butch called Jake earlier. He's been doing some poking around on the down-low, and the word in the state police is that Yarmouth isn't entirely averse to twisting witnesses' arms in order to make them say what he wants to hear."

"Are you going to keep Blair on?"

"Mom did some checking into him and his family. Not a bad kid who went through a wild stage when he fell in with the wrong crowd, is what they say. We had a long talk. I'm glad we did. He needs to control some of his inappropriate jokes and comments, and he needs to stop being so clumsy. If he can do that, it'll work out."

"I'm glad."

"That's not why I'm calling. The initial toxicology report on the cornmeal cake was released today. Someone had added ecstasy to it."

"I know."

"Everyone knows, sweetie. It's on Twitter."

"The police released the report on Twitter?"

"No, but some low-life reporter did."

I groaned. "Roguejourno222?"

"Yes. Who's that?"

"Judy Jensen's cousin. He's a recently fired newspaper reporter, trying to make a name for himself."

"The one we saw at the bakery the other day?"

"The same."

"If Jake finds out who he is, his life will not be worth living."

"Do you know Judy?"

"Sort of, but we're not friends. She did a nice feature on the bakery when I had my grand opening. I think her mom's in my parents' bridge club."

"She's embarrassed by him. She doesn't like his aggressive tactics. Let me see what I can do."

"The damage is done, Lucy. He's saying I poisoned my food. No one's ever going to come to my bakery again."

"Nothing on Twitter ever truly goes away, but we can do something about making sure he doesn't make any more unfounded accusations."

"How can we do that?" she asked.

"The Outer Banks bridge club grapevine."

"Worth a try. Talk to you tomorrow."

"Good night," I said.

My next call was to Aunt Ellen. If Judy Jensen was an Outer Banks native, and if her mom cared about the community, then a word in Mrs. Jensen's ear about what her nephew was up to wouldn't go amiss.

After I told her about Judy and Roger's visit to the library and Roger's Twitter reporting, Aunt Ellen growled into the phone, "Leave it with me, Lucy. I've heard Eileen Jensen complain more than once about outsiders interfering in Outer Banks business. She might have even had a thing or two to say about the gutter press when Jay Ruddle died at the lighthouse and the pack descended."

"Thanks, Aunt Ellen. Josie told me what you found out about Blair. Good work. It helps to know everyone in town, doesn't it?"

"Sometimes," she said. "But not when trying to pare down a wedding guest list."

Something Read, Something Dead

I was tempted to go to Twitter and see if anything new had been posted, but I decided not to. My blood pressure didn't need the stress. I returned my attention to Lord Peter and Harriet Vane.

Chapter Eighteen

We heard nothing more about the murder investigation for a few days. Josie's Cozy Bakery remained closed and all we could do was worry. Roger, aka @roguejourno222, finally gave up hanging around outside the bakery trying to get someone, anyone, to talk to him. He continued posting on Twitter, but as he had nothing to say, the posts were bland and without sensation. The news had moved on, as it does. Josie said she hadn't seen him again, and I suspected that had a lot to do with Aunt Ellen and the bridge club grapevine. If Roger was down on his luck and dependent on the goodwill of relatives, a stern word from Judy's mother might well have done the trick.

Detective Yarmouth came around to the library, once again, to talk to Bertie and me about the shower. He interviewed Gloria, Florence, and Mary Anna at some length and spoke to other shower guests. I heard nothing more from Sam Watson and worried that even if he passed all my information on to Yarmouth, the state police would dismiss it as gossip.

As if worry about Josie wasn't enough, we were on tenterhooks waiting for George Grimshaw's report.

Wednesday evening, before heading upstairs after the day's work, I asked Bertie if George had given her any idea of what would be involved in the repairs. She shook her head. "Too early for him to know the exact cost, and George never guesses. I don't suppose they told you anything when they were here?"

"No," I said. I didn't mention that the expression on Zack's face had made me want to run for the hills.

* * *

Minutes before closing on Thursday, Louise Jane came into the library, accompanied by Theodore Kowalski, rare book dealer and enthusiastic library supporter. "George Grimshaw sent his report to Bertie at four thirty," she said.

"How do you know that?" I said. "I didn't even know it." Come to think of it, when I'd gone into the break room at four forty-five, Bertie had been in there pouring herself a glass of tea from the pitcher she kept topped up in the fridge. She'd taken one look at me, grabbed her glass, and run out of the room. "Phone's ringing," she'd said, but I hadn't heard anything.

"My cousin works in Grimshaw Contracting's office," Louise Jane said. "I asked her to give me a heads-up when the report was ready."

"Is that ethical?" I asked.

She shrugged.

"Louise Jane suggested that as a longtime and highly involved library patron, I'd be interested in hearing the report firsthand as well," Theodore said.

Bertie came out of her office. The look on her face pretty

much said it all, and my heart sunk into my toes. "Imagine finding you two here," she said to Louise Jane and Theodore. "Oh, well, you might as well stay. Lucy, time to lock up. Then can you please call Ronald and Charlene and ask them to come into my office for a few minutes."

I picked up the phone.

It was a solemn group that gathered in Bertie's office. When she told us what George's report had said, it was enough to open up the Slough of Despond.

"A hundred thousand dollars!" Charlene said. "Where on earth are we going to find that much money?"

"As Connor can't be involved due to a potential conflict of interest, I've made an appointment to speak to Susan Barrington, the deputy mayor, first thing tomorrow," Bertie said. "We're owned by the town, and I'm hoping they'll agree to pay for most of the work."

"Susan's no friend of the library," Louise Jane said. "She's totally in the pocket of developers. I bet they'd love to get hold of some of our land for that luxury vacation accommodation they're after."

"Do you have proof of that, Louise Jane?" Charlene asked. "That she's being paid off, I mean."

"Everyone knows it."

"Not good enough," Charlene said.

"Surely the town will give us something," Theodore said. "And we can raise the remainder."

"How are we doing to raise tens of thousands of dollars?" Ronald said.

"Fund-raising efforts."

"You mean a silent auction or a bake sale?" Charlene said. "That might bring in a thousand bucks. If we're lucky."

"A thousand here, a thousand there," Theodore said. "Over time it adds up. How much time do we have, Bertie?"

"Not nearly enough. George says the damage is getting worse every day and is threatening the stability of the structure." She took a deep breath. "He adds that before too much longer, if the problem is not fixed, the building will be unsafe and have to be condemned."

I gasped. The faces of the people around me were studies in shock. Even Charles's little mouth formed a round O.

"I didn't read the whole report in detail, not being fully up on my engineering jargon, but I'll send it to my sister tonight and ask her to go over it. She's an engineer. George knows his business, and I expect my sister will confirm what he says, but I'd like to have it carefully explained to me."

"How about getting a second quote?" Ronald asked.

"We can do that, but I don't expect it will be much different. Everyone in the Outer Banks trusts Grimshaw."

"Are you going to tell the board?" I asked.

"I've composed an email already. I'll send it off when we're finished here. I've attached George's report, repeated the amounts he mentioned plus his urgency, and am asking for their suggestions for raising the money in the event the town doesn't come through. Tonight I'll start work on a grant request to the state. The lighthouse is a historic building of great significance and the library an important cultural center."

"I can help you with that," Louise Jane said.

"Thank you," Bertie said.

"What do you want us to do?" Ronald asked. "You know we'll do anything we can."

The rest of us chorused our agreement.

"Anything legal, that is," Theodore added.

Bertie smiled ever so slightly. "I was hoping you'd say that. We need to set up a bank account to receive donations and update our website with a way people can pay into it online."

Charlene raised her hand. "I'll take care of that. My cousin's a web designer. He'll do it for us free of charge. If he wants to ever be invited to my house for dinner again, that is."

"I've prepared a list of those who've donated to the library in the past and our other patrons and supporters," Bertie said, "along with a letter explaining the situation. If the town doesn't give us all, or most of, the needed sum, bake sales aren't going to amount to much. And we all know the state doesn't act quickly about anything. I'll divide the list between you and ask you to write a personal note introducing my letter."

"Happy to do it."

"Count me in."

"I'll start right away."

"I can contact the universities who've sent students here to work with our maps and papers," Charlene said. "It's a long shot, but some of them might be able to help. Those who wouldn't want to sweep in if we have to close and nab our documents, that is."

"Good idea," Bertie said. "As well as calling your list, get your thinking caps on. Hopefully the town will help us out and it won't all be up to us, but it doesn't hurt to be prepared."

Chapter Nineteen

Aunt Ellen phoned me Friday morning as I was getting ready for work. "I'm concerned about Josie. She's moping around her apartment all day, doing nothing but worrying. She needs to be kept busy. She's always been the sort who never sits down, even when she was a little girl. I can't invite her over here, because Gloria will say something about the wedding, and Josie'll get mad and storm out."

"She still doesn't have a wedding dress," I said. "Maybe we can go shopping tomorrow. I can take the day off, see if Grace and Steph are free."

"Would you, dear? I'd appreciate that. I can't go with her, not without Gloria tagging along. And that means Mary Anna and Florence too."

"Why are they still here? Have the police told them they can't leave?"

"No, but Gloria insists on being with us at, as she says, this difficult time. Mary Anna won't leave her mother. I don't know why Florence is hanging around. You'd think she'd have to get back to work."

"Maybe because you're housing and feeding her," I said.

"Oh, yes. That." Mary Anna and Florence had moved out of the Ocean Side and into the second spare room at Amos and Ellen's house. Things there were tense, I knew, not least because Florence had hinted to the police that Josie had reasons to want Mirabelle dead.

"I heard about the library needing funds for structural repairs," Ellen said. "The Friends of the Library have started making calls. Gloria's giving five thousand dollars."

"That's nice of her," I said. "Considering she doesn't even live here."

"I might have hinted that we'd be eating white bread and beans out of a can for the remainder of her visit if she didn't put her hand in her pocket. Gloria's not without funds, but she guards every penny as though it's her last."

"I'll ask Bertie for the day off tomorrow and let you know if the shopping trip is on."

"Thank you, dear."

* * *

Charlene kept watch over the lighthouse driveway from her third-floor office. When she saw what she was waiting for, she took the stairs two at a time, shouting to Ronald as she passed the children's library. I was on the ground floor and hurried to meet them.

The four (counting Charles) employees of the Bodie Island Lighthouse Library were at the door when it flew open and Albertina James marched in. She might have had a thundercloud hanging over her head. She'd come from the town hall.

"Ten thousand dollars and not a cent more," she said without stopping.

Her office door slammed shut behind her. Ronald, Charlene, and I looked at each other. "I'm guessing that didn't go well," Charlene said. Charles slunk away to bury himself under the table in the alcove.

I watched him go. "Do you think the crack's getting worse?"

"Yes," Ronald said. "You can almost see it grow minute by minute. Word's gotten out, and some of my parents are calling to ask me if the building is safe."

"Okay, people," Charlene said. "No use moping. We have calls to make and ideas to think over."

I gave Bertie time to calm down before approaching her with my request. "Would it be okay if I took a vacation day tomorrow? I'd like to take Josie dress shopping. That's if she'll agree to come. Aunt Ellen's worried about her moping around all day."

"That should be fine," Bertie said. "Ronald has a couple of children's programs, but between him and Charlene, the desk can be covered."

"Did anyone ever tell you you're a great boss?"

She didn't smile. "Let's hope I can keep being your boss."

* * *

Saturday morning dawned crisp and cool. The temperature was hovering around the freezing point and snow was in the forecast. Josie had agreed to the shopping trip, and Steph and Grace had been pleased at the suggestion. I'd arranged to pick everyone up and take them to a restaurant for breakfast, saying we needed to be well fortified for a day of wedding dress and bridesmaid attire shopping. As Josie's place was still closed, I didn't think a coffee shop would be all that appropriate, so we went to Shrimp Shack near Pirate's Cove Marina in Manteo, famous for its all-day breakfasts as well as the view over the small-boat harbor.

The moment we sat down, the waitress—scraggy gray hair, craggy face, sensible shoes, and a name tag that said Maggie—offered coffee and menus. The place smelled of bacon grease, rich coffee, fresh fish, and motor oil.

Josie studied the menu. "I can't eat anything they serve here, not before I try on my wedding dress."

I eyed her slim figure. "Go ahead, live a little." Something niggled at the back of my mind. I'd heard that expression recently and for some reason thought it might be important. No matter. I shoved the memory aside.

"I hope you have some idea of what you want, Josie," Steph said. "Did you look at the dresses on those websites I sent you the links to?"

"No." Josie studied the depths of her cup as she stirred cream into her coffee.

Grace, Steph, and I exchanged glances. Josie had sounded pleased when I called to suggest the shopping outing, but I feared she was getting cold feet and would want to go home early. The stress of all that had happened—and was still happening—was weighing heavily on my beloved cousin.

The waitress came back, pen and pad at the ready, and we placed our orders. I decided to go all out: two fried eggs, sausage, hash browns, toast. My friends ordered much the same, and the waitress laboriously wrote it down. She then repeated it back to us, equally laboriously.

She tucked her stub of a pencil in her breast pocket and started to turn. She stopped and swung back to face us. "Just so you know, Josie, we're all rooting for you."

The first smile of the day crossed my cousin's face. "Thank you so much. That means a lot to me."

"If someone from New Orleans got herself killed on the Outer Banks, then she brought trouble with her. The fool cops should know that and leave decent, hardworking people alone." Maggie harrumphed and went to get our meals.

"Who's she?" Steph asked when the waitress was out of earshot.

"I've no idea," Josie said. "I've never seen her before."

A phone rang.

"We agreed, no calls," Grace said. "This is our special day out."

Josie fumbled in her bag. "It might be important." She found her phone and read the screen. Blood drained from her face and she threw me a panicked look. She mouthed *Detective Watson*, and then she pushed the button and hesitantly said, "Hello?"

We couldn't hear what he said, but color flooded into her cheeks, a smile spread across Josie's face, and a spark returned to her eyes. She glanced at the faces of her three friends and gave us a thumbs-up and a big grin.

All the tension of the past week drained out of my body.

"Thanks so much for letting me know, Detective. I

appreciate the call." Josie hung up and put her phone away. She let out a long breath. "The bakery can open tomorrow."

"That's great," Grace yelled. We leapt to our feet and leaned in for a group hug. Maggie rushed over and wrapped her arms around us. The men sitting at the nearby tables grinned. One grizzled old sailor lifted his coffee cup in a salute. I doubt he'd heard what we said—they were too far away—but seeing happy people made him happy. And that made me even happier.

Funny how infectious happiness is.

"So they've concluded you didn't poison Mirabelle," Grace said when we'd sat down again. "I'll drink to that." We clicked coffee mugs.

"Not with anything prepared in the bakery, at any rate," Josie said. "If I'm going to open tomorrow, I have to get started on prep. Some of my ingredients are going to be past their use-by date and I'll have to order more. I have to call the staff and tell them to come in." She finished her coffee in one gulp. "Sorry, guys. Let's go."

"Absolutely not," I said. "You can do your prep tomorrow and open on Monday."

"Some of my suppliers don't make deliveries on Sunday."

"Then they'll deliver on Monday and you'll open Tuesday," I said.

Grace and Steph nodded. Grace picked up her knife and fork and gripped them firmly, one in each hand. "Not budging. I've planned a day of shopping with my friends—all my friends—and I'm not giving in."

"You didn't drive, Josie," Steph pointed out. "If you don't want to hitch back to Nags Head, you have to come with us."

Josie studied our faces. She broke into a huge grin. "You guys are the absolute best. Okay, you win. Shopping it will be."

Maggie plopped loaded plates onto the table. "That Sam Watson's got a head on his shoulders. Comes from being a true Banker, never mind he went to live in New York for all those years. I don't hold with bringing in outsiders to investigate what's Outer Banks business. Ketchup? Vinegar? More cream?"

"Yes, to all," I said. Detective Yarmouth had a strong North Carolina accent. If Maggie considered him to be an outsider, I wondered what she thought of me.

I didn't have to wonder for long.

"Now, you, Lucy," she said, "are an honorary Banker. Like old Ralph Harper said, you're a woman of the sea. Be right back with the coffee pot."

I leaned across the table and whispered to my friends, "She's got a heck of a memory. I've only been in here once, and that was back in the summer when I needed to talk to Ralph about the death of Will Williamson." I'd made an enormous effort to be seated next to his regular stool at five AM before Ralph finished his breakfast and got his charter fishing boat ready for a day on the water.

"Maggie's a Manteo legend," Grace said. "She can compete with Louise Jane for numbers of relatives and the depths of her roots. This place is gossip central. Everyone who wants the news comes in here."

"I must remember that," Steph said, "next time I have an uncooperative client or hostile witness and need to get the facts."

Maggie returned with the coffee pot and poured without asking if we wanted more. I like that in a breakfast place. "How's your mother these days, Stephanie? Recovered from that accident yet?"

"Fully recovered," Steph said. "Thanks for asking."

Maggie went to greet a group of new arrivals, and my friends and I exchanged looks. Then we burst into laughter. "See what I mean?" Grace said.

We dug into our breakfasts.

After the first welcome bites, Steph asked, "What's happening with the murder investigation? Did Detective Watson say anything about that?"

Josie popped a piece of bacon into her mouth. "He said I am not under suspicion *at this time*. Reading between the lines, I think he had to persuade Detective Yarmouth that, because the food to which the drug was added had been available to anyone passing, having been left in my car for a while, any good lawyer"—she grinned at Steph—"would argue that's cause for reasonable doubt. I want to call Jake." She put down her fork and got to her feet. "I promise I won't run off and hitch a ride into town."

Josie went outside in search of some privacy to make the call.

"I'm so glad that's over with," Grace said.

"Unfortunately," Steph said, "it's not. The police didn't conclude that Josie didn't kill Mirabelle, simply that such cannot be proven in a court of law. Not yet, anyway. The investigation will continue. They'll keep coming back with questions. The cloud of suspicion will hang over Josie for a long time. Maybe forever. As we're always hearing, Bankers have long memories, but when it comes to unsolved murder, the police have longer ones."

I glanced out the window. Josie was on the phone, pacing up and down the boardwalk as she talked. The winter sun cast a golden glow through her hair and the blue water sparked behind her. She was smiling, happy. She laughed at something Jake said. She'd realize, soon enough, what Steph had. This wasn't over.

The only way to clear the cloud of suspicion from Josie, I knew, was to find out who had killed Mirabelle.

Chapter Twenty

O ur shopping expedition was a great success.

The bridal shop Josie had chosen was small and beautifully appointed, not only for trying on and buying wedding attire but for entertaining friends. We flipped through the racks, each of us intent on finding the perfect dress. Our tastes turned out to be totally different. Tiny Stephanie who wore killer heels and power suits to work went for puffy dresses with enormous skirts and floor-sweeping trains. Grace, a public school teacher, wanted sleek and sexy with clinging fabric and plunging necklines. Maybe I'm more traditional than I thought I was, and the gown I favored had a boat neck, long sleeves, and full skirt. I thought it tasteful and elegant. "Stodgy," said Steph, as she admired a dress I thought was straight out of the 1980s.

But Josie knew her own taste, and she politely but firmly turned down all our suggestions. It didn't take her long to find one that suited her figure and her personality impeccably. We were made comfortable in armchairs with glasses of icy tea and bridal magazines while the shop assistant helped Josie to dress.

Our friend glowed with pure joy as she modeled the gown for us, and we agreed it was absolutely perfect. Any other woman would have needed tucks and pinches and hems taken up or let down. Her being Josie, the dress fit perfectly as it was, and she didn't need to leave it behind for alterations. We then went on to other shops and found a simple black knee-length, wide-skirted dress trimmed with black lace for me, shoes for both Josie and Grace, and a necklace and matching earrings for Steph to wear to the wedding. Josie wanted to keep her jewelry minimal. She'd wear only the small diamond earrings her mother had worn to her own wedding and leave her throat bare.

We'd eaten huge breakfasts at Pirate's Cove, but no friends' shopping day is complete without a lunch break, so we indulged in that too. Josie phoned the bakery staff to give them the good news and ask them to come to work on Monday. Other than those phone calls, she kept her mind off work and on her wedding, and I was glad of it.

At three o'clock we threw the last of the shopping bags into my full car and climbed in after them.

"That was fun, everyone," Josie said. "Thank you so much for forcing me to come."

"Are you going to tell your grandmother you snuck out and got your dress without her help?" Grace asked.

"I'll have to," Josie said, "the next time she brings it up. Which will be the next time I see her. I called Mom earlier and told her about Watson's call. I suggested she tell Grandma and the rest they can go home now."

"Do you think they will?" Grace asked.

"Probably. Grandma's complaining that her cat will be missing her, and her neighbor can't be trusted to water her plants properly, and she needs to go to her own doctor because her heart's been acting up with all this stress. On and on it goes. I don't think Aunt Mary Anna likes her mother's company any more than the rest of us do, but she won't leave without her. As for Florence, she's enjoying an all-expenses-paid vacation at my parents' house, but that can't last forever. She returned her rental car and has been helping herself to Mom's car whenever she likes. Mom had to hide the keys after one time when she needed to go out and found her car gone."

"What is it they say about visitors and fish?" Grace spoke from the back seat, almost buried beneath a mound of shopping bags. "They start to go off after three days."

"Can you drop me at the restaurant, Lucy?" Josie asked. "Jake'll be starting dinner prep about now and I can give him a hand."

"Aren't you supposed to be having a day off?" Grace asked.

"Helping Jake isn't work," Josie said, the light of true love shining in her eyes. "It's fun."

"What about your dress?" Grace asked. "If you're not going home, you don't want to be carrying it around for the rest of the day."

"How about I drop it at your mom's," I said. "It's on my way and you can pick it up later."

"Thanks, sweetie," Josie said. "But you have to swear you won't let Mom have a peek. Tell her to keep it locked up. I don't want Grandma deciding my dress isn't good enough for her granddaughter and taking it back to the store."

I dropped Grace and Steph off at their respective houses, Josie at Jake's Seafood Bar, and then drove to Aunt Ellen's. I parked my car and walked up to the front door, the heavy garment bag draped over my arms. The bag was fully opaque, and nothing of the beautiful dress could be seen.

"A peek. A quick peek," Aunt Ellen said, ushering me into the house after I'd explained what I was doing there.

"Absolutely not," I said. "If you can't resist the temptation, I have instructions to take it to the lighthouse."

"I'll be strong. Although it'll be mighty hard. Come with me. We can put it in the back of Amos's closet. No one will find it there, not even Amos. Quickly, before anyone sees us."

"Is that Lucy, Ellen?" Gloria called.

"Yes, it is."

"Invite her in. There's fresh coffee in the pot."

"No coffee," I said, once the dress was secure in the depths of my uncle's closet, "but I'll pop in and say hi."

Gloria was in the kitchen with Mary Anna and Florence. Mary Anna was typing away at her iPad and Florence was reading wedding magazines. Who knew such an endless supply of wedding magazines were available?

"That should do it," Mary Anna said as I came in. "Nothing's available tomorrow, but we're booked on flights to New Orleans Monday afternoon. It'll be so nice to get home. We should leave here around eleven thirty."

"As long as you're sure I'm not needed, Ellen," Gloria said. "I can stay if you want me to."

"If anything more comes up in the investigation," Ellen

said, "you're not far away, and the police have your phone numbers."

"I meant with the wedding plans. We never did discuss the expanded guest list. I wrote to my cousins in France with the news, and they'd be delighted to come. Provided they get an invitation, that is."

Aunt Ellen picked up a dishcloth and wiped down the immaculate counter tops.

"Do you think we'll ever learn what happened to Mirabelle?" Mary Anna asked.

"It's possible we never will," Aunt Ellen said.

"Maybe it was a random thing," Florence said. "Someone causing trouble and not caring who they hurt."

"I hate to think there are people like that in this world," I said.

The doorbell rang, and Aunt Ellen threw her cloth into the sink and hurried to answer. She was soon back, leading Detective Yarmouth. She gave me a worried look.

His rumpled suit was about ten years and ten pounds out of date and his tie was askew. His eyes narrowed as he studied each of us in turn. "Glad I caught you ladies all in one place."

"Not you again." Gloria thumped the floor with her cane. "We've told you everything we know. This is becoming most tedious."

"We heard the news," Ellen said. "Josie's bakery can reopen, and no charges are going to be laid. Thank you." In an exceptional breach of southern manners, my aunt did not offer her visitor refreshments or even a seat. She didn't even sit down herself. She just wanted him gone.

"No charges are going to be laid *at this time*," he said. "I've ordered the body released, and you can take Ms. Henkel home whenever it's convenient."

"My nephew, Mirabelle's father, is making those arrangements," Gloria said.

"Do you have anyone else in mind for the murderer?" Florence asked.

"If I do," Yarmouth said, "you will not be the first to know."

Florence flushed and ducked her head.

Gloria tut-tutted. "Don't ask such foolish questions."

"Don't presume Josie O'Malley's in the clear," he said. "The investigation remains open, and you'll be hearing from me again. I'll concede that the baked goods containing the drugs were left in such a place for enough time to allow almost anyone to tamper with them. Her staff confirms that she took them out to her car at quarter past eleven and then came back inside and worked until shortly before one. That doesn't necessarily mean Josie O'Malley didn't add the fatal ingredient herself."

Ellen's face tightened. "My husband is at the office, catching up on the work he missed being away last week. Shall I call him and ask him to come home?"

"That's up to you, Mrs. O'Malley, but I don't think I've accused anyone here of anything." Yarmouth turned to Florence, who'd once again buried her head in her magazine. "Do you have anything more to add to your previous statements that Josie was particularly angry with Mirabelle?"

"I . . . I . . . ." Florence said.

"Something about her having designs on Josie's fiancé and trying to disrupt her wedding plans?"

Florence looked at Aunt Ellen. She looked at me. Then she ducked her head, her bangs fell over her eyes, and she mumbled, "No."

"And you, Mrs. Bergman," he asked Mary Anna. "You said Josie and Mirabelle bickered constantly. Your words, not mine. Do you have anything further to add to that?"

"No, I do not," Mary Anna said. "As I told you before, bickering is what our family does. We think nothing of it."

"Christmas dinner at your place must be a ball of laughs. Ms. Richardson, you overheard Josie threaten to kill her cousin at least once. Have you remembered any other instances of threats being uttered?"

I turned to my aunt. "Perhaps you'd better call Uncle Amos. These questions are getting way out of hand. If anything, they're no longer accusations but attempts to put words in our mouths. What do you think you're getting at, Detective? You can't come here and start making these sort of ridiculous statements."

He raised one eyebrow. "I can't? Whatever makes you think that?"

"There are other suspects, you know," I said. "I hope Detective Watson told you about Toni Ambrose."

"Who's that?" Aunt Ellen picked her phone up off the kitchen counter, but she made no move to place a call.

"No need to call in the lawyers," Yarmouth said, "unless you know something incriminating you aren't telling me."

"She does not!" Gloria pounded her cane on the floor.

"In answer to your question," he said, "yes, he did tell me, and yes, I've spoken to Ms. Ambrose."

"Unlikely she confessed," I said. "But you have to agree she had a motive, not for killing Mirabelle but to cause trouble for Josie, and like any number of people she had the opportunity."

"Who's Toni Ambrose?" Aunt Ellen asked again. "Do you know someone by that name, Gloria?"

"Never heard of her, but then I'm always the last to know anything. For example, I didn't know Josie was going to buy her dress today, until I was returning from the restroom and saw Lucy carrying a bridal shop bag into Ellen and Amos's room."

"She did?" Florence said. "I didn't know that either. I thought Josie wanted my help."

Detective Yarmouth's eyes flicked back and forth between the women. He probably thought we were trying to distract him from his line of inquiry. Nope; we might be talking about murder and motives, but Gloria had something more important on her mind: her only granddaughter's wedding, and her place in it.

"Right now," Yarmouth said, "I don't much care who bought a dress when or why or why you think you need to be involved. Lucy, Detective Watson told me you think of yourself as some sort of hotshot private eye."

"That's nonsense. I doubt he said anything of the sort. I'm only trying to help by pointing out things you might not be aware of, not being familiar with the people involved."

"Getting familiar with the people involved is why I'm here, asking questions. I wonder why you object to that."

I bristled. "I object to that because you seem to be single-mindedly focused on Josie, to the exclusion of other viable suspects. You put some pressure on Blair, didn't you? To get him to tell you what you wanted to hear."

"Obviously you've spoken to the kid, and equally obviously you bought what he told you hook, line, and sinker. Let me give you a word of warning, Lucy. Some people are good liars."

"Who's Blair?" Gloria asked.

"Okay," I said. "Let's suppose he did lie to me. Have you then considered that when he told you about this so-called threat, he totally had a reason to point the finger at Josie: so she won't fire him for incompetence?"

I expected Detective Yarmouth to reply with a sharp, scathing retort. Instead, he laughed. "Now you see why we can't have amateurs doing the work of the police. If this man did what you suspect and accused Josie of murder to keep his job, he's not very smart, is he? If she's in jail, he doesn't have a job to be fired from."

I mentally floundered around, like a fish flopping on the bottom of Ralph Harper's charter boat, trying to sort out my thoughts. "That's not what I meant."

"You don't know what you meant," Yarmouth said. "And that's your problem."

Aunt Ellen was still holding her phone. She laid her other hand lightly on my arm. She said nothing, but let it rest there. I took a breath.

"You're very rude." Gloria's eyes flashed. "Did your mother raise you to behave like that?"

Aunt Ellen almost choked. Florence studied a picture of a winter wedding in her magazine with enough intensity that she might have been expecting a test later, and Mary Anna watched a sea gull who'd landed on the deck railing and was peering in the window, watching her in return.

"I like to think my mother would be proud of me," Detective Yarmouth said.

"Not if she knew you were badgering respectable ladies," Gloria said.

"I'll do what's necessary to get at the truth."

"As you see it," Gloria said.

"As the law sees it."

"You think they are one and the same?"

"Thank you for your time," he said. "I have your contact details if I need to be in touch." He headed for the door.

I jumped to my feet and followed him out. "What about Toni Ambrose? You said you spoke to her. What does she have to say for herself? What did you learn?"

"Not that it's any of your business, Ms. Richardson, but I'll tell you anyway. I learned that she was with Jake Greenblatt at the time in question. Have a nice day."

I opened my mouth. I closed it again. Toni had been spending time with Jake? While Josie was getting ready for her bridal shower?

I didn't believe it.

I had to believe it. If that was Toni's alibi, then Jake must have confirmed it.

Unless Yarmouth was lying, but why would he lie to me about something like that?

Maybe he was trying to cause trouble. Was that his detecting style? Stir the pot enough and see what rose to the top and leave the innocent to sort out the problems he'd caused? If so, I didn't think much of it.

And what did "spending time with" mean, anyway?

Fortunately, Aunt Ellen hadn't come with us to the door. She hadn't overheard that part of the conversation. I went into the kitchen to say goodbye.

"Don't you look at me like that," Florence was saying to Gloria. "I only told the police the truth. Josie *was* angry at Mirabelle. Mirabelle *was* flirting with Jake. Mirabelle and her over-the-top ideas *did* threaten Josie's wedding. You can't pretend that didn't happen, Aunt Gloria, just because you don't want it to."

I glanced at Aunt Ellen. She'd dropped into a chair and rested her elbows on the table. She saw me watching her and grimaced.

"The truth doesn't always have to be shared with outsiders," Gloria said. "We O'Malleys do not wash our linen in public. And certainly not in front of the police."

"Do I have to remind you," Florence said, "that Mirabelle is dead?"

"I have not forgotten."

"I never suggested Josie might have killed Mirabelle over it. I told them what I saw. What we all saw. It's my duty to help the police in any way I can, family laundry or not."

"Nonsense. You're enjoying being the center of attention. Having the detective listening to your every word. Taking you seriously."

"Will you two stop it!" Mary Anna burst into tears. "All you do is bicker, bicker, bicker. I can't stand it. I'm going for a walk." She ran out of the kitchen, sobbing.

"That girl always was too sensitive for her own good," Gloria said. "I'm going to have a nap before dinner. Help me to my room, Florence."

For a moment, Florence looked as though she might refuse. Then she let out a heavy sigh and stood up.

I kissed Gloria on her papery cheek and wished her and Florence a safe trip home.

"Not much longer until we'll be back for the wedding," Gloria said. "Although I do wish Josie would invite more of the family. Crystal is going to be crushed if she has to miss it. Josie and Jake are not still insisting on canapés at the reception, I hope." Her voice faded away as, leaning heavily on Florence's arm, the old lady made her way slowly down the hall.

When they were gone, Aunt Ellen let out a long sigh. "I honestly don't know if I can put up with this much longer. Amos never goes in to the office on Saturdays, but he was quick enough to escape this morning directly after breakfast. I should have known better than to let Yarmouth ask his questions without insisting Amos or Stephanie be here. But that man has a way of getting everyone defending themselves."

"Chin up. They're going home the day after tomorrow."

"And then they'll be back for the wedding. I might end up being the one who elopes."

I hugged her. "I bet my mom could handle Gloria."

A smile broke out across Ellen's face. "Do you know, dear, you might be right." When my parents met, my mom had been a girl from an Outer Banks fishing family with no more than a high school education who'd never been outside the state of North Carolina. She managed to make her way in the backstabbing, gossiping, one-upping, disapproving world of my father's blue-blood New England family and the Boston social elite. That life had made her hard, and although I loved my mother very much, sometimes I didn't like her.

"Do you think she and your father would want to stay here?" Aunt Ellen asked.

My mom always stays in a hotel when she visits Nags Head. She says she doesn't like to impose, but what she really wants is room service and housekeeping. She doesn't get that at Ellen and Amos's. Mom always comes alone or with her children; my dad hasn't been to the Outer Banks since the summer he met Mom. "Let me have a word with her. I'll tell her you need a buffer between you and your mother-in-law. Mom'll understand. Her mother-in-law was a tyrant." Suzanne Wyatt Richardson, I thought, could eat Gloria for breakfast.

"Your father, of course, is welcome here," Aunt Ellen said, somewhat begrudgingly. They've never gotten on. "I didn't get a chance to ask. How's Josie today? She must be very relieved."

"That's for sure. Our day out was a lot of fun, and we managed to keep her from rushing off to the bakery to dive head-first into work. She's opening Tuesday morning."

"I don't see why you're refusing to help!" Florence's voice came down the hallway, high-pitched, angry.

"Because you're a stupid, flighty girl, that's why," Gloria said. "You're exactly like your father, and I'm not throwing good money after bad."

A door slammed.

"What's that about?" I asked my aunt.

"Mirabelle's death has left Florence and her business in dire financial straits. She wants Gloria to give her a loan. As you can hear, Gloria refuses, but Florence can't take no for an answer. I suspect she stayed on here after Mirabelle died in hopes of bringing Gloria around. Instead, as I could have told her, Gloria has simply dug her heels in further."

Chapter
Twenty-One

It was coming up to five o'clock, closing time on Saturday, when I got back to the library. The only cars left in the parking lot were those of Charlene, Ronald, and Bertie.

I went inside, intending to slip up the stairs as little noticed as possible. I was having dinner with Connor tonight, and I wanted to have a shower and change before he picked me up at six.

"What's happened?" I asked. So much for remaining unnoticed. My coworkers were standing around the circulation desk. They did not look happy. Even Charles had an intense frown on his face.

"I'll leave you to tell her, Bertie." Charlene tossed her bag over her shoulder. "Good night, all. See you Monday."

"What's happened?" I asked again.

"I received an interesting phone call a short while ago," Bertie said. "One of the most faithful of our patrons asking for her donation to the restoration fund back. Her gift had been substantial."

"Did she say why?"

"She's discovered some unexpected expenses, so she can no longer afford it. Or so she said. I told her I was sorry to hear that and I'd see she got her money back. But then . . ."

"I've just gotten off the phone with Mrs. Peterson," Ronald said. "She wants her money back too."

"I don't understand," I said. "Surely, of all people, Mrs. Peterson recognizes the importance of this library."

"Someone's spreading rumors," Bertie said. "Rumors that say we'll never raise enough and all the donations we receive will be given to the town and be incorporated into the operating budget."

"That's ridiculous."

"Of course it is," Bertie said. "Since when did common sense have anything to do with the spreading of rumors?"

"Did Mrs. Peterson say who told her this?"

Ronald shook his head. "A reliable source is all she would say."

"Diane and Curtis." Bertie and I spoke in unison.

"We'll never raise the money," I said. "Not if our donors keep asking for their contribution back. What did you say to Mrs. Peterson?"

"I told her that wasn't true. If the project doesn't go ahead, all the money will be refunded, but we expect to be able to complete the work. She reluctantly agreed to let her donation stand. I got the feeling her husband wasn't happy with the generous amount she gave us."

"Keeping up with Mrs. Peterson's ambitions for her daughters isn't cheap," Bertie said.

"How's the fund-raising going, anyway?" I asked.

Bertie shifted from one foot to the other and her frown deepened.

"That good?" I said.

"People love this library, and they're contributing what they can, but times aren't easy for many. This is a tourist town in the off-season; people are biding their time until business starts picking up again."

"By which time it might be too late for us."

"I'm afraid so," Bertie said. "I have more bad news on that front."

"I don't want to hear it," I said.

"My contact at the North Carolina Department of Natural and Cultural Resources says he doesn't think our chances are good of getting a grant. Budget cuts are taking their toll, and there are other historic places that have been waiting for funding longer than we have."

"But our project is urgent."

A sad smile tugged the corners of Bertie's mouth. "As are they all, Lucy."

"On that cheerful note," Ronald said, "I'm off home. Enjoy your Sunday, both of you, and try not to worry."

"Like that piece of advice ever stopped anyone," Bertie said.

"Do you have any plans for tomorrow?" I asked her.

"Other than making phone calls to prospective donors? As it happens, I do. Eddie's coming to town and we're going to the Wright Brothers Memorial. I haven't been there in years."

"That's nice," I said. Eddie is Professor Edward McClanahan. I met Eddie when Bertie and I went to the university where he worked to investigate another murder that had happened in the library. He and Bertie had been a couple back in their grad student days. The relationship ended when he chose watching a TV program on the last days of Pompeii over traveling with her to meet her parents. They'd had no contact since until she and I walked into his office last October. Judging by the slight tinge of pink that touched Bertie's cheeks, their romance was being rekindled. I was pleased to hear it. "Have fun. And, as Ronald advised, try not to worry."

"On an outing with Eddie, I won't have time to worry about the library. I'll be too busy worrying that he'll try to get into the engine of one of the planes in order to examine the workings."

I laughed.

"Good night," she said.

"Good night, Bertie."

I went upstairs, Charles running on ahead, and let myself into my Lighthouse Aerie. It was just an apartment; plenty of apartments in this world. But not many overlooked the marshes and the beach and the wild Atlantic Ocean. Not many had curved whitewashed walls and a single window set into blocks of stone four feet thick, protected by sturdy iron bars, with a cushion-covered bench seat perfect for reading.

It would be nice, I told myself, to have more space. A proper kitchen, a table big enough to have friends over for dinner. Not to have to run up one hundred steps every time I realized I'd forgotten something.

I felt moisture on my cheek and brushed at it angrily.

"It's just a place," I said to Charles, "and just a job."

He sat on the bed and watched me. The cat seemed to have

shrunk, pulling into himself, his fur losing the excessive fluffiness that gave him so much presence.

"If worse comes to worst, you'll always have a home with me," I told him.

He buried his face in his paws. Yes, Charles could live with me wherever I went, but Charles was a library cat. Charles was *this* library's cat.

And I, I realized, was *this* library's person.

Whatever happened to the library, I reminded myself as I had a quick shower and got dressed for the evening, was insignificant compared to the good news Josie had heard today. Her business was saved, and most important of all, she wasn't going to be arrested for murder.

* * *

I was waiting downstairs when Connor knocked on the library door. I opened it with a smile. Light snow had begun to fall, and behind him I could see flakes dancing in the light above the door. His hair was damp as the snow on his head melted.

He gave me a kiss, and I returned it.

"Ready to go?" he said when we separated.

"Yes." I lifted my coat off the hook on the wall, and Connor helped me put it on. Charles had leapt onto the shelf by the door. He hissed once, and then he reached out and swatted at Connor's hand.

Connor yelped. "Hey, big guy, watch it. That hurt." He studied the back of his hand. A small scratch broke the skin.

I plucked Charles off the shelf. "What's gotten into you?"

He twisted his head, spat at Connor, and fought to get out

of my arms. I put the cat down quickly. "He's in a bad mood today."

Charles lifted his head and walked away.

Charles loved Connor. That is, I'd always thought Charles loved Connor. I had no idea what had come over him. Perhaps my talk about having to move out of the lighthouse had upset him.

I locked the door behind me, and Connor and I walked to the car. Fat flakes of snow fell all around us, and it was beginning to stick to the ground, turning everything white and clean.

As we drove into town, I told Connor about my day.

"That must have come as a heck of a big relief," he said.

"To Josie, and to us all. I don't like that they haven't arrested someone else for the murder, but at least Josie can get back to work. The bakery is so important to her."

"Give the police time, Lucy."

"I'm prepared to give Sam Watson all the time he needs, but I'm not so sure about that Detective Yarmouth. I don't trust him one little bit. Gloria O'Malley told him his mother would not approve of the way he spoke to us."

Connor chuckled. "I can see her doing that. You need to be careful about this, Lucy. You don't trust him, and if he doesn't trust you in return, he can cause trouble for you. All the more reason for you to stay out of it."

"I'm not getting involved," I said, deciding not to mention the fishing expedition to the Blue Lagoon I'd dragged my friends on. As we drove past Jake's Seafood Bar, I let out a long breath. It was one thing to get involved in the murder investigation in an attempt to clear my cousin. But what, if anything, should I do about what Yarmouth had told me about Toni Ambrose's whereabouts the afternoon of the shower? That Jake—Jake!—was her alibi?

No one, least of all Josie, would thank me for interfering in that. But if Jake was seeing Toni on the sly while planning to marry Josie, my cousin needed to know.

"Earth to Lucy," Connor said.

"What?"

"I asked you if that new Italian place is okay for dinner tonight. I've been wanting to give it a try."

"Sure. Sounds good."

I tried hard not to ask Connor about the lighthouse restoration project. The more I tried not to talk about it, the more I thought about it. I ordered a garden salad and steak for dinner. I thought the salad greens limp and the tomatoes picked before they were ripe. The steak was overdone, the fries that came with it were underdone, and the "roasted fresh root vegetables" had only minutes before emerged from a freezer package.

Or maybe I wasn't enjoying my meal because of my increasingly darkening mood. Connor pushed his empty plate to one side. He'd had the spaghetti Bolognese. "That was great. I'm definitely going to recommend this place." He eyed my plate. "You didn't eat much."

"Not too hungry," I said. "I had breakfast in Manteo and then lunch in Nags Head. Shopping requires lots of fortification."

"Did Josie get her dress?"

"Yes, and it's absolutely beautiful. I bought mine too. It

cost more than I wanted to spend, but Josie loved it, and my favorite cousin only gets married once."

"Would you like to see the dessert menu?" the waiter asked.

"Sure," Connor said.

"Just coffee for me, please," I said.

When the small menu arrived, Connor examined it carefully. He had quite a sweet tooth, that man. "The carrot cake sounds good. I think I'll have that."

"The library's fund-raising efforts are being sabotaged," I blurted out.

"What do you mean, sabotaged?"

"Someone's going around telling potential donors that if we don't raise enough money for the necessary work and the library has to close, the funds will be absorbed into the town budget."

"That's absurd. Even if we wanted to, we couldn't do anything like that. Who's saying so?"

"I don't know. No one will tell us who their source is. It has to be Diane and Curtis. Connor, you know how important the library is to the town, to the entire area. Surely you can do something. There's no way we can raise the money we need in the time we have only by asking our patrons. As generous as some of them have been, we need too much."

A veil settled over his face. "I can't talk about this with you."

"But it's so important."

"I won the election comfortably, but not every one of the commissioners is my friend. We've got a lot happening this year with the proposed development projects along the beach and the Monaghan family's project that threatens to intrude on the dune environment. I can't . . ."

"Here you go." The waiter put a plate on the table between us. He smiled at me. "I brought two forks. Just in case."

The cake was a deep golden brown, rich with spices and dotted with shredded carrots and pieces of walnut, the icing thick and creamy. My stomach rolled over.

Connor made no move to pick up his fork. "I can't give anyone the opening to claim I'm spending town funds to save my girlfriend's job. Bertie knows this. I thought you did too."

"But . . ."

"No buts, Lucy. I'm sorry, but that's the way some people will paint it if I do try to intervene with the decision. The town's offering what the councilors have decided we can afford. I might not agree with that, but I had to recuse myself from the discussion and the vote, and even if I wanted to, which I don't, I can't now go back and tell them we're authorizing more money. You'll have to pump up your fund-raising efforts."

"We're trying as hard as we can. What can we do, if someone is out to see us fail?"

"Unfortunately, that's not the town's concern. The decision has been made. I said I'd do what I can to help in my personal capacity, but I'm afraid that's not much. I can't even help you raise money, as that would potentially blur my roles as mayor and private citizen."

"That's . . ."

"That's the way it is, Lucy." He dug his fork into the cake and broke off a hunk. He stuffed it into his mouth and chewed rapidly. A cloud had moved in behind his eyes, and he ate without pleasure. "Can we have the check, please?" He shoved his plate aside, unfinished, and hailed a passing waiter.

We drove back to the library in a silence as chilly as the snow falling around us. Connor parked at the bottom of the path. "I've an early start tomorrow, so I won't invite myself in."

I undid my seat belt. "I'm sorry I brought the subject up. I don't want this business to come between us."

"It is between us, Lucy, and we can't pretend it isn't. I care about the library, you know I do, but I can't help you. I'll wait here until you're safely inside."

A soft blanket of pure white covered the ground. I walked up the path, barely noticing the flakes drifting to the ground. I opened the library door and turned to wave at Connor. He flashed his lights in response and then drove away, headlights illuminating the falling snow. The line of footprints I'd left in my wake marked my passage. As I watched, they began to slowly fill in as more snow fell.

I shut the door and twisted the lock. Charles's amber eyes glared at me from the top of a shelf.

"I couldn't have handled that much worse if I'd tried," I said. "Nor could you. Don't attack Connor again. It's not his fault."

Charles's tail moved, and he made no further comment.

Chapter
Twenty-Two

Sunday morning, I opened my curtains to a true winter wonderland. The snow had stopped overnight, the skies were clear, and the sun was cresting the watery horizon. Everything was calm and still, covered by a blanket of fresh snow tinged orange in the light of the rising sun.

I'd tossed and turned all night, absolutely furious with myself. I knew Connor would be trapped in a potential conflict-of-interest allegation if he tried to intervene in the matter of money for the lighthouse restoration. I knew it, and I also knew he cared very much about the library.

But I'd argued with him anyway.

The library's closed on Sundays, and I always look forward to my day off. Today I wasn't looking forward to spending the day brooding. I considered calling Connor and apologizing for ruining our evening, but I decided not to. I'd probably be unable to resist telling him, one more time, that the future of the library was in doubt.

I put the coffee on and popped a bagel into the toaster. When it was ready, I took my breakfast and *The Busman's*

Honeymoon to the window seat and curled up to read. The view outside was so beautiful—blue sky, dark ocean, sparkling white ground, a light dusting of snow covering the bushes and trees—that I felt some of my anger—directed totally inward—fading away. A good number of people were out in the marsh this morning, searching for birds and wildlife and enjoying a hike in the crisp cold air.

I read for several hours and finished the book. When I emerged back into the real world, I felt much better for it. Lord Peter and Harriet Vane had solved the case, their honeymoon was over, and all was right between them. I stretched mightily, shooed Charles off my lap, and stood up. I had my shower and dressed for the day. I thought I'd go to the beach and take a long, peaceful walk.

Instead, I found myself passing the entrance to the Coquina Beach parking area without slowing and continuing on to Nags Head.

Last night my foolish mouth had gotten me into trouble. *In for a penny, in for a pound*, as the saying went.

At one thirty I pulled into the spacious lot of Jake's Seafood Bar. Jake's is a busy place Sunday lunchtime, with the after-church family crowd and people returning from a morning's outing, and I hoped the rush would be dying down by now.

The hostess gave me a smile when I walked in. "Good afternoon, Lucy. Are you on your own today or meeting someone?"

"I'm not here for lunch, thanks. I was hoping to have a chance to speak to Jake. Is he in?"

"Yes."

"I'll pop into the kitchen, if that's okay."

241

"Go on in."

I found my prospective cousin-in-law up to his elbows in fresh green herbs. Pots bubbled on the stove, cooks stirred and chopped, and waitstaff ran in and out, grabbing laden plates or dumping empty ones.

"Hey, Lucy," Jake said as he chopped. He wore the standard white chef's double-breasted jacket with high collar, black trim, and short sleeves above baggy pants with gray and white checks. No tall starched white hat, though. "What brings you here?"

I breathed in the scents of basil and oregano, with maybe a hint of rosemary. "I was hoping you had a minute to talk, but you seem to be busy."

"Don't know why, but everyone came in late today. Something to do with the snow, maybe." He put down an enormous cleaver. "I've always got time for you. Things are pretty much under control here."

I'd rarely seen anything less "under control" in my life. Pans sizzled, steam rose, knives slashed, flame flashed, smoke blew.

I have trouble making dinner in my microwave if the instructions on the packet aren't detailed enough.

"Take over here, Meg. I'm stepping outside for a couple of minutes." Jake wiped his hands on a cloth and led the way through the kitchen and out a small door at the back while I nervously dodged cooks wielding pots of boiling water and vicious-looking knives. We emerged onto an edge of the deck that ran around the back of the building to form the summer outdoor bar and public seating area.

"Aren't you going to be cold?" I asked. Jake wore a short-sleeved indoor jacket, whereas I had on my winter coat, scarf, and gloves.

"Nah. It's nice to cool down for a bit. What's up? I hear you had a good shopping day yesterday. Thanks for taking Josie out. She needed to be with her friends. Although Josie will never admit she needs anyone." He grinned. "Today she's at the bakery. Which is what she needs most of all."

I shifted my feet and stared over the Sound. A few boats drifted on the water, carrying hardy winter fishermen. Snow and ice clung to the trees on the far shore. "I'm not going to say this is none of my business, because I know it isn't. I love Josie."

"Goes without saying." He leaned on the railing next to me.

"And I love you too, Jake. I'm sorry, but I have to ask. Are you still involved with Toni Ambrose?"

He let out a bark of laugher. "You're kidding, right?"

I turned to face him. His expression, surprise mixed with amusement, was all the answer I needed.

"Toni says you're her alibi for the time the baked goods Josie prepared for the shower were left unprotected in her car."

"I should be surprised you know that, but I'm not. Josie says you seem to have a way of getting people to tell you things they shouldn't."

"It wasn't Sam Watson, if it matters. Or Butch either."

"Yarmouth, I'd guess. But it doesn't matter. Yes, I'm Toni's alibi. That's true. Shortly before Christmas, she came into the restaurant looking for me. I assumed she was passing through, maybe heading to Florida on a winter vacation, so I invited her to join me and have a drink at the bar, expecting she'd be on her way soon enough. But that wasn't why she was in Nags Head at all. She was here, she told me straight out, to ask me to come back to New York City with her. Why she'd think I'd want to do that, I have no idea. We weren't that much of an item. Not as far as I was aware, anyway. We dated a few times, but nothing serious was ever said between us. When I told her I was breaking up with her, she cried and threw things, but I got the impression she did that because it was expected, not because her heart was really into it. I left New York, came here, made plans to open the restaurant. Shortly after that, I ran into Josie at a party—I'd known her in school—and all of a sudden, standing there that night, I knew what love really is." He smiled at the memory. "I never heard another word from Toni, or gave her so much as a thought, until she showed up here. She'd heard from mutual friends I'd gotten engaged, decided I must be on the rebound from losing her, and she came here to stop me from making a mistake. Or so she said. I told her, politely I thought, she was wrong. I guess she didn't believe me. I swear, Lucy, I did nothing, I said nothing, to make her think I want to be with her again. Because I don't. We finished our drinks, and I told her I had to get back to the kitchen. She gave me a kiss on the cheek and left, and I assumed that was the end of it. Next thing I knew, she came in to tell me she'd found an apartment and gotten herself a job and was, and I quote, waiting for me to come to my senses."

"What did she mean by that?"

"To break it off with Josie and get back together with her. She said she'd understand if I didn't want to return to New York, so she's willing to move here permanently."

"You told Josie about this?"

"Not at first. But before long Toni starting coming in here once or twice a week, having a drink at the bar, asking the staff about me, and I was afraid she'd start bothering Josie, so I had to warn her. So far Toni seems to have been staying well away from Josie."

I said nothing about what Josie had told me: that Toni had been hanging around the closed bakery the other day, watching her. "What happened the afternoon of Josie's shower?"

"Toni came in here, around eleven. Marched into the kitchen, all charming and flirty. She said she wanted a job. I told her I don't have any openings and she needed to get out of my kitchen because we were busy. She said she'd wait until I had my break, and then we could talk. She loaded the word 'talk' with all sorts of significance. She went into the dining room, took a seat, ordered herself a drink and lunch. And there she sat until almost two. I know she was there the whole time, because I asked Ruth, the hostess, to keep an eye on her for me. I cowered in the kitchen, hoping she'd give up and leave. Finally, around two o'clock when the place was mostly empty, I went out and told her to leave and not to come back. I made sure my staff were listening and watching when I talked to her. I told them Toni is no longer welcome here, and she's not to be allowed in. I said that in her hearing."

"What did she do?"

"She left, quietly and peacefully. She said she understood that I had obligations and she'd be waiting for me."

"You're sure about the time? If she was here from eleven until two, then she didn't poison Josie's baked goods."

"My staff spoke to Detective Yarmouth as well as me. We might be off the time by five or ten minutes either way, but no more than that. We run by the clock in here, particularly on Sunday lunchtime. Speaking of the clock." He glanced at his watch.

"I'll let you get back to it. Thanks for talking to me, Jake."

He smiled at me, and I gave him an impromptu hug.

"I haven't seen or heard from Toni again," he said. "I'm hoping the death of Mirabelle and her being questioned by the police—as a suspect—scared her off."

"Don't count on it. She's still in town, still waiting. I think she's biding her time, hoping Josie'll be arrested and she can console you in your grief."

His handsome face twisted in anger.

Chapter
Twenty-Three

Speak of the devil, as they say. I dodged boiling water and knives and left Jake's kitchen. I watched a waiter carry plates of lobster ravioli and grilled flounder into the dining room and thought about what I was going to have for dinner. I had next to nothing waiting in the fridge at home.

"Thanks," I said to Ruth as I passed the hostess station.

"Everything okay, Lucy?" she asked.

"Sure. I just wanted to talk to Jake for a minute."

She glanced around. People were leaving, no new guests arriving. "I mean, is everything okay with Jake? It's been tough on him, and that means on us, what's been happening with Josie and all."

"That's over. The police have cleared Josie and she's opening the bakery on Tuesday." That might be a mite optimistic of me, but I was determined to be optimistic.

"I'm so glad to hear that. Jake's a great boss, none better, but he's a chef, and a good one. Top restaurant chefs aren't known for their calm patience under stress."

"Been tense around here, has it?"

"Oh yeah. To put it mildly. I'm so looking forward to the wedding. It was nice of Jake to invite us all."

"I'll see you there. I'm going to duck into the ladies' room for a minute."

"Sure."

The restrooms were down a short corridor off the hostess station. I nipped inside. A few minutes later, when I opened the door to leave, I heard the hostess talking. Her voice had turned sharp and angry. "You're banned. I'm sorry, but those are my orders."

"Nonsense. You've misunderstood the situation."

I peeked around the corner. Toni Ambrose, all spiky black hair and metal. "You don't need to bother," Toni said. "I know the way. I'll just pop into the kitchen and say hi to Jake."

"You will not." Ruth picked up the phone.

Toni's face tightened. "I'll see you fired."

"Yeah, that's going to happen. This is private property and you're not allowed in here. If you don't leave right now, I'm calling the police."

"You wouldn't dare."

"Try me."

"Everything okay here?" The bartender, a young guy who didn't look like the sort you'd want to mess with, appeared at Ruth's side.

"This woman refuses to leave," Ruth told him. "The boss said she's not to come in."

"Yeah, I know. I heard him too. Why don't you take a hike, lady?"

Toni bristled. "I'll have you both fired over this."

"Whatever," the bartender said.

I kept in the shadows close to the wall. No one needed my help here.

Toni took a step forward. The bartender stepped in front of her. He made no move to touch her but said, slowly and calmly, "Call the cops, Ruth."

"Calling 911 now," Ruth said.

"Jake!" Toni yelled. "Jake, it's me! I need to talk to you. If you marry that woman, you're making a big mistake. Jake!" She made as though to run past the people blocking her way.

The bartender put his hand on her arm. "If you know what's good for you, you'll leave now, quietly, before the cops get here."

"They're on their way," Ruth said.

Toni shook him off. "Okay. I'll go. Now. When Jake and I are together again, I'll see you're both thrown into the street."

"Lady," the bartender said. "Take my advice and get out of town before you land yourself in a whole mess of trouble. I'm Jake's friend. He's marrying a good woman. Nothing you can do will mess that up."

"We'll see about that." Toni whirled around and marched out of the restaurant.

I let out a long breath, peeked around the corner to make sure she'd left, and stepped out from the corridor.

"I'll tell the cops to cancel the call," Ruth said. "I'm sorry you had to see that, Lucy. That woman's as nutty as Jake's pecan pie."

"But nowhere near as sweet." The bartender shook his head. "I'm sorry she left."

"Why's that a bad thing?" I asked.

"She needs a ride in a cruiser and a night in the cells to get her head straight. I miss the old days when we could run troublemakers right out of town." He was about twenty-five years old. "Looks like Jake didn't hear what was happening out here. I'll tell him she's been in again. He's going to be madder than . . ." His voice faded away as he headed for the kitchen.

*　*　*

My phone rang as I was on my way home from Jake's. I answered with Bluetooth to keep my hands on the steering wheel. The snow had stopped falling and the sun had come out, but the roads were slick. The good people of North Carolina aren't all that good at driving in snow. "Grace. Hi."

"Hope I didn't catch you at a bad time?"

"I'm in the car, but using hands-free so I can talk."

"How about an impromptu hot tub party? My place, tonight?"

"That sounds like fun."

"They're calling for more snow, and we can sit out on the deck and watch it fall. I was going to suggest a girls-and-boys party, but when I spoke to Josie, she said Jake had a thing with some friends planned for tonight, and she thought Butch was working. So that takes two of the boys out of the equation. Can you manage an evening without Connor?"

I thought of the previous evening I'd spent with Connor and the fact that he hadn't called me today. If I invited him, he might not even want to come. I didn't say any of that. "Sure. What time?"

"How about seven? After dark."

"See you then."

I decided not to say anything to my friends about what I'd witnessed at Jake's. It was up to Jake if he wanted to tell Josie or not. It had been an ugly incident, but it could have been a lot worse. Aside from the other day when Toni had been spotted outside the bakery, she didn't seem to be bothering Josie. And that was definitely a good thing.

Toni was a strong suspect for the killing of Mirabelle, if it had been done to cause trouble for Josie. Too bad she had such a cast-iron alibi. An alibi from the last person in the world who'd have reason to lie for her.

When I got home, I made myself a mug of hot tea, settled at the kitchen table, pulled out the list of library patrons I'd been assigned, and continued making calls. Most of the people I spoke to said they were happy to make a contribution to the restoration fund, but a few sounded reluctant, and they eventually told me they'd heard they might not get their donation back if the repairs didn't happen. No one could say exactly who'd originated that rumor. It was always something like: "My sister's son's teacher, or maybe it was his hockey coach, said . . ."

By the time I finished my calls, I was thoroughly despondent. People were eager to see the library saved, upset at the thought that it might have to close, and happy to contribute, but most of them offered something in the range of twenty to fifty dollars. They were being as generous as they could, but it would take a lot of twenty-dollar donations to amount to the sums we needed to save the library.

I studied the phone. I could ask my parents. They could fund the entire restoration project without a second thought if they wanted. I was afraid they wouldn't want to. Or my mom wouldn't want to, which amounted to the same thing. Dad wouldn't much care, and Mom handled their personal finances. My mother hadn't wanted me moving to the Outer Banks, and she hadn't wanted me ending my never-formalized engagement to Ricky Lewiston, son of Dad's law partner and a junior attorney in the highly respectable, highly lucrative, long-standing firm of Richardson Lewiston.

Mom would like the idea of the library closing, if it meant I'd lose my job and move back to Boston.

I decided to wait. Mom and Dad would be here in a few weeks for Josie's wedding, along with my brothers and their families. Aunt Ellen was a keen patron and volunteer at the library. It might be best if she approached the subject while everyone was in a happy, celebratory mood.

I didn't bother making anything for dinner. Knowing Grace, she'd have a ton of food waiting for us beside the hot tub.

At quarter to seven, I put my bathing suit on under my clothes and threw a towel into my beach bag and headed out.

Traffic was light on the way into Nags Head. Thick clouds had moved in and the snow had resumed. A few houses still had their Christmas decorations up, and they added light and color to the dark night.

Josie's car was parked outside Grace's house. Grace lived in a small but nice duplex in Nags Head, to the west of the Croatan Highway, meaning away from the ocean. Not that anything in Nags Head is very far from the ocean. She met me at the door and handed me a glass of sparkling wine before I'd even stepped over the threshold. She wore a long black wrap over her bathing suit and her hair was tied into a knot at the back of her head. "Come on in. The gang's all here. By gang, I mean Josie. Steph couldn't make it. She'd forgotten she was supposed to be having dinner with her mom tonight. She might drop by later if it's not too late."

Grace led the way through the living room and out the French doors to the backyard. A wide wooden deck ran along her half of the rear of the house. A hot tub, emitting clouds of steam into the cold night air, took up about half the deck, and a round table and four chairs occupied the rest. A fence separated her from her neighbor, but otherwise the yard was open to the large, heavily treed property of the house behind.

I peered into the veil of steam and saw my cousin waving her glass at me. "How did things go today?" I asked. "Are you going to be ready to open on Tuesday?"

"Ready and eager," Josie said. "Spread the word at the library, will you?"

"I've already sent an email to everyone on my work list," Grace said, "and many of them replied to say they're glad to hear it." Grace is a primary school teacher. She took off her wrap and stepped into the hot water. "Come on in, Lucy. If you want something to eat, help yourself." Platters of cheese, individual savory pastries, and bread and crackers were laid out on the table.

I put my glass down on the edge of the tub, pulled off my jeans and T-shirt, threw them onto a chair, and slowly ventured into the hot water. I sat down and leaned against the side of the tub, found my glass, took a sip, and closed my eyes. The warm water cradled my body as the snow drifted down onto my hair. "This is truly heavenly."

"Exactly what we need after a hard week," Josie said.

"Is your grandmother still planning on leaving tomorrow?" I asked.

"Yes, thank heavens. I don't think Mom's nerves can stand another minute of her in the house."

"Is Blair coming to work tomorrow?"

"He is."

"I'm glad. He likes you, Josie. He likes working for you, and he really wants to put his past behind him. That's what he told me, anyway, and I believed him."

"You believe the best of everyone, Lucy. But in this case, I agree with you."

"You're too nice for your own good sometimes," Grace said. "I would have fired him for what he said to the police."

"No, you wouldn't," Josie said. "You're too nice too. We can't blame him; he told the police what he'd overheard, like a good citizen should. If Detective Yarmouth threatened him into making the situation sound worse than it was, Blair felt he didn't have a lot of choice. Blair apologized and I accepted his apology. We had a good talk. That is to say, I talked and he listened. I told him he has to do something about his attitude toward the customers and toward me and the rest of the staff if he wants to stay on. I asked if he was prepared to do that, and he said he was. As far as I'm concerned, that's the end of that."

"Is there anyone else you've had trouble with before, Josie?"

I asked. "Someone who might be out to get revenge on you? Norm Kivas was angry with you for a while, but he seems to be behaving himself these days."

"I'm glad to hear it."

"Why are you asking about that?" Grace said. "Mirabelle was killed, and she had nothing to do with Josie's bakery."

I explained my theory that someone had added the drugs to the baked goods not in an attempt to kill anyone but to discredit Josie and ruin her reputation. "After all, from what I know, the amount added wouldn't have been fatal to a person in good health. It killed Mirabelle because she had an iffy heart."

"Her heart"—Josie wiggled further down in the water—"was one size too small."

"Isn't that two sizes too small?" Grace said.

"I'm being charitable. As for anyone else, I honestly can't think of anyone who hates me that much. Of course I have rivals in business and disgruntled employees, that comes with the territory, but poisoning someone's food's a pretty drastic step."

I was on the verge of bringing up Toni, but changed the subject before I could blurt out what I'd overheard earlier today. "Your mom and I have come up with a plan to keep Gloria under control at the wedding." I went on to tell them about involving my mother. Josie's light tinkling laugh rang out through the steam and the snow. "That'll work. When it comes to old money, the Richardsons are the real deal, although theirs is tainted Yankee money. That'll impress Grandma no end. Yankee money or no."

Grace put the plates of food around the edges of the tub so

we could help ourselves, and we nibbled on snacks and sipped our wine and talked about nothing much at all.

Eventually Josie said, "This is fun, but I'd better be on my way." She rose out of the water like an emerging sea-goddess. "Busy day tomorrow, and I have deliveries arriving starting at five AM. I hope I'm not wasting my time. I'm worried the bakery's reputation has been totally ruined and no one will come, being afraid I'm going to poison them."

"Nonsense," I said.

"Rubbish," Grace said. "You don't have to leave yet, do you, Lucy? Have another glass of wine."

"I can stay for a bit, but nothing to drink, thanks. I have to drive home and I'm already feeling mighty sleepy. I'd enjoy some more of this cheese, though." I cut myself a hunk of brie and put it on a cracker with a touch of red-pepper relish.

Grace got out of the tub and walked inside with Josie to say good night. The drapes were pulled back, and when Grace switched on a light, I could see them chatting and then Josie heading down the hall to get dressed.

I leaned back and let the water wash over me. I was facing the house, my back to the yard and the trees behind. Josie emerged from the bedroom. She and Grace hugged, the door opened, Josie left, and Grace closed the door behind her and came outside.

"Nothing nicer than a snowy night," Grace said.

"Everything's so calm and peaceful."

"I'm so glad things worked out okay with Josie and the bakery, but it's not good that they haven't arrested anyone for Mirabelle's murder, is it?"

"No, it's not. Suspicion will stick to Josie until they do. If it was a malicious prank gone wrong, they might never find out who did it."

"Is Ronald working tomorrow?"

"He should be. Why?"

"I'm worried about a boy in my class. He's falling further and further behind in his reading. His parents are supposed to be helping him at home, and they say they are, but I don't think that's true. I want to talk to Ronald about it."

Grace and Josie had been friends since the first day of kindergarten. I'd never spent any time alone with Grace, and tonight we enjoyed having the opportunity to get to know each other better. We chatted casually and easily about our lives.

Eventually Grace said, "We should be drinking plenty of water out here. I'll be right back."

"Umm," I said. "And then I should probably go."

She clambered out of the tub and went into the house. I sank further down and let the hot water caress the back of my head and soak into my shoulders. *Heavenly*. I wished Connor were here. Connor. What was going to happen between Connor and me? The library restoration issue hung over our relationship like a noxious cloud. Because he was involved with me, he couldn't intervene with the council's decision. I'd briefly considered breaking up with him to save the library, but that wouldn't help. It was too late to end our relationship now. People might think that was nothing but a ploy to free him to intervene in the decisions concerning the library.

Out on the street, a car door slammed. A dog barked in response. Then all was quiet as the snow fell silently. I'd trust in the feelings I had for Connor, and the feelings I believed he had for me, and everything would be all right in the end.

Through my hot-water-and-glass-of-wine-induced mental fog, I heard a board creak on the stairs leading up from Grace's lawn. I felt something touch the top of my head, and then, before I knew what was happening, I was struggling to breathe. My face was underwater, the pressure on the top of my head and my right shoulder intense. I tried to push myself upright, but something held me down. I opened my mouth in a scream and swallowed chemical-laden hot water. I was pushed deeper into the water. My arms flailed. I struck something solid and firm behind me, but I couldn't get a grip on it.

I struggled for breath and swallowed more hot water. My lungs strained and my throat burned.

My last thought before passing out was that I was sorry I'd argued with Connor.

Chapter
Twenty-Four

"Lucy!"

I coughed. My stomach heaved and I leaned forward and spat up a good portion of the water from Grace's hot tub. I sucked air in as rapidly as I could. Strong arms were wrapped around me, holding me firm, keeping my head above the water. Cold clean air rushed into my heaving lungs.

I spat again.

"Say something, Lucy," a voice said.

I coughed. "Something."

"I've got you. Try to stand. Steady now, no hurry. There's a girl."

I planted my feet on the bottom of the tub and struggled to find purchase. The arms around my chest lifted me, helped me to rise. My butt hit the side of the hot tub and I fell backward onto the wet tile.

I looked into the night sky. Snowflakes fell to earth, landing on my cheeks and my lips. I coughed again, turned my head and brought up more water, and then I tried to sit.

"Stay still."

"I'm okay." I struggled to pull myself into a seating position. Yellow light poured from the back of the house, and steam rose from the hot tub as snow continued to fall all around us.

I heard running footsteps crossing the lawn, the creak of the boards on the step, and I flinched. Then I heard Stephanie's voice. "Gone."

"Nothing?" Grace said.

"They had a car. I didn't get anything." She crouched beside me and peered into my face. "How you doing, honey?"

"I've felt better."

"Let's get her inside and dressed," Steph said. "I called 911."

I was lifted to my feet. I looked at my friends. They were both in their bathing suits and bare feet. "What are you doing here?" I asked Steph.

"I finished at Mom's and thought I'd swing by and see if you were still here."

"Good thing you did," Grace said.

They helped me into the house and settled me on the living room couch. Grace went back outside and got my clothes. When she came in, steam rose off them. "These are almost frozen. I'll find you something to change into. Get that wet bathing suit off."

She ran down the hallway, and Steph helped me out of my suit.

Grace brought a thick fleecy blanket. I accepted it gratefully, and the two women wrapped it securely around me. Shock was beginning to settle in and I was freezing.

Sirens sounded outside. "I'll let our visitors in," Steph said.

Butch Greenblatt was first through the door. He gave Steph an anxious look followed by a private nod, and then he took in the whole room. "Are you all right, Lucy?" He crouched on the floor in front of me, his eyes wide with concern. "Do you need to go to the hospital?"

I shook my head. "I'm okay." I burst into a coughing fit.

When I finished, he said, "You don't sound okay."

"I swallowed a lot of hot water."

"Lucy was outside," Steph said. "In the hot tub. He took off through that patch of trees in the property behind."

"Check the yard," Butch said to the officer who'd come in behind him. He pushed himself to his feet. "Tell me what happened."

Grace and Steph exchanged glances. "I scarcely know," Grace said at last. "Lucy and I were in the hot tub. Josie was here earlier, but she left about twenty minutes, maybe half an hour, ago. I went into the house to get us glasses of water and the doorbell rang. It was Steph."

Stephanie nodded. "I was late."

"I showed Steph to my bedroom so she could change into her bathing suit," Grace said. "Then we talked in the kitchen for a couple of minutes."

"We heard splashing and thought Lucy was getting bored out there all by herself, so we went to join her." Steph shook her head. "I still can't believe what I saw. Something . . . someone . . . was couched over the tub, holding Lucy down. It was awful. Horrible."

"Did you recognize this person?" Butch asked.

"No. We yelled, and he looked up and saw us, then he let go of Lucy and took off. He had a hood pulled over most of his face, so I couldn't see hair or anything."

"You think it was a man?" Butch said.

"Figure of speech," Grace said. "I have no idea. It could have been a woman; I couldn't tell."

"Me neither," Steph said. "But there was only one person. I'm sure of that."

"I had trouble getting the door open," Grace said. "It sticks sometimes and I was panicking and all thumbs. By the time it finally opened and we got outside, they were heading into the property behind."

"I told Grace to see to Lucy and took off after them." Steph looked down at herself. The tiny, trim figure in a bright-pink bikini, bare feet. She blushed. "I didn't get far. Can I get my sweater?"

"Sure." Butch appeared calm and in control of the situation, but I thought it a sign of how disturbed he was that he didn't even turn his head to watch Steph and her pink bikini walk away. Her feet were blue with cold, a dead leaf stuck to one foot, and she limped, ever so slightly, while trying not to.

"Grace, is that what you saw?" Butch asked.

"Yes. Lucy was underwater, not moving, when I got to her." She wrapped her arms around herself. Her bathing suit was a black-and-brown one-piece. "We got to her in time."

"Why don't you get a robe on?" Butch said. "I've called Detective Watson."

"That's not . . ." I said.

He lifted one hand. "Someone tried to kill you, Lucy. I think a detective's required."

"Butch is right." Steph had changed quickly into a thick oatmeal sweater and jeans. Her feet were still bare, showing toes painted a sparkly gold. "This wasn't someone playing a stupid prank. If we hadn't heard you splashing and come out to check on you . . ." Her voice trailed off.

"The suspect ran off when you arrived," Butch said. "Then what happened?"

"I chased him. Or her," Steph said. "Into that patch of trees. I wasn't wearing shoes, so I was too slow. When I emerged onto the street on the other side, all I saw was a car disappearing around the corner. Going fast. No lights."

"I don't suppose you got the plate?"

"Not even the model of car. A compact, dark color. That's all I can say. As for the person, I saw a heavy winter coat, knee length, with a hood pulled over the head, and legs in dark clothing. That's it. I'm sorry."

He touched her shoulder briefly and stared into her eyes. "You shouldn't have tried to chase them. You were unarmed. Not to mention undressed."

"Instinct, I guess," she said.

They exchanged soft smiles, and then Butch turned back to me. "Lucy?"

"I saw nothing and no one. One second I was enjoying the evening, and the next I was underwater struggling to breathe."

Sam Watson walked into the room. His gaze swept over us. Grace with her hair hanging in long wet strands, wrapped in a blue terry cloth bathrobe, Steph dressed but in bare feet, me huddled on the couch, hair wet, eyes red, clinging to a security blanket.

Butch pulled his flashlight off his belt. "I'm going to check outside. If we're lucky, they dropped their driver's license or something."

He left by the sliding door, and my gaze followed him. Lights bobbed across the lawn and among the trees. The back door of the house behind opened and a man called out, asking what was going on. An officer was on her hands and knees examining the edges of the hot tub.

"Lucy, want to tell me what happened?" Watson said. "I got the gist when Butch called me. You were attacked in the hot tub?"

I nodded.

"I'm sorry, sir, but . . ." a woman's voice said from the front door.

"I'm the mayor. Let me in!" Connor burst into the room, his eyes wide, his hair mussed. He dropped to the floor in front of me and gathered my hands into his. "Lucy. Are you okay? What happened here?"

"Take a seat, Mr. Mayor," Watson said. "We're about to find out."

"What are you doing here?" I said.

"The 911 operator called me because your name was mentioned in the call. There's at least one advantage to being the mayor of this town." Connor touched my cheek ever so lightly and stared into my eyes. Then he dropped onto the couch beside me, lifted my blanket-wrapped legs, and tucked them onto his lap. I was suddenly aware that I had no clothes on underneath the wrap. My body, shivering with cold and shock only moments before, almost burst into flames.

Steph, Grace, and I told the story once again. A deep line formed between Sam Watson's eyebrows. When Steph said they'd seen someone holding me under, Connor let out a low growl.

Butch came back inside. "Boot tracks in the snow, both coming and going between this house and the street behind." He glanced at Steph, and a slight smile lifted the edges of his mouth. "And a set of bare footprints, about a size six. For once we won't have trouble distinguishing the tracks of the suspect from his or her pursuers."

"Anything interesting about the prints?" Watson asked.

"Size average, I'd say. Could be a man or a woman. Nothing else I could see, but it's dark out there. I'll talk to the immediate neighbors now, and we can search better in the morning."

"Do we need a dog?"

"No point. The prints ended at a set of tire tracks. He got into a car and drove away."

"Lucy," Watson asked, "were you able to tell if this person was wearing gloves?"

I thought. All I could remember was hot water and fear. "I don't know, sorry."

"It's cold out tonight, so they likely were, but we'll try to get prints lifted from the edge of the tub anyway."

"Lucy needs to get herself on home," Steph said. "She needs a hot drink and then into bed."

"I'll take her." Connor rubbed my legs through the blanket.

"Lucy," Watson said, "do you have anything to add tonight? If not, I'll come around in the morning to talk to you further."

"I saw nothing. I heard nothing. Do you think this has something to do with the killing of Mirabelle?"

"That's entirely possible. You've been asking questions, as is your habit. Perhaps I should have done more to stop you."

"Like that would help," Grace muttered.

"I have been asking questions," I said. "But I've not been getting any meaningful answers. If someone tried to kill me because they think I know who killed Mirabelle, they've wasted their time."

"Did anything about this person seem familiar, Lucy?" Grace asked.

I shook my head. "It might have been a big black bear for all I know." I chuckled. "Except they didn't have claws. I would have noticed if there had been claws." I laughed again. The idea of a bear tiptoeing stealthy through the thin line of trees with the intention of drowning me in a hot tub seemed dreadfully funny.

Grace handed Connor a glass of water, and he held it to my lips. "Take a drink. Sam, we're leaving."

"That's a good idea," Watson said. "Ms. Stanton, you can be going as well. Ms. Sullivan, I'm afraid we'll be in your way for a while longer. We'll be back again tomorrow, soon as it's daylight, to search further."

"Take all the time you need," Grace said. "Lucy, let's get you something to wear on the way home."

Connor helped me to my feet, and Grace and Steph each took one of my arms while I clung to the blanket.

"My car," I said.

"Come back for it tomorrow," Grace said.

"My clothes," I said.

"You can get them tomorrow." Connor tucked the blanket around me. "Do you have pajamas she can borrow, Grace? I'll jack the heat in the car up high. She'll need shoes, too."

Grace and Steph walked me into a bedroom. They pulled the blanket away, and Grace helped me into a loose-fitting fleece top and comfortable bottoms. Steph knelt in front of me and slipped a pair of sandals on my feet. I felt rather like a queen with people to help me dress.

When I was ready, Sam Watson held the front door open, and Connor held me close as he led me outside. "I'm okay," I said. "I can walk."

"I want to help. Oh, Grace, Lucy'll need her bag. Her keys should be in there."

Grace handed it to him.

He half-carried me down the steps. His car was parked in the driveway, behind mine. Steph's was on the street, surrounded by police cars, marked and unmarked. Snow continued to fall, softly and gently, illuminated by flashing blue and red lights. Neighbors stood on their porches or at their windows, watching. Connor held the door for me and guided me inside.

"Home, James," I said when he'd started the engine.

"Yes, madam," he replied.

"I'm so dreadfully tired all of a sudden, but I'll never get to sleep . . ."

267

Connor gently shook me awake. "We're here. Let's get you inside and upstairs."

*　*　*

When I next awoke, sunlight was pressing hard against the back of the heavy drapes covering my single window. Something heavy lay on my chest; someone breathed into my face. Panic flooded into me and I screamed. I scrambled to push off the weight. My eyes flew open to see Charles's blue ones staring into mine. I collapsed in relief. "Good morning."

He jumped off the bed and headed into the kitchen.

I looked around the room. A red blanket was thrown over a chair. *Where did that come from?*

And then it came flooding back. My head dropped into my pillows, and I stared at the ceiling. Grace's house. The hot tub. Sparkling wine and snacks and fun times with good friends. An attempt on my life. Police flashlights moving through the snowy trees.

"Hello?" I called. "Anyone here?"

All was quiet. A water glass sat on the night table, next to my phone and my book, a slip of paper tucked under it. I pulled the paper out and read.

You're sleeping well. I'm going home and leaving Charles to watch over you. Call if you need anything. It was signed with a crudely drawn heart.

I leaned back with a smile. Then I picked up the phone to check the time.

Ten o'clock!

On a working day.

Something Read, Something Dead

I leapt out of bed and headed straight for the shower. Half-way there I realized I was in a pair of unfamiliar pajamas. Oh, right. Grace's.

I peeled them off and studied myself in the mirror. I could see no sign of last night's trauma. I touched the top of my head and felt sore, soft skin where I'd been held down. I turned to check out my upper back and neck. A small mark was cut into the skin high on my right shoulder. I remembered the hand on my head, pushing me further and further into the water. Another hand on my shoulder, adding more pressure and some stability.

The cut was oddly shaped. I strained to see it properly, but the angle was wrong. I dug in the cupboard for an old makeup mirror and used it to create a reflection I could see.

The cut wasn't deep, and if there'd been any blood, it had been washed away last night by the hot water.

The outline of a triangle was embedded in my skin.

Chapter Twenty-Five

Ronald jumped up from behind the circulation desk the moment he saw me. "Lucy! You shouldn't be out of bed."

Obviously they'd been given the news.

"I'm okay," I said.

"And if you weren't, you'd say you were anyway."

Mr. Snyder, who comes regularly to read magazines and enjoy some companionship, leapt out of the wingback chair with a speed that belied his age. "Take my seat. Sit here."

A patron grabbed a book off the nonfiction shelf and shoved it into Ronald's hands. "This will tell you what to do about head trauma."

Bertie ran into the room.

"I'm sorry I'm late," I said. "I didn't set my alarm last night and slept in."

"Nonsense," she said. "Upstairs you go, young lady."

"No, I'm fine. Really."

"In that case," she said, "my office. Ronald, bring us some of my special tea."

I almost cried, "No, not the special tea." But I didn't. I meekly followed Bertie down the hall. Charles followed me.

"She looks okay," the patron said, "but you never know with head injuries. When my Bobbie . . ."

"I don't have a head injury," I said to Bertie.

"Perhaps not, but you did experience a traumatic incident."

"Need I ask how you know about this?"

"Connor called me. He stayed with you most of the night, in case you woke in distress, and left when I arrived. I've been upstairs to check on you a couple of times. You were sleeping peacefully, so I let you be. Sit."

I sat.

Ronald brought a mug of Bertie's special tea. A particularly foul-smelling, -looking, and -tasting beverage that seems to have magical powers of recovery. At the first whiff of the drink, Charles ran out of the room so fast he was nothing but an indistinct blur of tan-and-white fur.

Ronald handed me the mug. I held my breath and took a sip. As nasty as I remembered. I tried not to gag as I forced it down.

They watched me as if expecting me to keel over at any moment.

"I really am okay," I said.

"Then I'll get back to work," Ronald said.

"Take the day off, Lucy," Bertie said. "You may think you're fine, but you did have a terrifying experience."

"Thanks."

"Keep drinking that."

I took another sip. The horrible beverage spread through-out my body. Surely it was nothing but my imagination, but I immediately felt my mind clearing and strength returning to every muscle. "I'll take some time off, but not to go back to bed. I have a pretty good idea what happened."

Bertie studied me. "You shouldn't go out alone. Whoever tried to kill you might still be out there. Sam Watson also phoned me this morning. I'm to call him as soon as you appear."

"I won't go alone."

"Sam and Detective Yarmouth," Bertie added. "They're thinking this is related to the death of Mirabelle."

I cradled the mug and thought. "Let me do what I have to do first."

"Lucy . . ."

"I'll take care," I said. "Promise. Can I use the office phone?"

"Go ahead. It's almost time for toddlers' story hour. I'll relieve Ronald and he can get ready."

Bertie left me alone and closed the office door behind her. I called Steph at the law office.

"Lucy! Are you okay?"

"I'm fine." I eyed the remains of the tea. "Can you get away for a couple of hours?"

"When?"

"Now."

"As long as I'm back by three. I have a court date at three thirty."

"We won't be long."

"Where are we going?"

"I'll tell you on the way. You'll have to pick me up. My car's still at Grace's."

"On my way."

"I heard that." Charlene came into the office, carrying a small, foil-wrapped package. "You shouldn't be going anywhere."

"I'm fine," I said. "Particularly after a few mouthfuls of Bertie's special tea."

"I thought I smelled something rotten in here." She shoved the package into my hand. "First, eat."

"What's this?"

"Tuna sandwich. White bread, lots of mayo, slices of green onion. The best."

"This is your lunch, Charlene."

"So it is. You need something in your stomach before you go haring off in all directions. Eat."

I wanted to refuse, but I realized I was ravenous, and I *was* planning to go haring off in all directions. "Thanks." I unwrapped the foil.

She gave me a smile and left.

I ate the sandwich (willingly), finished the tea (reluctantly), and then went upstairs for my bag and coat. When I got back down, Steph was coming in. She looked court-ready in a camel coat, dark stockings, and red patent-leather pumps with four-inch heels.

"What's up?" she asked as we drove into town.

"I know who attacked me, and I know why."

"Then we should be going to the police station."

"I'm not ready to talk to them yet. I'd be fine with telling

273

Watson my theory, but not that Yarmouth. He'll either accuse me of trying to drown myself for the attention or wasting police time. Probably both."

"Lucy . . ."

"Bear with me. All I want to do is sound out the person I'm thinking of. If I learn anything, I'll call Watson and let him take it from there. I've invited you because I'd like to have a witness if they say something incriminating. Turn right at Whalebone Junction. We're going to the Blue Lagoon."

"You think Toni did this?"

"Yes." I told her about the mark on my shoulder.

"Why? What does she have against you?"

"She has nothing against me. Nothing at all. As far as I know, anyway. Perhaps by attacking me, maybe even killing me, she hoped to cause grief for Josie. Maybe she wanted to somehow make it look like Josie had done it."

It was five minutes after eleven when we arrived at the Blue Lagoon. The light in the window telling us the bar was open glowed red. Two vehicles were in the parking lot. One was a white van, the other a dark compact.

"What if she's not here?" Steph asked.

"Then I'll get her home address and we'll go there."

"They won't give you her address."

"They will if I have you with me. Looking like a female Perry Mason."

"In my nightmares," she said. "I've seen that show. It was popular with my class at law school. Do I have to point out that Perry didn't do the grunt work himself? Wasn't it Paul Drake who investigated on Perry's behalf?"

"Do you have a private eye on permanent retainer?"

"No."

"I rest my case, councilor."

She shook her head. "The things you talk me into."

The Blue Lagoon was empty, and I called out. A door leading to the back swung open, and Toni emerged.

She gave us her professional smile. She didn't gasp when she saw me, turn pale, or try to run away. She just picked two menus off the hostess stand and said, "Table for two?"

I hesitated. This woman had tried to kill me last night. I'd have thought she'd have had *some* reaction to seeing me standing in front of her this morning. I glanced at her hand. The large heavy silver ring with the intertwined triangles was on her right thumb. A reproduction of one of those triangles was firmly impressed into the skin of my right shoulder.

"That's a nice ring," I said. "I noticed it when we were in the other day."

"Thanks," she said. "My boyfriend gave it to me and I never take it off. Table for two?"

"Don't you recognize me?"

"Sure I do. You were in here the other evening with your friend who was recovering from a bad breakup. I hope she got home okay."

"She's fine."

Steph was looking at me, waiting for me to do something, to say something. I shrugged. Thank heavens I hadn't dragged Watson or, even worse, Detective Yarmouth down here to listen to me accuse Toni of attacking me.

It was possible Toni was such a psychopath she felt no

emotion at being confronted by someone she'd recently tried to kill. I didn't know how a real psychopath would react, but if that was the case here, I was obviously wasting my time.

It was also possible someone else owned a ring similar to Toni's, although that seemed like a heck of a big coincidence. Then again, perhaps my mind, desperate to find answers, had created a pattern where none existed. It was just a triangular mark on my right shoulder, after all.

"I've changed my mind," I said. "I'm not hungry after all. Let's go, Steph."

Toni put the menus down. "Okay." She didn't seem to care that we were leaving.

I started to head for the door, tail firmly between my legs, when I had a thought. I turned back to her. "You know my cousin, Josie O'Malley."

All the blood faded from Toni's face. She gripped the side of the hostess stand. The skin around her ring turned white. "What of it?"

"She was attacked last night. She's in the hospital in serious condition. They say she might not make it."

"Sorry to hear that." Toni couldn't keep the triumph out of her voice. A smile touched the edges of her mouth.

"I'm surprised Jake Greenblatt's not more upset about it," Steph said. "They were supposed to be getting married soon. Guess that's off."

Toni's hand moved toward her pocket. No doubt she was anxious to make a phone call.

"Why don't you call Detective Watson, Stephanie?" I said. "He'll be interested in what's happening here."

"Nothing's happening here," Toni said. "Nothing that would interest the police. Sorry to hear about your cousin, but it's got nothing to do with me."

"Actually," I said. "I lied. Josie's not in the hospital and she's not about to die. She's at the bakery this morning, hard at work. She plans to reopen tomorrow morning."

Toni studied my face, searching for a trap.

"You got the wrong person," I said. "I'm the one who had a sudden immersion into a hot tub last night."

Toni's eyes darted around the room. "You're lying again."

"I was at Jake's restaurant yesterday when you came in and tried to see him. They threatened to call the police and threw you out. Before doing that, they reminded you he's about to get married. I think you decided it was time to do something once and for all to derail his wedding plans. You've been following Josie. She saw you lurking outside the bakery one day, and there were probably other instances when she didn't see you. Last night you followed her to our friend's house. You watched the house for a while from your car, and then you drove around to the street behind, parked the car, and crept through the trees. I don't know if you were planning all along on attacking Josie, or just decided to do so when you saw you had the chance to get rid of her. It doesn't much matter in a court of law, does it, Stephanie?"

"Not if the result's the same and a person dies."

"You saw three women last night, Toni. What you didn't realize was that the three women were not the same three at all times. Josie left, probably when you were moving positions, and Stephanie here arrived. The curtains were open and you would have seen Grace and Stephanie in the house, and one person alone in the hot tub. You thought that one person was Josie. It wasn't. It was me."

"You're off your rocker," Toni said. "I don't have to listen to this."

"Hi, Detective Watson." Steph spoke into her phone. "Stephanie Stanton here. We need you at the Blue Lagoon, and it's urgent." She glanced at Toni's right hand. "Tell your fingerprint techs to be ready."

"Ah, yes," I said. "Fingerprints."

Steph put her phone away. "It was a cold night. Anyone would be wearing gloves. But most people will almost instinctively take their gloves off when shoving their hands into water. Thus the imprint of your ring is on Lucy's neck. And, most important of all, your fingerprints are on the edge of the hot tub. Prints don't wash off with water. Did you know that, Toni?"

"I . . ."

"You killed Mirabelle to make it look like Josie did it, didn't you?" I said. "How'd you work that alibi? Getting Jake Greenblatt, of all people, to vouch for you?"

"Now you really are around the bend. Get out." She turned her head and raised her voice. "Tom! I need help out here."

A heavily bearded man, all piercings and tattoos, came out of the kitchen, wiping his hands on a towel. "What's happening?"

"We'll wait for the police in the parking lot," Steph said. "They'll be here any minute."

"You got the wrong person last night, Toni." I sucked in a breath as a thunderbolt hit me. I whirled around and grabbed Steph by the shoulders. "Louise Jane was right."

"Louise Jane? What on earth has she got to do with anything?"

"What's the time?"

"Ten past eleven."

"We might get there in time, if we leave now. Let's go. Call Sam and tell him to meet us at Aunt Ellen's. Toni and her petty jealousy can wait. Mirabelle's killer cannot." I ran for the door.

"You gonna tell me what's goin' on here?" Tom asked.

"I quit," Toni said.

"What about lunch service?" Tom said.

"Tough," Toni said.

"Back soon," Steph called as she followed me outside.

I jumped into her car and fumbled for my phone.

"You thought of something, Lucy. What is it?" Steph started up the engine.

I lifted one finger, telling her to hold on. I called Detective Watson's number. Yes, I have that in my contact list.

"Almost there, Lucy," he said.

"Turn around."

"What?"

"We're on our way to Ellen and Amos's house. Meet us there. I know who killed Mirabelle."

"Who?" he said.

"Who?" Steph said.

I hung up.

Steph tore through the streets. "If a cop car ties to pull you over," I said. "Lead them on. We haven't got time to stop and explain everything."

"Which is good, because I can't explain anything."

"I thought Toni tried to kill me last night to somehow frame Josie. I had no idea how she'd think that would work, as you and Grace were around and I hadn't been fighting with Josie, but I didn't really care. I thought it possible she killed Mirabelle for the same reason, to frame Josie, but her alibi for that appears to be solid. As soon as I saw Toni was totally uninterested in me when we came in, I realized she hadn't tried to kill *me*. She'd wanted to kill Josie, but mistook me for Josie. Superficially, Josie and I look nothing alike, but we are first cousins, so sitting down, as I was, with my hair soaking wet, there might be something about the shape of our heads or our posture that made her get the wrong person."

Steph took a corner on two wheels.

Chapter
Twenty-Six

We screeched to a halt in front of the beach house. Uncle Amos's car was in the driveway, the trunk open. He stood in the midst of a cluster of suitcases and travel bags, mentally scratching his head as he wondered how he was going to fit them all in.

"I have no physical evidence," I said to Steph. "Nothing the police can take to court. I need you to keep your eyes and ears open for anything that can be used."

"I have absolutely no idea what's going on."

"Good. That way you have an open mind."

"So open," she said, "everything I know is in danger of falling out."

We got out of the car as a cruiser containing Sam Watson and Detective Yarmouth pulled up behind us.

"I don't like being given orders by civilians." It would appear Yarmouth had been called away from his coffee break. Crumbs and a sprinkling of colored sugar dotted his shirt front. A gust of wind lifted the strands of long hair off his head. "First we're being told to come to some bar, and then we're yanked around and ordered to come here. If you're wasting my time, Ms. Richardson, I'll have you arrested."

"Assisting the police by providing information pertinent to a crime is never a crime, Detective," Steph said.

He took in her expensive coat, her shoes, and most of all her tone of voice and demeanor. "And you are?"

"Stephanie Stanton, attorney and partner in O'Malley Stanton."

"What are y'all doing here?" Uncle Amos said. "We're about to leave for the airport."

"I'm afraid your guests are going to miss their plane," I said. "Are they all here?"

"Inside with Ellen."

"Let's not keep them waiting. Detectives, will you join us, please." I marched up the path, willing the others to follow. I tried to make my steps strong and determined, to look as though I was fully confident of my facts.

I was anything but.

I knew what had happened to Mirabelle. I knew why. Proving it was another matter entirely, but once the Louisiana Mafia, as Josie called them, had gone home, I'd not get another chance.

The group was standing in the front hall. Gloria, Mary Anna, and Florence had their coats on and purses in hand. Gloria leaned on her cane. Aunt Ellen and Josie were with them.

"You're in time to say goodbye," Aunt Ellen said as I came in. She blinked when she saw the crowd behind me. "Goodness, what are all these people doing here?"

"How's everything going at the bakery?" I asked Josie.

"We'll be ready to open tomorrow. Hello, Detective. Uh . . . Detectives. Is there a problem?"

"Not with the bakery," I said. "Shall we go into the living room? Gloria, at least, should sit down."

"It's nice to see you, dear," Gloria said, "but we don't have time for a visit. We're late as it is. Florence misplaced my pocketbook and I can't fly without identification. Once, the word of a lady would have been . . ."

"I did not misplace anything," Florence said. "I told you I'd look after it for you, but you insisted on keeping it. And then you lost it."

"If you must blame me for your carelessness, dear, go ahead." Gloria patted her hair; her rings flashed in the light from the hallway lamp. Not many people dress up to fly these days. Florence wore jeans and Mary Anna was in a loose blouse and skirt. Gloria sported a baby-blue Chanel suit with pearls.

"Enough, please," Mary Anna said. "You know full well you had it last, Mama."

"I know nothing . . ."

"Living room," I said. "Now. New evidence has been uncovered in the death of Mirabelle, and the police are here because of it. If you have to miss your plane, so be it. There are others."

"But then I'll have to pay for another ticket," Gloria said.

"At least you can afford it," Florence said. "Some of us can't."

Mary Anna groaned. "I just want to go home."

Aunt Ellen rolled her eyes. She seemed to be doing a lot of that lately.

"Let's hear what Lucy has to say," Uncle Amos said.

"Might as well," Yarmouth said, "as long as I'm here. Before I arrest the lot of you."

I led the way into the living room and everyone followed. Gloria sat in Amos's leather chair, and Mary Anna and Florence took the love seat. Aunt Ellen sunk onto the couch with a deep sigh, and Steph joined her. I tried to give Ellen an encouraging smile. Unfortunately for my aunt and uncle, if my plan worked out, at least two of their guests would be staying a few more days.

Uncle Amos, Sam Watson, Detective Yarmouth, and Josie leaned against the walls. Yarmouth planted his feet far apart and crossed his arms over his chest with a scowl that would frighten small children. I told myself he didn't frighten me. I don't think I convinced me.

I took a deep breath.

What would Lord Peter Wimsey do?

He'd lay out the facts as he knew them, calmly, professionally. He'd draw logical, inescapable conclusions from those facts, and allow others to do the same. He would then instruct the officers of the law to arrest the culprit, and they would do so.

I glanced at Stephanie, sitting primly on the edge of the couch, her knees together, hands in her lap. She could be my Harriet Vane, ready to leap in and support my Lord Peter when a point needed clarification.

Perhaps I should have told Steph ahead of time what I was thinking so she could do that.

"Get on with it," Yarmouth said. "We haven't got all day here."

"Louise Jane McKaughnan was right," I said.

"Lucy," Watson said. "You suffered a traumatic incident last night. If you're going to tell us the ghost of a Civil War bride or a lighthouse keeper's son killed Mirabelle Henkel, I'll excuse you on the grounds that you aren't thinking straight."

"Bear with me, please," I said. "As some of you probably know, Detective Watson is referring to an attack made upon me last night."

Aunt Ellen and Uncle Amos nodded. They knew about it, probably from Connor. Gloria gasped. Florence said, "What happened?" and Mary Anna said, "This town isn't safe. I want to go home."

Josie's face was a picture of shock. "When did that happen? Where? Who? Have they been arrested?"

"It happened shortly after you left Grace's place. Someone tried to drown me in the hot tub. As you can see, they were not successful. And no, they have not been arrested, not yet, but the police know who it was."

"We do?" Yarmouth said.

"You will when I tell you," I said. "But this is more important."

"More important than an attempt on your life?" Uncle Amos turned to Watson. "Sam, what do you know about this?"

"No more than you," Watson said. "As is increasingly becoming the norm when Lucy's involved."

"Which is all too often the case," Aunt Ellen said.

Everyone began talking at once. I seemed to be losing control of the narrative. I didn't recall that ever happening to Lord Peter Wimsey.

"Let Lucy continue." Steph used her court voice to cut through the chatter. "Everyone has questions, but you won't let her talk."

"Thank you, Harriet," I said.

"Who?"

"Never mind. Where was I? Oh, yes, last night. At first, I thought the attack on me was related to the murder of Mirabelle. When I confronted my attacker . . ."

"What do you mean, at first?" Josie asked.

"When did you do that?" Aunt Ellen asked.

"That was not wise," Uncle Amos said. "Stephanie, were you with her?"

"Don't look at me," Steph said. "You try stopping her."

"You concluded that the events of last night were not related to the killing," Watson said. "Not directly anyway, thus the abrupt turnaround."

"That's right. Toni Ambrose attacked me . . ."

Josie groaned. Several people said, "Who?"

"You might want to go around to her place soon as we're finished here." I spoke to Watson. "She's about to do a runner. Her attack on me had been a case of getting the wrong person."

"You mean she was after me?" Josie asked.

"Yes, I do."

Josie groaned.

"Who is this woman?" Aunt Ellen asked.

I didn't answer. "Steph and I paid a call on Toni this morning. She never intended to harm me; she didn't even realize I'd been the one in the hot tub. Last night, she thought I was Josie. When I understood that, I remembered what Louise Jane said about the death of Mirabelle. That the spirits of the lighthouse intended to kill the bride-to-be, but they got the wrong person because they don't know what gluten-free means."

"Okay," Yarmouth said. "I'm outta here. Detective Watson, I suggest you place this woman under medical supervision."

"Not so fast," Watson said. "I think she might be onto something. Although it's taking her forever to say it. Go ahead, Lucy."

I looked around the room. Everyone was watching me, but one person in particular had gone very pale.

"When they first got here, Florence, Mary Anna, and Mirabelle were staying at the Ocean Side Hotel, where they had separate rooms."

"That's right," Mary Anna said.

"Florence and Mary Anna arrived at the shower together, and you, Gloria, came with Mirabelle."

"Yes," Ellen said. "I came early, so someone had to pick up Gloria."

"That means the three of them—Florence, Mary Anna, and Mirabelle—had rented two cars, not one."

"Which is correct," Gloria said. "Total waste of money. I told them that, but young people these days . . ."

"What of it?" Mary Anna said. "Amos, please put a stop to this. I want to go home. If we leave now and drive quickly, we might still be able to catch our flight."

"I want to hear what she has to say," Gloria said. "Carry on, young lady."

"Thank you," I said. "Three hotel rooms and two rental cars meant one person had the opportunity to go out on Sunday before the shower without the others knowing. Perhaps she went to Josie's bakery to have an early lunch. Maybe for a chat. Or it might be that she was simply out for a drive. Regardless of her reason for being there, she saw Josie putting the baked goods she'd prepared for the shower into her car and leaving them there. She decided to have a peek. The plate of gluten-free desserts was in a separate box and clearly marked as such."

"You're telling us what we already know," Yarmouth said. "The outlines of it anyway. Who's the important thing, and you don't seem to be getting anywhere with that."

"Mirabelle had switched to a gluten-free diet only a week before she died. It was therefore logical for us . . . I mean the police, to conclude the drugs added to the food on the special plate were intended for her. But someone else in this room had recently given up gluten-free in favor of Josie's baking."

Gloria lifted her hand to her mouth.

I turned to look directly at Florence. "You and Mirabelle were business partners, but you weren't at all close. You didn't like each other."

"You're right about that," Florence said. "I couldn't stand her. I wanted her out of my business, but she'd managed to dig herself in so deep, I'm in desperate straits without her. No way did I want Mirabelle to die."

"I agree, you didn't. You had no reason and no desire to kill her, but you weren't aware she'd begun eating gluten-free."

Florence glanced around the room. She let out a broken laugh. "Of course I knew. Can you imagine Mirabelle not talking about something like that?"

"I can't imagine her not making a big deal of it, but I can imagine you not hearing her. You told me you tuned her out most of the time. I suspect you tuned out a lot of things. On the other hand, you didn't know Gloria had given up gluten-free, did you?"

"Everyone knew that."

"No, they didn't. Not until after Mirabelle's death. Josie told me her grandmother has an 'ever-changing diet.' She follows every fad out there until the next one becomes popular. I thought nothing of it until this morning. Then I remembered that Gloria asked for crackers, not bread, when we had dinner at Jake's the day after the New Orleans group arrived. Mirabelle thought Gloria had done so on her behalf, but . . . pardon me, Gloria . . . I don't think Gloria's that . . . considerate. A few days later, I encouraged Gloria to try one of Josie's pecan squares."

"And she did," Aunt Ellen said. "She had another at the shower because she enjoyed the first one so much."

"Ellen told Gloria to go ahead and live a little. At the time, I thought she meant not to worry about the calories. I said the same thing to Josie when we had breakfast on Saturday. But putting two and two together . . ."

"Lucy's right," Aunt Ellen said. "When Gloria arrived, she told me she was on a gluten-free diet. Frankly, it made things difficult for me. I had no idea what to prepare for meals. When we were at the bakery a few days before Mirabelle's death, before Gloria could ask what was gluten-free, Lucy recommended the pecan squares."

The two spots of red rouge on Gloria's cheeks stood out like a clown's makeup against her pale face. Her lips were a tight red slash, and she gripped her cane firmly. "Josephine's pecan squares are what must be served in the dining room in heaven. I do not *follow every fad*; I attempt to take care of my health as befits a lady of my age. However, I decided then and there to forget about this gluten-free nonsense and enjoy myself in the few years I have left." She glanced around the room, waiting for someone to tell her she had plenty of life still in her. No one obliged. They were all looking at me.

"And that," I said, "was the case of mistaken identity. The killer poisoned the gluten-free desserts expecting Gloria, not Mirabelle, to eat them."

"They could have gotten anyone who'd been at that party," Yarmouth said. "Anyone or everyone. That's a mighty desperate act."

"Except GHB isn't normally fatal in the dose consumed," I said. "You have a bad heart, don't you, Gloria?"

"Yes, I do. That's no secret. My family knows about it."

"So they do. Even I know. The GHB could have killed you. But Mirabelle had a bad heart too."

"That's what the autopsy showed," Watson said. "We don't think she even knew about it. She didn't have any record of taking medication for a heart condition."

"Mirabelle," Mary Anna said, "was such a drama queen. She complained constantly of having every ailment going around. She never went to the doctor in fear he'd tell her she was imagining things and she should be exercising more and watching her diet."

"Let me get all this straight," Uncle Amos said. "Lucy, you're saying someone in this room intended to kill my mother? But they killed Mirabelle by mistake."

"I'm saying Florence did precisely that. Didn't you, Florence?"

"I don't have to listen to this nonsense." Florence got to her feet. The look she gave me blazed with such sheer malice, I was glad I was in a room full of people. "If Amos won't drive me to the airport, I'll call a cab. The rest of you can do what you like."

"Hold on there," Watson said. "Stay where you are. Let's hear Lucy out."

"Talk about a drama queen. You're not seriously listening to her, are you?" Florence glanced toward the door. Uncle Amos moved ever so slightly to block the exit.

For once Gloria was silent. She sat stiffly in her chair, her hand on the brass head of the falcon on her cane, stunned.

"Why?" Josie said what everyone was thinking.

"Gloria's always insulting Florence," I said. "Criticizing, nitpicking, making snide comments."

"Gloria talks to everyone that way." Aunt Ellen ducked her head. "Sorry, but it's true."

"Not entirely," I said. "From the moment I met them, I noticed an extra dig when Gloria's talking to or about Florence, an extra degree of pure nastiness."

Gloria stamped her cane. "What an outrageous thing to say. I never!"

"What of it?" Florence said. "I can't stand the miserable old bat. No one can."

Gloria gasped.

"My father says she's always been a joke, with her southern plantation fantasies, and Jackie O suits, and dreams of past greatness, but we have to be nice. Because she's family, he says. What he means is because she's rich and we want to be in on the inheritance."

Watson took a half step forward. Yarmouth still looked confused.

Florence lifted a hand to her mouth as she realized what she'd said. She tried to cover up, and the words spilled out of her mouth. "If you want to arrest everyone who wants to kill her, you'll have to take us all in. I should have known better than to come here, with *her*, but Mirabelle insisted the trip would help our company make some important contacts."

"My mother's not rich," Uncle Amos said.

"Perhaps not as in multimillionaire status," I said. "But she does have money, doesn't she? She donated generously to the library restoration fund. She has enough to help Florence get out from under the thumb of Mirabelle and save her company. Florence asked you for money, didn't she, Gloria? I overheard her doing so just the other day."

"Constantly and repeatedly," Gloria said. "Of course, I refused. I believe young people have to make their own way in the world."

Florence glared at her.

"As I recall," Gloria said, "I recently told her she could wait until I was in my grave for her share of the inheritance, like the rest of the family."

"Oh, Mama," Amos said.

"Gloria wouldn't give you the money you needed when she was alive," I said to Florence, "so you decided you'd have to do something to hurry that inheritance along. And get rid of the woman you hated at the same time."

No one said a word.

"That," I said to Florence, "is why you were so distraught at the death of Mirabelle. Not because your cousin and business partner, someone you didn't like in the least, died, but because you got the wrong person." I held my breath. I had not the slightest piece of evidence to back up any of my statements. I'd studied all the evidence, and I'd come to the only logical conclusion.

For several long moments, no one moved. Then Gloria rose from her chair in a swift sudden action that belied all her claims of aches and pains. She lifted her cane high and brought it crashing into the back of Florence's right leg. Florence screamed and fell to the floor.

"Mother!" Amos yelled.

Watson and Yarmouth leapt forward, but then they hesitated. They didn't seem to know what to do when the aggressor was a woman in her eighties.

But Florence did. She grabbed the cane, wrenched it out of Gloria's hands, and pushed herself to her feet. Gloria fell back into the chair with a cry. Florence shifted the cane and held it like a baseball bat above Gloria's head. "You miserable old woman. You couldn't even die when you were supposed to."

"Careful, Ms. Fanshaw," Watson said. He and Yarmouth had their hands on their guns. "Don't do anything reckless. It's all just talk so far. Don't make the situation worse."

I don't think Florence even heard him. She stared at Gloria. "Not so high-and-mighty now, are you?" Madness, hatred, and rage had twisted the younger woman's face into something almost unrecognizable.

Gloria cowered in her chair, shriveled and old and frail and frightened. She whimpered, "Amos, do something."

"Careful now." Watson's voice was calm and in control. Everyone else was frozen into position, shock written across their faces. If Florence made another move toward Gloria with the cane, Sam Watson would shoot.

What have I done?

"Florence Fanshaw, you are a guest in my house and you will put that cane down this very instant," Aunt Ellen said. "It does not belong to you."

Florence blinked and slowly lowered the cane. Watson leapt forward, grabbed her arms, and swung her around. He pulled cuffs off his belt and snapped them on. Yarmouth shook his head and lifted his hand from the butt of his weapon.

My legs gave way and I dropped into a chair.

Chapter
Twenty-Seven

"Something must be happening up ahead," Connor said. "A traffic accident, maybe. Let's hope it's nothing serious."

It was seven thirty on Tuesday morning. A light dusting of snow had fallen overnight, giving everything a fresh, clean feel. Connor and I were on our way to Josie's Cozy Bakery to get coffee and muffins for breakfast. We planned on having a walk through the marsh before going to work, and rather than me making the coffee, we'd decided to pick it up at Josie's as a show of support on her reopening day.

Traffic heading into Nags Head was almost at a halt on the other side of Whalebone Junction. We inched forward, one in a long line of slow-moving cars.

"I hope this isn't going to last too long," I said. "If it does, we might miss our walk. I have to be at work at nine."

"Do you want me to turn around?" Connor said.

"No," I yawned. "Being at Josie's this morning is important."

He smiled at me. "Tired? You had quite the night last night."

I hadn't gotten home and into bed until late. Watson had arrested Florence and charged her with the murder of Mirabelle Henkel. The family had been in shock, Gloria most of all. Aunt Ellen had hustled her weeping mother-in-law off to bed while Stephanie got on the phone to find a lawyer to represent Florence. Mary Anna went for a long walk, and Amos and I followed the police and Florence to the station.

I'd been there for hours, making my statement, repeating all my observations and conclusions.

The only thing I didn't mention was that I'd been thrown off the scent by Charles's actions at the bridal shower. Charles, I'd always believed, was a good judge of people. Except for the attack on Connor the other day (which might be excused on the grounds that he knew Connor was not helping save the library), he'd never steered me wrong. But at the shower, the big cat had been affectionate toward Florence. He had, I decided, felt sorry for her.

The town offices are next door to the police station, and Connor had arrived at a run as we drove up. Once he'd seen I was fine and not under arrest, he'd gone back to the meeting he'd dashed out of without excusing himself. Amos had been permitted to stay with me while I was interviewed and gave my statement.

At last I'd been allowed to leave. Watson walked us to the door. I hadn't seen Detective Yarmouth since we left the beach house.

Watson thrust out his hand. "Good job, Lucy."

Startled, I took it in mine.

"You put everything together well."

"What would Lord Peter Wimsey do, I asked myself."

"Ah, yes, him. CeeCee brought that book home to read for your book club. I thought I'd give it a try, but I soon gave up. I couldn't stand it. Couldn't stand Wimsey either. Hope you're not going to start wearing a monocle, of all things."

"I don't think it would suit me."

"It wouldn't. And neither does detecting. You were an enormous help to us, Lucy. This time. Please don't interfere in any of my cases again. You are not Lord Peter, or even V. I. Warshawski. You put yourself in unnecessary danger sometimes."

"Strangely enough, an attempt was made on my life, which turned out to have had absolutely nothing to do with the death of Mirabelle or my so-called detecting. Danger happens."

"So it does," he admitted.

While Watson had been charging Florence, and Amos and I were cooling our heels in an interview room, officers had been sent to Toni Ambrose's apartment. They'd found her throwing her things into suitcases. She'd been arrested for the attempted murder of me.

"Unlikely that charge will stick," Uncle Amos said. "She's claiming it was a prank and no harm was done. Which clearly is the case."

"We'll get her on something," Watson said. "Mischievous endangerment or some such."

"I don't care," I said. "As long as she leaves the Outer Banks and never comes back."

"We can attempt to make that a condition," Watson had said.

Slowly and painfully, Connor's car approached the strip mall where Josie's Cozy Bakery was located. He leaned out the window to get a better view of what was going on. "The accident must be right around here. Traffic coming toward us is clogged up ahead. I don't see any flashing lights, though."

"Traffic patterns have a life all their own," I said. "No one can ever figure them out."

"This time, I think I can. The tie-up's at Josie's."

Every space near the bakery was taken, and vehicles were half parked on the sidewalk. Cars had illegally parked on the other side of the road, and traffic was backed up in all directions as people searched for parking or tried to get out of the lot. At Josie's, a line of patrons stretched out the door, along the row of shops, and curled onto the edge of the road.

"Oh my gosh," I said. "Look at all those people. This is incredible."

"I checked Twitter first thing this morning," Connor said, "like I usually do, looking for anything that's happening around here I need to know. Your friend Roger . . ."

"Roguejourno222 himself."

"That one. He put up a post saying Josie's would be open today. He called it 'Nags Head's famous bakery' and attached a publicity picture of a pile of croissants."

"I'm surprised he could be so gracious. I bet Judy Jensen or her mother was standing over him slapping a rolling pin into her palm while he typed."

"That red car's backing out. I can grab their spot if I cut off the van that's trying to edge through the oncoming traffic. Better not do that; they might be a voter. One of the disadvantages of being the mayor. Do you still want to go in?"

"Oh yes."

"Jump out here. I'll park across the road and join you."

I opened the door and leapt out of the car. I fell in at the back of the line. "Good morning, Lucy," a man said to me as I wrapped my scarf tightly around my neck. Good thing I was dressed for our hike if I had to stand out here in the cold.

I didn't know him, but I said, "Morning, sir," anyway.

The line moved slowly but steadily forward. Everyone was wrapped up against the winter weather and in a good mood. I was halfway to the door when Connor trotted up.

"Hope you've left some for us, Frank!" a woman called to a group of people leaving.

Frank rubbed a generous stomach. "Not a crumb remains. Sure was good, though."

We took another few baby steps. Some people recognized Connor and greeted him warmly.

A woman, bearing a takeout latte, saw me and hurried over. "Lucy, I'm so glad I ran into you. Do you have information on where I should send my donation to the library restoration fund?"

I reached into my bag and pulled out the sheet of paper Bertie had prepared for just such an emergency.

"Thanks." She stuffed it into her pocket and turned to Connor. "What's this I hear about the town being unwilling to save the Lighthouse Library?"

"A council budget decision, ma'am," Connor said.

"You ought to be horsewhipped. The lot of you." She stormed away.

My stomach hurt from trying not to laugh.

"Speaking of which." Connor lowered his voice. "How's the fund-raising going?"

"Slowly. People care about the library and they're giving what they can. Charlene's organizing a bake sale for next weekend, and Ronald's making plans for a silent auction. Bertie's trying to get a big-name mystery author to make an appearance that we can sell tickets for. But all of that won't make up anywhere near enough."

He put his arm around my shoulders. "I'm so sorry."

I smiled up at him. "I'll be okay. Whatever happens. If you're here."

"And I will be."

"Hurry it up, Mr. Mayor," an old man said. "Haven't got all day here."

"You leave him alone, Karl Sugarman. The man's gotta do his courtin' sometime," his companion said.

We reached the door and stepped over the threshold to be enveloped by a warm blast of freshly risen dough–, sugar-, and coffee-scented air.

When we'd almost made it to the front, I noticed a woman accept her change and drop it into a clear plastic box on the counter. The box was stuffed full of coins and bills, many of them twenties. A sign had been taped to it, which read LIGHT-HOUSE LIBRARY RESTORATION FUND.

I struggled to swallow the lump in my throat. Beside me

Connor opened his wallet, pulled out two twenties, and put them in the box.

"Attention, everyone!" Alison called from behind the cash register. "We're out of muffins. Josie and her crew are working as hard as they can to make more. We still have a few other delicious treats prepared for you until they're ready."

"What on earth is happening here?" I said when it was our turn to be served.

Alison wiped a lock of hair out of her face. "Never seen anything like it. You'd think the end of the world was nigh and everyone needed one last coffee or muffin before going to their reward. What can I get you?"

I ordered a latte and Connor asked for a black coffee. The display case was almost completely empty. One lone slice of banana bread remained on the shelf next to two almond croissants.

"Everyone wants to show their support for Josie and let her know they're happy we're open again." Alison beamed. "Isn't it great?"

"And you're collecting for the library too. Thanks so much."

"Thank Josie," Alison said. "It was her idea."

"Coming through." Blair emerged from the back, bearing a tray loaded with fresh cherry Danishes. Behind us, the crowd cheered. "Hey, Lucy," he said.

"Hi. This is amazing," I said.

He arranged the pastries on the shelf. "I'll tell Josie you're here."

"That's not . . ." I said, but he was gone.

My cousin came out of the kitchen, wiping her hands on her apron. Her face was flushed and dotted with flour, and more flour and a piece of what looked like butter was stuck to a section of hair that had escaped its net.

I gave her a hug. "This is unbelievable."

"Hey!" Someone shouted. "Josie's here!"

Everyone cheered.

Josie broke away from me. Her eyes were wet. "I . . . I . . ."

"Speech!"

"Speech!"

I gave her a nudge. "Say a few words."

Connor stepped surreptitiously back, taking himself away from the center of attention.

"I . . ." Josie cleared her throat. "I can't thank you good folks enough for coming. The people of the Outer Banks truly are the best."

Cheers.

"Please be patient. My staff are working as hard as they can. Muffins are almost ready."

More cheers.

"Oh, and please do what you can to support the Lighthouse Library restoration fund." She disappeared into the mysterious depths of her kitchen.

Connor and I took our drinks and left. I would have loved one of those Danishes, but I thought I'd better leave them for the ravenous hordes behind me.

Chapter
Twenty-Eight

The wedding of Josie O'Malley and Jake Greenblatt was the highlight of the winter. The night air was cold and crisp and the sky full of stars. The bride was radiant, the groom handsome, the couple's parents beaming with pride, their friends jubilant. The father of the bride made a toast to absent friends. We momentary bowed our heads in memory of Mirabelle and gave a thought to Florence. Steph, Grace, and I had converted Jake's Seafood Bar into a winter-wedding wonderland with silver and ice-blue decorations. Josie's bouquet of pale-peach roses, leaves of dusty miller, and stems of silver brunia was reproduced in the flowers on each table, which had been nestled into mason jars tied with silver ribbon. The supply of canapés was seemingly endless, and the tower of cupcakes, iced in various shades of blue, stood on a side table, waiting to be cut. Steph and Butch's signature cocktail, a classic drink of gin with elderflower liquor and club soda, had been a huge hit, and I might have had a glass or two more than was good for me.

"Gone." Jake, who looked very elegant despite not wearing

a morning suit in the style of Lord Peter, led me onto the dance floor.

Josie was dancing with her brother Aaron, handsome in his brand-new suit. Josie herself positively glowed. She and I had been to the hairdresser this morning, and her hair was gathered behind her head in a loose bunch interwoven with tiny white flowers. She wore no train or headpiece, and her dress was the very definition of elegant simplicity: an A-line design featuring a cap-sleeved, close-fitting lace bodice with a scooped neckline, cascading in a waterfall of sleek chiffon from her thin waist to the floor. The back was pleated, edged with lace, and featured a small bow.

"What's gone?" I asked the groom.

"Toni. The police." He jerked his head to indicate Sam Watson, who was huddled with Butch, no doubt talking shop, while CeeCee dragged Connor onto the floor. "Said they wouldn't press charges for the assault on you if she left town. She's gone back to Buffalo, where her family lives."

"I knew Sam was going to do that, and I approved, but do you think she'll stay away?"

"I do. She didn't even call me to say goodbye."

"Good riddance."

"Josie's grandmother seems to be bearing up." We took a quick peek at the circle of tables pushed against the walls. Gloria knocked back another glass of champagne, munched on an endless supply of salmon and crab canapés, and told everyone who stopped to talk to her that she didn't care for sit-down dinners at weddings.

"She's been surprisingly well behaved, Aunt Ellen tells me,"

I said. "She thought Josie's dress could do with a lot more beading and a little more fabric around the neckline, but that was all the criticism she had. I didn't even have to call in my mom with the heavy artillery."

My parents swept past us. Mom looked great in a pale-green Versace cocktail dress and diamonds. Dad gave me a grin. They were staying at Ellen and Amos's along with Gloria, and the visit was going well. No one had offended anyone else. Not yet, anyway.

"Thank you." Jake gave me a deep bow when the song ended. He escorted me back to the library table and asked Nan, Ronald's wife, for the honor of the next dance.

"Great wedding." Ronald watched them move around the floor. His tie for the evening was neon pink scattered with red hearts.

"Great people," Charlene added. "They deserve to be so very happy."

"Speaking of very happy," Bertie said. "Gather around, everyone. Consider this an emergency library staff meeting. Connor, you can stay as long as you promise not to tell the commissioners before I send in my report."

"I can do that," he said.

We pulled our chairs closer and leaned in.

Louise Jane and Theodore were chatting to Professor Edward McClanahan, Bertie's date for the evening. She waved them over.

"Is it time for us?" Louise Jane's eyes shone with excitement and maybe a bit too much champagne and cocktails.

"Time for you to what?" I asked.

"I'm so excited," Theodore said. He'd dressed almost as formally as the groomsmen in a three-piece gray suit with starched white shirt and gray tie.

"In a minute," Bertie said. "You'll want to hear what I have to say first. Then Louise Jane and Teddy, you can make your announcements. Jake says to give him the signal when we're ready."

"Signal for what?" I asked.

"An anonymous benefactor has made a donation to the restoration fund of twenty thousand dollars."

Ronald whistled, and Charlene punched the air with her fist. "That's great," I said.

My parents danced past our table. Bertie looked at me and wiggled her eyebrows, and I understood who this mysterious benefactor was.

"In addition, I got word this afternoon that a donation of five thousand will be made in the name of the late Jonathan Uppiton."

That came as a shock.

"How on earth," Charlene said, "did you manage to get Diane to agree to that?"

Bertie preened. "I did a bit of investigative work of my own while Lucy was busy solving a murder. Why don't you tell them, Eddie?"

"I made a call." Professor McClanahan looked very pleased with himself. "To a representative of the board of the Bodie Island Lighthouse Library. I might have accidentally let it slip that I am a professor at Blacklock College, and I might have mistakenly given the impression that the college was considering donating to the library in order to keep its valued rare book collection open."

"Misunderstandings happen," Charlene said.

"Quite so. Fortunately, the board member I spoke to had little knowledge of the inner workings of academe." His bow tie was at the approximate angle of the Titanic as the great ship went down. He straightened it. It immediately began to tilt toward the stern once again. "As if my college would spare as much as a cent to save another organization's valuables. We'd be more likely to want to see the library closed and the collection dispersed in order that we might grab some of it at a discount."

"Let me fix this and then you can continue with your story." Bertie leaned over and gave the tie a couple of twists until it was straight.

"Thank you, my dear," Eddie said. "The . . . uh . . . gentleman I spoke to thanked me for my call, but said the restoration fund would not be able to meet its goal and thus my donation would be wasted. He sounded very sad at giving me such news."

"That rat," I said.

"When I next see Curtis Gardner—" Charlene said.

"Did we mention names?" Bertie said. "We did not. Fortunately, Eddie just happened to be recording the phone conversation . . ."

"My bad," the professor said.

"And I played it back," Bertie said, "when I called the person or persons in question. I might have mentioned that I was going to give it to the local radio station. People who generously opened their wallets and checkbooks in support of the library might not be pleased to hear it."

"We have twenty thousand from the anonymous donor," Charlene said. "The five in memory of Jonathan, about ten thousand from various library friends and patrons, including those who gave at Josie's reopening, five thousand from Josie's grandmother. That plus what we all gave, and the proceeds of our bake sale and silent auction, comes to a nice sum, but still not enough."

"We got this far." I tried to sound optimistic. "We can keep going."

"I don't know how many more cupcakes I can bake," Charlene said.

Jake escorted Nan back to our table, and Josie joined him.

"Are you ready?" Jake asked.

Bertie looked at Theodore and Louise Jane. "Are you two sure about this?"

They nodded enthusiastically. "Totally."

Ronald, Charlene, and I exchanged confused glances.

"Let's do it," Louise Jane said.

Bertie stood up. Between Jake and Josie, she walked with Louise Jane and Theodore to the front of the room. Jake signaled to the band and they stopped playing. Jake took the microphone.

"First," he said when he had everyone's attention, "on behalf of my beautiful wife"—the room erupted in cheers—"and myself, I'd like to once again thank y'all for coming. The band will be here for a long time yet, and I sense something good about to come out of the kitchen—" More cheers. "Now, a special announcement on behalf of the Bodie Island Light-house Library, which is dear to all our hearts." Jake stepped back and Bertie took his place.

"She's up to something," Ronald said. "I recognize that grin."

"The same grin I fell in love with," Eddie said, "the day I dropped my stack of books on the stairs going into the lecture hall, so long ago. She tripped over them, as I remember, and swore a blue streak at me for my clumsiness. When her leg came out of the cast, she told me I was forgiven."

"Shush," Charlene said.

"It's my great pleasure to be able to announce here tonight," Bertie said, "that thanks to extremely generous gifts from two of the staunchest library patrons, the library has exceeded the amount needed for the restoration fund."

I gasped and turned to my friends. Mouths hung open. Connor had a spark in his eye. "You knew about this?" I asked.

"I'd like to take the credit, but I can't. Once Bertie had secured the promise of enough funds to get the work started, she approached the town again. The commissioners were impressed by the devotion the people of this town have to the library and agreed to double our initial offer."

Theodore stepped up to the microphone. He tapped on it. "Is this thing on?"

"We can hear you, Teddy," someone called.

Theodore leaned over and spoke loudly and clearly. "Thank you." He stepped back.

"What are you thanking us for?" Butch called.

"Oh, didn't I say?"

"No, you did not."

Bertie took his place. "Theodore sold a signed first edition of *Live and Let Die* by Ian Fleming for a price of twenty-five thousand dollars, and he has donated the full sum to the library."

"Oh my gosh," I said. "He got that book from Julia Ruddle in thanks for saving her life. Giving it away is a huge sacrifice for him."

Bertie continued. "Louise Jane McKaughnan's great-grandmother is, as many of you know, in ill health and not able to travel, but she has instructed me to tell you that at Louise Jane's suggestion, she sold a collection of letters received by Captain Thaddeus Clark of the *Rebecca McPherson* in 1753. Included among the letters is one from the captain's mother's neighbor, discussing local matters of the day." Bertie paused.

"That's probably worth something to a naval historian," Charlene said, "but I can't see that anyone else would care. I know about Clark and his ship, and what happened to it, but nothing about his family life."

"She has that look," Eddie said. "Wait for it. Something's coming."

"Captain Clark's mother's neighbor at the time," Bertie said, "was a young gentleman by the name of George Washington."

Charlene gasped. The room burst into cheers.

"Mrs. McKaughnan has sold this packet of letters to the Historical Foundation of the Carolinas, and has agreed to donate the proceeds of fifteen thousand dollars to the Light-house Library."

Ronald, Charlene, and I leapt to our feet and gathered each other into a group hug. Connor hugged Nan, and Eddie applauded vigorously as the band struck up the next song.

"You did it!" I said to Bertie when she joined us.

"We did it, Lucy. All of us. Together. I've told George to enter our job into his schedule and start applying for the necessary permits."

Louise Jane and Theodore joined us. I thought Charlene was about to cry. Ronald slapped Theodore heartily on the back, and I threw my arms around Louise Jane. "That was unbelievably generous."

"I told you, Lucy, the Lighthouse Library is important to me too. Wouldn't it be exciting if they find something long buried under the lighthouse? Like pirate treasure or a dead body?"

"Don't be fanciful," I said. "That only happens in books."

"This calls for a celebratory dance." Eddie bowed deeply to Bertie. "May I?"

She laughed and took his hand. Theodore escorted Louise Jane onto the dance floor, and Ronald and Charlene joined them.

"Care for this dance?" Connor asked me.

"I'd love to."

He took my hand in his, and we walked onto the floor. He folded me into his arms. The band struck up "Love Me Tender" by Elvis Presley, and we danced close together, moving gently to the music. "A perfect night," he said.

I murmured agreement and settled myself deeper into his arms. Then I had a sudden, horrible thought. "Oh, no!"

Connor pulled away and looked into my face. "What is it? Are you all right? Did I step on your toe?"

"I'm fine, but I remembered something. In my rush to get ready to leave for the church in time, I forgot to feed Charles. When I get home, my life won't be worth living."

Connor laughed and pulled me close.

"Love me tender, love me true," the singer crooned.

And that, I realized, is what I would be doing with this man for a long time to come.

Author's Note

The Bodie Island Lighthouse is a real historic lighthouse, located in Cape Hatteras National Seashore on the Outer Banks of North Carolina. It is still a working lighthouse, protecting ships from the Graveyard of the Atlantic, and the public are invited to tour it and climb the two hundred fourteen steps to the top. The view from up there is well worth the trip. But the lighthouse does not contain a library, nor is it large enough to house a collection of books, offices, staff rooms, two staircases, and even an apartment.

Within these books, the interior of the lighthouse is the product of my imagination. I like to think of it as my version of the Tardis, from the TV show *Doctor Who*, or Hermione Granger's beaded handbag: far larger inside than it appears from the outside.

I hope it is large enough for your imagination also.